foursight

foursight

Graham Joyce
James Lovegrove
Kim Newman
Michael Marshall Smith

Edited, and with an introduction by
Peter Crowther

VICTOR GOLLANCZ
LONDON

'Andy Warhol's Dracula' first appeared online
on Event Horizon: Science, Fantasy, Horror
(/http://www/eventhorizon.com)/

First published in this omnibus volume in 2000 by
Victor Gollancz
An imprint of Orion Books Ltd
Orion House, 5 Upper St Martin's Lane,
London WC2H 9EA

To receive information on the Millennium list,
e-mail us at: smy@orionbooks.co.uk

A CIP catalogue record for this book
is available from the British Library

ISBN 0 575 068701

Typeset by SetSystems Ltd, Saffron Walden, Essex
Printed in Great Britain by
Clays Ltd, St Ives plc

The Long *and* the Short of it

An Introduction by Peter Crowther

I think I probably came across the term 'novelette' in the early 1960s through the pages of *Astounding Science Fiction*: if one had to be precise (which, I accept, I do not), I'd guess it was Clifford Simak's 'The Big Front Yard' from the October 1958 issue (it appeared in the UK edition a few years later) but, as I was to discover much later when I bought up huge truckloads of magazines from the good old days, the term had been around in that magazine much longer.

As I recall, the appearance of the word on *Astounding*'s contents page gave me some initial (if short-lived) confusion: there were some short stories – right there, beneath the 'Novelette' heading – and I knew all about those. I'd already consumed several stacks of anthologies and collections by that time and I had grown to love the short-form narrative (a love affair that has remained passionate and fresh to this day). And, of course, I knew about novels – I'd also read a lot of those, but I didn't like them nearly as much as the short stuff. That preference, too, has remained pretty constant.

But I was a bright if not particularly academic child and I quickly decided that a novelette must be a short story that was maybe a little on the long side . . . or a novel that was maybe a little too short. Now, for anyone thinking that they had to be a *lot* short to qualify for that second slot, remember that we're talking here about the days when buying a novel didn't require you to possess either a boxer's biceps or a wheelbarrow just to get the book home. Novels then were around one hundred and sixty to two hundred pages and, if it was a good one, you could crack it in a night . . . or a couple of days max.

I kept checking the contents pages of the mags I bought – far more in those days than I do now – to see if the term cropped up anyplace else. It did, here and there, notably in the various tomes supposedly edited by Alfred Hitchcock that my parents used to buy for me in hardcover (a real treat) for birthdays and Christmas. These literary oddities were usually sandwiched between runs of short stories, probably as much for the aesthetics of the contents pages as for anything more profound.

Novelets had been a staple of Horace Gold's *Galaxy* since it appeared on the scene in 1950 but the October 1955 edition was the first to feature a novella – Robert Sheckley's 'A Ticket To Tranai'.

They didn't appear in my favourite magazine – *The Magazine of Fantasy and Science Fiction* – until the January 1966 edition, which was the first one edited by Ed Ferman (previously it had been Ed's father, Joe, the magazine's founder, but Joe stepped down in January 1966 to assume the position of Publisher). There were two novelets (note the dropped 'te' favoured by John Campbell, trivia buffs) in that edition – Robert Young's 'L'Arc De Jeanne' and Robert Green's wonderful 'Apology To Inky' (check it out if you can find it – lovely story) – and I was now firmly won over.

There was something slightly more solid in a novelette (I'll use Campbell's spelling from here on) than in many of the short stories I read, most of which tended to run to maybe six or seven thousand words at the outside. The novelette usually came in around the twelve thousand word mark, which offered a little more space, or so it seemed, for the author to round out his or her ideas into a complete piece. But, of course, it didn't stretch to the novel-length works, many of which, even then, were like gangly kids who had outgrown their strength.

But, as novels lengths started to increase, the space between them and novelettes grew too wide; this had clearly been noticed for several years by Ed Ferman, who had already been featuring 'short novel' on *F&SF*'s contents pages (and even 'novel', which is pretty implausible given the magazine's overall length) before, in July 1973, the word novella appeared as a description of Michael Bishop's 'The White Otters of Childhood'. (Aren't you glad you've got geeks like me to find all this stuff out for you? Even so, I sometimes think I should get out more . . . meet people . . .)

The die was pretty much cast from there on in, although the ground-rules have been modified from time to time. My own take on the situation is this: short stories run to ten thousand words; novelettes start there and run to, say, twenty thousand words, at which point novellas take over until you hit forty thousand words; novels go the full distance from there.

So, what you have here is a collection of four stories, two of which – in strict definition terms – are novelettes and two novellas. But for ease, we're breaking the rules and calling them all novellas.

Whatever you call them, the pieces that occupy the wilderness between short story and out-and-out novel are considered by some to be neither the sand nor the sea, while for others they're the best of all possible worlds. Certainly the novelette or novella, as a literary artform, rarely enjoys (or suffers) the indecisive or merely non-committal middle ground.

There are great novelists and there are great short story writers – we all have our favourites in each category. But we tend not to think of great novella writers . . . especially not within the relatively specialist fields of science fiction and dark fantasy (and I include the much-maligned nomenclature of 'horror' – a word which the literati would have us believe strikes as much fear in the hearts of publishers as the work which it describes is intended to instill in the hearts of readers – in that catch-all).

Well, this specially commissioned series of novella quartets – the individual stories in which will initially appear, as the four stories in this book have already done, as very limited-run standalone books with guest introductions, under my and Simon Conway's PS imprint – aims to redress the balance. And this first time out, we're looking specifically at the realm of dark fantasy . . . though with a few surprises thrown in along the way to combat complacency. Because one thing's for sure: none of these stories will prepare you for any of the others . . . for how could Graham Joyce's war-torn Leningrad filled with doppelgängers possibly prepare you for James Lovegrove's lonely commuter belt cellar where a successful man keeps a whipping-boy clone of himself, or Kim Newman's vampire-ridden New York City in an alternative 1960s, or Michael Marshall Smith's vision of a modern-day Florida where alien races, Government agencies and underworld hoodlums vie daily for control?

Yes, if anything could possibly link these stories it would be strange places . . . strange goings-on, agreed, but *strange* places.

'They' say, those faceless and identity-less people who seem to be the collective *vox pop* of Society at large, that books of short stories don't sell. And they would probably say – given half the chance – the same about books of novellas (or even novelettes). But they used to say, the antecedents of those same people, that the Earth was flat . . . and in some quarters there are those who say – maybe the very same sour-voiced and sour-minded folks – there's no such thing as the perfect pint of Guinness. Well, we all know the shape of the Earth now, and there's this wonderful little pub on Wicklow Street in Dublin . . .

So, maybe they're wrong about everything, just as a matter of course. I certainly hope so. Because here in this book, and in the volume of science fiction novellas that will follow it next year, you've got a quartet of fine writers playing in a medium that doesn't appear so often that we can afford to ignore it. I hope you enjoy it.

Peter Crowther
September 1999

graham joyce

leningrad nights

This is the story of a city so old and so beautiful and so terrifying that no one knows its true name. That is, it has many names, but they refuse to harden or fix and set. Every few decades the City fathers have the task of thinking up a new name, one which will last no longer than the others. And each time the name is changed, the city sheds a skin. The skins litter history, and the cities of the old names hover like ghosts, in a time and space of their own.

But what a city it was when Leo was a boy! Where even puberty passed him by, because he was too busy trying to stay alive.

Before it happened, he was a boy happily playing one summer, in a great mythical city of slender golden spires and dazzling cupolas and secret waterways. He fished, all the time; he could talk the fish on to his line. Then the sky darkened and there was the nine hundred days siege. Then he was a man. The nine hundred days taught him everything this world had to teach him, and by then he was still only fourteen years old.

His father was killed very early in the war. It crushed his mother so deeply that it crippled her spirit and she surrendered the will to live. She was one of the first victims of the siege, contracting dysentery and dying of infection. Later he would thank the guts of the martyrs that all Russians were not so weak, or the nine hundred days would have been the ninety days and the Nazis would have been swilling vodka in the Winter Palace before the end of the first Autumn.

'Weak,' croaked Uncle Yevgeny, as they buried her. They were still burying people properly at that stage. He made a minimalist gesture with his hand. 'She was weak.'

When Yevgeny croaked like that, it was not out of sentiment.

Uncle Yevgeny was a gnarled, bitter old Russian with a face carved from a bulb of knotted pine. He drank tea soaked in tincture of opium and lived alone up by the Museum of Atheism. His throat had been corrupted by smoking thick twist low-grade Turkish tobacco; now he only ever croaked or growled, or more typically abandoned speech altogether. Mother had disapproved of him, but now he was all Leo had left.

'What must I do, Uncle? What must I do?'

'Do?' Yevgeny said, turning from the fresh grave. 'What must you do? You must stay alive.'

That was the only advice or help he ever got from his uncle. Everyone else was preoccupied with surviving the siege. He stopped going to school and no one seemed to notice.

He was already accustomed to shortages. There had always been a shortage of this or that and rationing had been introduced long before the Nazis were hammering on the gates. He'd been raised with an ability to improvise, to eke out whatever was there, and he could barter like a Cossack. But nothing could have prepared him for what was to come.

Vast guns, hunkered like grey wolves on the dark horizon, pounded them from the German lines; usually with clockwork regularity, and then sometimes at any hour, just to keep the Russians on their toes. Sometimes it seemed they were making a joke out of the bombardment. Every day they would shell precisely at six o'clock for one hour, over several days. It was like waiting for the rain to give over before you could go about your business. Then one day for laughs they would start an hour early, or pause before slipping in an extra burst and everyone would be sent scurrying like rats. The guns taught Leo a lesson in the absolute laws of uncertainty.

The people would crawl out of their houses to assess the damage: this family's house demolished, or a cinema gone forever. And while everyone was full of sympathy and patriotic anger, they were secretly relieved that it was not their own miserable hovel that had sucked in the whistling shells. There would be smoke everywhere. Ribbons of dirty blue or yellow smoke suspended, unmoving, in loops and coils three feet above the street, or hanging in the blasted doorways and broken windows of the wrecked houses.

Leo did what he'd been told to do. He concentrated on staying alive. He prayed, and not to God, but to the blind justice of The Whistling Shell, that he and his house might be spared but that it might take the Godenuvs because they were dirty and known thieves, or the Kuprin family because their eldest boy now fighting on the lines had bulled Leo at school. And if he was right – and sometimes he was – he thanked the blind justice of The Whistling Shell with a selfish heart, and promised to offer up another prayer the next day, if only he might be spared.

He hoarded; anything he could get his hands on: food, firewood, matches, salt, anything which he saw was becoming scarcer. In the streets people were selling their watches, their jewellery, whatever might bring in a crust, but Leo hoarded. It go so bad that the people ate their horses. Then when they had eaten the horses, they ate what the horses ate. They ate rough oats. They even boiled up grass with the oats to make it to further. Leo learned about the colour of shit after he had eaten grass.

In desperation he turned to Uncle Yevgeny. Even though there were things about the district which scared him, he made his way to Yevgeny's apartment to beg for help.

There was no electricity to light his way as he clambered over rubble and squeezed through the blocked stairway to Yevgeny's freezing apartment. A rat scuffled on the steps, and on the third floor the handrail on the stairs swung out over the stairwell, and Leo went with it. Somebody had taken the banisters for firewood, and Leo swung out over the dark stairwell and back again as the handrail opened and closed over the death drop like a pair of shears.

Already in a state of shock, he stumbled into Yevgeny's apartment, finding the door open. Yevgeny was seated in his usual chair, gazing out of the frozen window at the ice-bound river Neva and the Museum of Atheism.

'Uncle?'

Uncle didn't stir. His eyes were open, but the frost on the window had jumped across the room to ice his blue eyes. His hands rested in his lap, bearing a shred of cardboard. Another piece of cardboard was in his mouth, but dry. Leo wondered how many hours his uncle had been sitting there.

'What do you do, Uncle?' Leo tried to imitate Yevgeny's guttural inflections. He stood behind the seated corpse and nudged Yevgeny's elbow so that his dead uncle's bluish hand flicked in a tiny gesture. 'You survive.'

Leo left Yevgeny gazing at the golden dome of the Museum of Atheism.

There was nothing edible to salvage from the apartment. Instead Leo went to the cupboard where he knew his uncle kept the samovar. What a vessel it was! It had been in the family for generations, and it had always been a matter of chagrin to Leo's mother that the samovar had fallen to Yevgeny. On the few occasions when the family had visited, Yevgeny used to take down the samovar for all to admire, and, Leo observed, to annoy his mother.

'It's too fine to make tea in!' his mother would protest.

'I agree,' Yevgeny would growl, proceeding to do so anyway.

But it was true: it was too unique an object to spoil with use. The silverwork was a delight and the porcelain was decorated with pictures of serpents harried across the earth by the fiery sword of a winged saint. 'Everything that makes our family special is written on that samovar,' Leo's mother would complain bitterly after every visit. 'All my memories of childhood. Your babushka, Leo, and even my own grandfather. All my memories kept alive under the engraved silver lid. I wanted it for the family ashes, and Yevgeny cooks up his stinking brews in it!'

He would no longer. Leo took down the samovar from the shelf and wondered what he might get in return for such a beautiful object.

'Bye, Uncle,' he said, bearing the samovar out of the apartment.

'Uggh,' he croaked on his uncle's behalf, a passable personation of the old boy's minimal salutations.

Leo had no misgivings about parting with the object. His guts were clawing with hunger and besides, everyone in his neighbourhood had made sacrifices of their most personal possessions, and he felt a pleasant righteousness in joining the people in communal suffering. It was fitting. He could hold up his head.

After bearing the samovar home, he waited indoors until the pounding of the guns was over, so that he could go out when most of the people would be out of doors. Then he carried the samovar proudly into the street, plainly affording everyone equal opportunity to view this splendid artefact before they put in their bid.

He found a knot of old men and women on a street corner. They were surveying a building that had sucked in a shell. It had been a tailor's shop, and now it was a pile of rubble. Grey smoke writhed like a serpent over a broken tailor's dummy, and thence along the litter of plaster and broken lath and smashed masonry.

He marched confidently up to the whispering crowd. 'What will you give me for this rare and beautiful samovar?' he asked, thrusting the object under their noses.

They looked, first at the samovar, and then at him. Then they looked at each other. Then they laughed in his face. 'What's the use of a samovar without any tea?' cackled one of the old women.

Stung, Leo advertised the ceramic drawer at the back of the samovar, where he had seen Yevgeny keep his opium-soaked tea.

One of the old women peered into the drawer. 'What's that? Mouse droppings? The lad's trying to pass mouse droppings off as tea!'

'Here!' said another. 'Come into my house. I'll give you some mouse doings.'

One of the men inspected Yevgeny's tiny twists of tea. 'You sure it's not your own doings?' he said. They all laughed again.

'It is tea!' Leo roared. He felt his cheeks flame and his eyes water. Hunger gnawed his bowels like a rat. He had marched out to make a sacrifice of his family's most treasured possession, thereby to join the suffering of the people, and the people had laughed. He was paralysed with humiliation. He couldn't even make a move to run away or hide his face.

One of the old men approached him and steered him away from his tormentors. 'No one wants a samovar,' he said gently. 'Take it home.' Leo only looked at him angrily. 'Wait here,' the man said, before going into one of the nearby houses, returning with a rough biscuit.

'One small biscuit for this?' Leo stammered.

'Look,' the man said, 'I'm only trying to save your face in front of these old women. A samovar is worth less than nothing in this city now, and maybe never will be again. Give it to me and take the biscuit; then at least you can walk home with your head up. What do you say?'

But Leo thought he was being cheated. He couldn't see that the man was acting out of kindness, and that things were going to get even worse. 'Peasants!' he shouted. 'You're all too stupid to see the value of this samovar!'

The mood of the small crowd turned. He now realised he'd made a mistake in drawing attention to himself. 'You make sure you eat that biscuit,' said another woman, 'because tomorrow it'll be your turn to go to the line. Make yourself useful and kill a few Germans.'

'Give me a gun and I'll go now,' he said, his thirteen-year-old voice cracking.

'You'll have your gun soon enough. This tailor,' she said, indicating the still-smoking ruins of the shop, 'was already measuring up your uniform. Now we'll have to find you another tailor.'

He didn't know at the time, but they didn't have any guns; and that if they had, then he would already have been sent up on the line.

'Meanwhile,' said another of the old women, for they'd rounded on him now, 'why don't you take a leaf out of o' those Young Pioneers' books, and stop whining about self self self all the time.' She was referring to a band of boys and girls who went around the city trying to help people in their suffering. 'Don't think we haven't noticed you scurrying in the shadows like a canal rat, trying to pass off samovars to folk for what little they've got. Don't think it hasn't been noticed. Get out and help folk if you can't fight and you've got nothing to do with your time.'

He was stung with tears. He ran from them, ran back to his house with the wretched samovar, and flung himself on the bed, sobbing, the breath gone out of him. His heart was lacerated with shame. He hated the old crones. He wanted to die. Hunger tore at his belly and the reproach of the old women echoed cruelly in his ears.

He regretted not accepting the biscuit, for he'd nothing left. Leo opened the ceramic drawer and surveyed the tea ruefully. Soaked in Yevgeny's tincture, it had indeed been compressed into tiny pellets. He used one of the pellets to brew himself a cup in the beautiful samovar, and when he drank the cup of tea he'd made, his hunger pains subsided almost immediately.

Tea-coloured; and gold; and immeasurably older than ever he'd suspected the city to be. That was how it appeared to him when he went outside. The entire city gone the colour of, well, if not tea, then perhaps stale chocolate, but with a soft pulsating under-radiance. And a double-image, as if there were now a second Leningrad, this one inaccurately superimposed over the first one he had known; but he knew without doubt that this new version was the real Leningrad.

He took with him a flask containing more of the tea. He floated through the streets like a wraith, marvelling at the architecture still standing and the demolished buildings equally, seeing a rhythm in the spaces between, an exceptional order to the dispensations of The Whistling Shell. And the staircases revealed by half-blasted walls were everywhere, proliferating and multiplying until he could see through walls to all the staircases in the entire city, vertiginous stairways, flights of steps, dizzying ladders, criss-crossing fire-escapes, comprising a kind of music and proportion. Astonishing to see so many hundreds and hundreds of staircases running up and down. He walked until his neck ached from gazing up at them.

He found a small girl, maybe four years old, grubbing in a pile of bricks. She wore a dirty blue smock and was half-starved. Her eyes were disproportionately large for her face and she looked at him with suspicion as he approached. When she asked him for something to eat he offered her a sip from his flask, which she took before running off into the shadows like an alley cat.

The act of dispensing that drop of narcotic tea made him feel whole again. Unable to shake the image of the girl from his thoughts, he returned home, his heart in shreds for love of her dirty blue smock and her hunger. He saw it very clearly: a new Leningrad had been triggered, in which he could be a new person. He resolved from that moment on to spend his time looking for people to help, to seek out suffering and to do what he could wherever he could. He'd been stung into action by the bottomless eyes of a tiny girl. No longer would his own hunger, safety or comfort be the motivating principle of his life.

And there was suffering. Everywhere. His eyes had suddenly been opened. The people were dying like flies. Winter had locked in the very breath of the city and the lung-cracking cold was unbearable. If they weren't dying of starvation, the people were freezing to death. In one street he encountered the body of a woman solidly frozen in a standing position: she had leaned against a wall, exhausted, snow-covered, no food to keep her going, and had fallen asleep on her feet. She just never woke up.

He went about the city trying to do good, helping here and there, finding a stick of fuel for this old person, scratching a bite of food for this family. He became well-known: they called him the red-faced angel. In the places he visited, he was very glad to see a rat. He became an expert rat-catcher, skinning them and stewing them, perhaps with a potato. With melted snow he made pans of stew this way and took it to hungry people.

'What is it?' they would invariably ask.

'Best steak,' he would say without a wink, and they thought it wonderful.

He ventured out every day, fuelled only by the occasional sip from his tea-flask. The houses were dead. The city was becoming choke-full of ghosts, smoke hanging in the air and the reek of death and piss and shit everywhere in the sreets. It was not unusual for him to stumble across corpses lying in the snow. The apartments stood like grey tombs in a necropolis, all intersecting with tracings of weird staircases. Sometimes he had to break down doors to find if anyone inside was alive.

The fact is that half the population was lost. A million people. By the end of the nine hundred day siege the body-count would be nearer a million and a half. He moved through the dying, seeing the spirits of the recently dead ascending from the bloated or frozen corpses without egress. Ectoplasmic forms stuck to ceilings and door lintels like deflating grey helium-filled balloons. He talked to them, whispering encouragement, suggesting routes through the flickering and ethereal morass of staircases.

He had one good coat but he gave it away and adopted a soiled blanket, clasped at the neck with a talismanic twist of shrapnel. He thought if he wore a piece of The Whistling Shell, the dermis of the Kruppsteel God, then he might be passed over. He was himself surviving on next to nothing. He consumed very little of the meagre food he turned up; he was running on another fuel, the light and heat and energy of the inner flame, the fire of the soul. It seemed enough, and it got him from house to house, day to day. He was inspired by love for the suffering people, by self-sacrifice and untiring hard work. It goaded him on through the ghost city, through the slums and ghettos, grey smoke weaving and coiling about them like worms. All this suffering, the Germans, the smoky serpents; they fused together in his mind to represent a single common enemy launching all these attacks from a platform high above the city, an enemy which could be defeated if only it were possible to keep the inner lamp burning.

And he had an ally in his work. On the radio, they continued to broadcast the sound of a metronome ticking, an act of defiance, to show that the city still had central control somewhere, a heart beating bravely. Ghost broadcasts crackled over the airwaves to be followed by the dull relentless ticking of the metronome. Loudspeakers set up in the glacial streets carried the eerie rhythm. Sometimes he kicked open the doors of houses to find only corpses, or old people weak beyond speech; but the radio would be turned on and the metronome ticking. It was like the numinous presence of a minor god; Tempo, trailing audial banners the length of the march of time, reminding him that even the grey wolves at the gate would turn to fur and bone and dust. If he could out-survive them.

And his ally came in the shape of the stirring words, broadcast over the airwaves, of the boy-poet. Whatever Leo was doing he would stop and listen to his inspiration. The people talked of the boy-poet, said he was only eleven years old, but his poems rang with courage and patriotism, with defiance and exhortation. His words fell like a momentary sweetness amidst all the rot and despair and the decay. They were food and fuel to the soul. It didn't matter how deep into the hell they were falling, the poet's words were a parachute for the heart.

Leo loved the boy-poet, whoever he was. When he was weary and heartbroken from going about his business, the boy's words reminded Leo of his mission. He envied his spirit and faculty. Such wisdom in such youth! Leo carried his words with him like a flag wherever he went, memorising them and discussing them with the people he helped. The boy-poet betokened Leo's faith, his certainty that one day they would win through. Leo, who had never before written a word of poetry, found himself scribbling pale imitations of the poems he heard on the radio.

Then suddenly one day the boy-poet stopped broadcasting. Leo listened for an explanation, some report of the boy's circumstances amid the diminishing bulletins. There came no word. After a while he went to the radio station clutching a sheaf of his own poems to show the boy-poet and to find out why he had ceased broadcasting. He was received there by a gruff, consumptive, unshaven man who wore one half of a pair of spectacles over his right eye. 'The boy-poet? Maybe he's dead.' There was the rot of vodka on the man's breath. 'What have you got there? Let's have a look.'

The radio-station manager squinted through his single lens, giving Leo's poems the once-over. 'Hmmm. Maybe he's still alive after all. Listen tonight.'

That evening the same boy's fearless young voice crackled over the airwaves, but this time Leo recognised the words as his own. Leo brewed himself the last of Uncle Yevgeny's tea, and wondered how that could be. Then the answer came to him. The boy was not any one individual, but the living heart and soul of the city itself, choosing with arbitrary conviction to speak through this person or that. And the man from the radio station had told him that he, Leo, had brought the boy back to life. Leo threw himself into the enterprise of poetry with augmented passion.

*

Though he dreaded the idea of returning, something propelled him back to his Uncle Yevgeny's apartment. He needed to make a search of the place, even though he would have to climb over the man's putrefying corpse. He had no idea of what conditions he might find it in.

Though there were patrols, there was little looting going on in Leningrad. What was the point, when everyone was trying to get rid of their material possessions in return for a bit of bread? The door to Yevgeny's apartment stood ajar, exactly as he'd left it. The wind whistled through a window where the glass had been blown out by a shell, casting flurries of snow inside the room.

Leo was astonished to find Yevgeny's cold body in fine condition. Certainly the skin was the blue colour of heated steel, but there was little evidence of decomposition. Someone had explained to him that this could be caused by the creation of a micro-climate. Leo felt the cold air circulating around the room and sniffed the body for evidence of decay.

'I'm still here,' Leo croaked with uncanny accuracy. He had to suppress a smile at his own talent for mimicry.

It was true. The old man's glassy eyes were still fixed ahead on the ice-bound Neva and the Museum of Atheism. 'So I see, Yevgeny, so I see.'

'*Uncle* Yevgeny. Show a bit of respect. You're still a pup.'

'I'm a different person now, Uncle. I'm doing some good.'

'You think you can do good? No one can do good. You'll find out. What are you doing? Keep off my things.'

'I'm looking for your tea, Uncle. You must have stashed it away somewhere.'

'You stole my samovar, you little whelp. I'll come after you.'

'You'd better not. I've been around a bit since we last spoke. I've seen a few things.'

'You've seen nothing. When I was in the trenches fighting for the Tsar we had to cook and eat the enemy before we were through.'

'And I'll take this old army coat of yours if you don't mind. You won't be needing it.'

'Put it back, you dog. I saluted the Tsar while I was wearing that coat, and I saluted Lenin. None of them were any good. Keep your grubby little praws out of those pockets.'

'Ah, tea! Magnificent! I had a feeling it was in here. And medals, Uncle! I didn't know you were decorated. Mother never told me you were decorated!'

'Your mother was weak little slut with a runt offspring.'

Leo turned and fisted Yevgeny hard in the face. The impact forced the frozen head to the side. Yevgeny looked downcast. 'Don't ever speak of my mother again in that way, Yevgeny.' He re-aligned the head so that Yevgeny could continue to gaze upon the Museum of Atheism. 'I'm sorry to have be part of your moral re-education, Uncle, and I regret not having time to complete the job. But I have important work. I may not be back this way for some time.'

Leo pulled on the greatcoat, took the tea and decorated himself with the medals.

'And your slack-mouthed juvenile poetry is piss in the wind,' Yevgeny shouted as Leo left the apartment.

Leo went about the city doing good wherever he could, seeking out opportunities to help people. He never disclosed to anyone the fact that the radio station had chosen to broadcast his words, fearing it an arrogance. But he encouraged discussion of the boy-poet's passionate appeals. Yes, they agreed, his words are a source of unflagging inspiration to us all, and no, he had lost nothing in nobility of thought or in the power of his invective.

Leo was almost delirious with a mixture of humility and pride on hearing the suffering people speaking about his poems as they came over the radio. Humility and pride. And perhaps that was when the split first occurred.

Sheltering one day from the early evening chorus of The Whistling Shell, he sipped at his tea-flask and composed poems of metronomic metre with a tiny stub of pencil as the agents of pride found their way in. Hiding behind the crump of gunfire and detonations, they winged in on the mortars and infiltrated with the stealth of grey smoke. Leo wrote a line and scratched it out; wrote and scratched. But he was already lost. The whispering of these unseen agents had already found ear. If he could bring the boy-poet back from the dead, they reasoned, could he not also restore life to others? There is no death, he wrote in his notebook. Humility scratched it out. Pride wrote it in again, this time in a firmer hand.

When the evening bombardment had given way to the canticles of the howling wind, Leo ventured out again. From that moment on he went from house to house, seeking out the worst cases, the near-corpses, the death-in-life situations, the most hopeless conditions in which he could work.

The cold and ice raged. That winter of 1941–42 had fangs of crystal and steel. The people he passed in the streets wore full-face masks to protect their skin from being stripped by the wind: red masks, blue, green, black. Lustreless eyes looking back at him from the peepholes cut in the masks. The trolleybuses stood dead on their tracks, hung with ice, creatures of extinction. Leo had to give up poetry when the ink froze in his inkwell and his last centimetre of pencil vanished in his hands in the middle of a sprung rhythm. He was still finding bodies, stiff as sticks frozen in the street having given up the ghost on their way home after collecting water from holes hacked out of the Neva ice.

His search for the worst cases took him to the Haymarket district. Around the Haymarket the scum and cut-throats of Leningrad plied their business. He was afraid, that was certain. He was, after all, still a boy and at that time rumours of cannibalism were rife. Everyone would claim that they knew someone who had a friend who had had one of their children abducted by the cannibals. Everything at that time was believable. Was there cannibalism in Leningrad during the nine hundred days siege? One does not ask questions to which one already knows the answer. And the stories insisted that the cannibals prized child-meat above all other. It was dangerous to wander around at night. But guided by the inner flame, he was drawn to the worst areas of the city.

Perhaps the ghouls left him alone because they thought he was mad. A filthy thirteen-year-old boy, shuffling along in Yevgeny's over-sized greatcoat, decorated with pre-revolutionary honours. And he argued with himself as he went about his way. Impassioned debates ostensibly to keep himelf awake or to prevent himself from drifting into the gold and sewer-brown narcotic mist of the alternative Leningrad. Sometimes it happened that his tiring spirit would lose an argument with himself, and the humble spirit within him would shelter under a broken stairwell, to sleep, to dream, while the proud and angry spirit would split away, racing contemptuously from one phantom staircase to another in the massive over-arching gallery of the transparent city.

But while the humble spirit dozed, the split would not endure for long and the haughty spirit would return, apolegetic, having found from somewhere a meaty, savoury stew, hot and steaming, with which to revive his brother. And the humble spirit, not knowing if this was real or an apparition of the fuel of Good Work, would accept it anyway. 'What is it? Is it rat?'

'Best steak,' the haughty spirit would reply without a wink. 'We can do nothing if you die on me.'

So perhaps the ghouls left this mad boy alone as he made his way through the corrupting shadows of the Haymarket. Maybe some race-memory of the deranged antics of the shaman scared them off. For whatever reason the scum and the spivs, the pimps and the detritus of the worst of all wars in the coldest of all cities eyed him suspiciously and with polluted eyes, but allowed him to pass unmolested.

Then, in one apartment, lying on a bed of filthy rags, he found a young woman, skinny and dystrophic, but pregnant and very close to her time. She couldn't even move from her bed for sickness and cold and hunger. Another twenty-four hours, Leo figured (and how he'd become expert in making these assessments as he moved among the sick and the dying), and she would have joined the one and a half million.

What was miraculous was that the baby was still alive inside her. He placed his hand on the woman's distended belly and felt it move. This he took as a special sign: this one was for him. The woman's eyes failed to register him as he kneeled by the bedside. Her spirit had already died and only her feeble body anchored it to this world. Exactly what he was looking for. He, Leo Shapoval, thirteen-and-a-half years old, would take it upon himself to bring both her and her baby back from the dead.

He took her hand. She was grey with cold. She couldn't have been much older than eighteen or so herself. He tore down some old curtains and piled them on the bed. Then he went out to pillage neighbouring houses for anything that would burn. While levering a door from its frame he was spotted by a looter patrol, and fired upon. They gave chase but he escaped. After an hour he returned with several strips of broken lath, made a fire and boiled up some water.

His first act was to trickle some drops of opium tea into her mouth, before taking a sip himself. Then he set about changing the bedding. It was soiled and filthy, so he burned all that and put down fresh bedding for her. Her clothes stuck to her body. He undressed her completely, took a rag soaked in the boiling water and washed her like a baby from head to foot, hoping that some feeling might be restored to her limbs, or that some lustre would return to her eye. There was not a flicker of hope.

He rushed out into the street again. He desperately needed to make her a thin broth, something that would revive her. He was confident that of all of the people he had helped, someone would now come to his aid. But he found no one who would part with so much as a grain of flour. They had nothing; or they pretended to have nothing, and they turned their shamed faces away from him. Now they could no longer look him in the eye, those who had once laughed at him. He was frantic. He went about for three hours. Then he found a man baking bread. Bread! He watched the man bake his 'bread' from sawdust and glue. Sawdust and glue and a fingerful of flour. The man promised Leo a slice – and one slice only – when it was baked. After a fight someone gave him a potato.

He made a soup of the potato. Then he went back to collect his promised slice of sawdust loaf and crumbled that into the soup. He dipped his finger and let the soup trickle into the girl's mouth. She coughed, but eventually she swallowed it, and then she took some more. What was left he set aside for later, but he knew it was hopelessly inadequate. He needed meat. Just a little. Just enough to give her and her baby some strength.

Ground meat was available at the Haymarket, at fantastic prices. Three or four hundred rubles for a few patties. It was always patties, for who knows what goes into a patty? The people who sold the patties were always big men with heavy boots. And they were invariably fat, with soft, pink cheeks, while everyone else around them was a floating wraith. Something about the soft, pink and yet leathery texture of their skin gave rise to speculation. But it made no difference. The price was utterly beyond his reach. He despaired.

'It's no good,' he said aloud. 'She's too far gone.'

The proud boy sniffed from across the room and tossed another stick of wood on the fire. 'Not this one. This one is mine.'

'I'm sick of it,' said the humble boy. 'I'm too tired. I can't do this any more.'

'And I'm sick of your constant whining. Why don't you stay here. I'm going out.'

'Don't!' The humble boy's head was nodding. 'I know what you do.'

'Stay here. Look at her. Write a poem. Get some sleep.' And with that the proud boy ran up a flight of tea-and-gold coloured stairs, and was gone.

'What do you know about pregnant women, Uncle? What can you tell me about childbirth?'

The late winter sunlight lanced off the golden dome of the Museum of Atheism and reflected from the icy crystals of Uncle Yevgeny's eyes. The effect was one of the remarkable iridescence. 'I don't care about pregnant women,' Yevgeny wept. 'Look what they did to my leg.'

Leo glanced down and winced. Someone had amputated Yevgeny's left leg at the knee. Neither was the amputation a surgical operation. The job had been performed frantically, perhaps with an axe.

'You won't be needing it, Uncle. You're not going anywhere.'

'It's not right.'

'I've got more important things to worry about. What can you tell me of childbirth?'

'What do I know? Have your boot laces ready.'

'My boot laces? What for?'

'You'll figure it out.'

'You're an old shit, Uncle. You know that? A frozen turd.' Leo stood behind the corpse of his uncle and sniffed. Still no signs of decomposition. He aligned himself with Yevgeny's view of the Museum of Atheism. 'What do you see there? Tell me what you see every day.'

'I see Isaac.'

'Who?'

'You're an ignorant little communist-reared brat. That is the cathedral of St Isaac. I see the saint rising out of the dome, an inch at a time. One day it will be a cathedral again. Oh, my leg! My leg!'

When he returned to the house his small fire was winking out in the grate. He fed it the last of his fuel and tossed whatever he'd found into the pot. He was shivering with exhaustion, and knew that he had to find a way to keep both of them warm. Stripping off his own damp clothes he climbed into bed beside the skinny woman. She was the first woman he'd ever seen naked, and she was not a pretty sight. Undernourished, feeble, sickly, skin hanging on bone and an ugly swollen belly like a pig's bladder. It was not an erotic experience for young Leo.

Finally he fell asleep, cradling her to him, trying to think warmth into her. He refused to let her die. He knew that if she died, then it would also be over for him. Once in the night he woke up and thought she had finally let her spirit go, but no, she breathed again. The wind outside moaned and complained at a soul dropped in transit, a spirit fumbled, but the woman had chosen to come back to him. All through the night he rocked her, holding life into her, keeping her just centimetres from the dark precipice.

The next day the same. He washed her with hot water and trickled some of the meat broth – yes it was meat – into her mouth, and he fancied that he could see some colour coming back into her sore limbs. The second night he embraced her to him. This time he woke in the freezing night to find her arm locked tightly around him. Her clinch was unbreakable, but he knew that the impossible had been enacted: he had loved her back to life.

That next day something sparked in her eye, a brief flare, tiny, but in the cosmos of her iris a comet travelling across the loneliness of space. She took in his presence and looked about the room. She placed her hand on her belly to feel if the baby was still there, and seemed dismayed to find that it was. He gave her a little more broth, perhaps too much, or maybe it was too strong for her, because she vomited it up again.

'Come on,' he said, 'that's my best steak.' But she was too weak to smile, let alone answer. Her rejection of the food notwithstanding, after a week of tender nursing she was coming back to life.

Later he gave her more of the broth and this time she kept it down. Leo looked out of the window with satisfaction. Down in the smoky, tea-coloured, snow-shrouded street stood a boy in an army greatcoat bedecked with campaign medals. The boy waved back at him.

He had other things to worry about. The baby was about to arrive.

The girl shuddered and wept and uttered the name of some saint he'd never heard of. Then she spoke her first words to him. 'Go and get someone who knows what to do.'

'I'm your only hope,' he told her.

She cursed him. Her second words to him were a volley of filth. He'd never heard anyone speak quite that way, alternating between appeals to saints and demons. He didn't mind in the least: wasn't he her saviour? She groaned as a contraction came and he tried to comfort her with lines from one of his poems.

'Believe in the future, because the future for us is the present.'

She stopped groaning when she heard that, squeezing her eyelids together as if trying to focus on him. Then she threw back her head and cackled manically. Her laughter unnerved him. There came a scratching at the window, and there, outside in the dark, floated the doppelgänger-boy in his army greatcoat, shaking his head in dismay.

He ignored the apparition suspended at the window. 'Tell me what to do,' he said, 'because there's no one else.' In truth he could have gone to find some old woman to come and boil water and administer to the whole messy business, but he was committed. She was his, and the baby was his.

Yet he knew nothing of life other than what the siege had taught him. He knew how babies got to be where this one was, and he wouldn't have minded the opportunity to practise with someone to make another. But the business of how they emerged, or how to get them out . . . He was utterly ignorant.

But he had with him the blessed elixir, the divine poppy juice. Already schooled in its best effects, he let her sip tea from his flask in judicious doses, and though she still moaned with pain she was able to ride her contractions like a small boat on the barrel of a wave. A gelatine-like fluid formed over her eyes and her manner softened. 'What's in that tea?'

'Never mind that.'

She reached out a hand and tousled his hair. 'Whatever it is, you little runt, you're a fucking saint.'

He took a pull on the tea himself, and the first ten hours was easy enough. He swabbed her and held her hand. He recited lines which he told her soared from the pen of the boy-poet. She tolerated this for a while until she exploded from within her opium cocoon to protest, 'Give it a rest, will you?'

'I thought the words of the boy-poet would be a comfort to you.'

'That radio-fuck? I hate the whining little milksop. I always have hated him – him and his piss-quick doggerel. I can't believe you remembered his words just to bring them to my maternal bed! What fucking abominable luck! In the name of Judas give it a rest!'

'Don't you like poetry?'

'Fuck! Jesus and Judas! Mary's milk! Not another line, please!'

'Fine. I won't say any more.'

She was the first person he'd met ever to claim open hostility to his free verse. It was a salutary lesson in literary criticism. But he had little time for authorial sulking, because her contractions increased and her waters broke.

'More tea, little brother, more tea!'

Like a tempted saint, he had so far managed to keep his eyes averted from her vagina. Now as she drew up her knees and opened it to him, he was terrified. It was as if he'd secretly hoped that the baby might be spewed up from her mouth, but as he squinted in horror at her distended labia he felt he was peering at the Gates of

Life: smooth, living and pulsating pillars of pink, mottled porphyry, veined with marble and grown around with a rampant ivy. It was the notion of what lay within or behind these gates that intimidated him, for he knew that they gave passage into a shadowy damp cavern glistening with the mercurial rivulet, the herald trickle, and that the cavern itself gave way to a roaring cosmos in which solar blizzards buffeted and shrieked with cold hard energy and blinding starlight. He backed away.

But the baby was coming, and he was gripped with an irrational terror that when it arrived it would be demonic, but resembling him exactly, fully formed at his present age and that there would be an exchange of souls where he would have to take the baby's place sheltering in that solar blizzard of energy, waiting for the next opportunity to be born.

He saw a purple bulge appear, and there and then he made a prayer and a poem and a dedication and a promise on that baby's head and on the safety of his own soul that he would spend the rest of his life devoted to doing good. How was he to know it wasn't the baby's head he was looking at, but the distended tissues of vagina and anus. He'd sworn his most profound and dizzying oath on the spare flesh of an arse and a cunt.

But the baby did come, and when it did it shot out of her and right into his hands, milky with vernix. It was so slippery he almost dropped it. The energy blizzard, the shrieking of the raw cosmos behind the Gates of Life, got louder in his ears. He hadn't been prepared for the baby's colour, which matched the tone of Uncle Yevgeny's cadaver; or for the slightly conical head, which, even as he stared at it, seemed to be resetting in orthodox fashion; or for the small black lakes of its eyes which fixed on him and blinked with unconvincing cinematic animation. Moreover there was a membrane on the baby's face, a caul. It didn't seem right and, instincts taking over, he stripped the caul away with his fingers.

The woman lay groaning on the bed. He knew that the umbilical cord couldn't stay there holding the two together so he plunged his knife in some water he had boiling and made to chop it.

'Not yet!' she panted.

He waited. The afterbirth eventually slithered out like a sack of blood and tripe. The shrieking and roaring from the aperture of life went on unabated, louder even.

'Tie the cord in two places,' she said above the noise he was hearing. 'Where is your string?'

String was the last thing he'd thought of. String was for preparing parcels for the post office, not for equipping babies for life. Then he remembered something Uncle Yevgeny said, and he unlaced his boots.

'Tight,' she said, 'tie it really tight.'

He tied one of his laces near the baby's abdomen and the other further down the umbilical cord. She motioned that he should cut. He cut, and the shrieking stopped. But for the breathing of the new mother, and the soft feathering of snow at the window, there was no sound. He held the baby in his arms and it blinked at him with an expression of perplexed relief.

'What is it?' the woman wanted to know.

He looked at its blue-grey skin, its bruised head, and said, 'What do you mean?'

'Is there anything between its legs, you fool?'

He peered hard, and for a long time. 'Only the usual.'

She laughed hard, and sat up. 'Give me the baby. Here. It's a boy.' She fell back laughing, holding the baby to her breast. 'Only the usual.'

Leo was shocked by the sound of laughter. He couldn't remember when last he'd heard it. He too laughed, and he ran to the window, opening it to the soft billows of snow. 'May I, Leo Shapoval,' he shouted joyfully to the dark street, 'announce Only The Usual.' Then he closed the window again.

But the laughter stopped for both of them, because there was more to do. 'I must get clean,' she said.

The maternal bed was a hideous mess. Leo stared at the sack of afterbirth, almost as big as the baby itself. Perhaps it was because she was starving, or maybe she knew it was good for her: whatever, she stuck her hand into the afterbirth and stuffed some of it into her mouth, gagging on it at first, but then swallowing. It made Leo want to vomit, but she didn't even seem to think about it as she wolfed down another handful of the stuff.

After she'd told him to dispose of the rest of the placenta, he cleaned them both. First the baby, which he wrapped in one of his mother's traditional babushka scarves he'd brought from the house. Then he cleaned up the mother. She'd had a bowel movement during the delivery and the blankets were soiled with blood and shit.

'Pretty messy,' he said.

'You try it sometime.'

'I'm not criticising. I was just thinking: it's a pity everyone can't be a mature witness to their own birth. After all the shit and blood, everything from this moment on is progress.'

She looked at him hard, and stroked his cheek. 'You're all right, kid. I don't know who the hell you are, but you're my guardian angel. Thank you, Heavenly Father, for sending him! What did you say your name was?'

'I'm Leo. Are you of a religious bent?'

'I'm Natasha. I think we should call this baby after you.'

He looked at the babushka-wrapped miracle of warmth and breath. He was beautiful. 'Can we call him Isaac?'

'Sure we can. Isaac. What day is it? Do you know? Does anyone still know?'

He had to thumb through his notebook to work it out. 'It is December 21st.'

'Longest night. Now the days will get longer and the nights will get shorter. Leo, I feel our luck is changing.'

She made him keep the caul.

Leo could see that Natasha was a very rough kind of woman, hard-bitten and coarse-mouthed, even at her young age. But all that counted for nothing. Natasha was his sleeping princess. She was the property of fable.

'Who are you, Leo?' she asked him repeatedly.

'Can't you see it doesn't matter who I am? I've brought both you and the child back from the brink. Together we have cheated death!'

'Listen, Leo. I'm going to have to disappoint you now. I'm afraid you've saved a whore and a whore's brat. Do you know what a whore is? It means you've saved less than nothing.'

'Nonsense!' he cried. 'It doesn't matter what you were before the war. The past is all aflame. The march of future will be our present – '

'Fuck the saints! Will you please stop speaking to me in poetry! I can't stand it!'

'What I mean is, things can be different now.'

'You're young. Very young.' The baby started to cry. 'Look, Isaac can't get enough milk. I'm not strong enough to be a mother to him.'

Leo looked across the room. There his doppelgänger waited, nodding his head. 'I'm going out to get something to eat. You'll be all right.'

'Promise you'll come back, Leo? Promise?'

'I promise.'

Leo went directly from there to the Haymarket vendors. Patties were still on sale at mythical prices. Natasha had told him to take the caul with him.

'What on earth for?'

'If you put it about that you have a baby's caul, someone might give you something for it. It's considered good luck, especially to the sailors. They believe it's a charm to prevent them from drowning.'

But no one was much interested in a caul. The fat, soft-skinned spivs looked at him with contempt, wrinkling their noses. One bald-headed trader of expensive furs and shrunken beetroots leered at him. He had the eyes of a dead fish. 'But a good-looking boy like you can always earn himself a patty in five minutes.'

'How?'

The spiv stuck out a blue slug of a tongue, waggling it lasciviously.

'Fuck your mother on a dark grave,' shouted Leo's doppelgänger from over his shoulder. The fat spiv only shrugged and stamped his feet against the cold.

Leo made his way to Uncle Yevgeny's. Someone had made a fire in the downstairs doorway. He had to step over the wet ashes. 'Ho, Uncle,' he cried, when he got upstairs. 'You don't look too good.'

'My arm is gone,' Yevgeny protested. 'And how am I suppose to balance if I lose my other leg?'

'Hey, that reminds me. Your advice about boot laces. Came in very handy. Got any more tips about child-raising?'

'Drown them at birth. They'll never do you any good. One day they'll break your heart.'

Leo put his nose close to Yevgeny's neck. 'Oh! I do believe you are finally on the turn, Uncle. You'll be no good to anyone. Still, it was good while it lasted. I wonder what changed.'

'They burned the door, downstairs. It affected the through-draft.'

'Why are you talking to a stiff?' asked the doppelgänger.

'He's a better conversationalist now than he ever used to be,' Leo protested.

'Hey! Less of the abuse!' growled Yevgeny.

'It makes me sick to hear you chattering away to a decomposing corpse.'

'I agree he's on the turn,' Leo said, 'but just occasionally he has a useful contribution to make.'

'Get what you came for and let's go.'

'Ow! My last leg!' Yevgeny shouted.

'Damn it, I cut myself,' Leo said.

'Get out of here,' said the doppelgänger. 'I'm going to torch the place.'

'Is that necessary?'

'Of course it is. With that front door burned off you don't know who's going to walk in and find this old bugger. There will be questions asked.'

'Before you go,' Yevgeny groaned, 'look in the drawer. Something for Natasha. Not that it will do you any good, for you're beyond all redemption.'

Leo opened the top drawer of the writing table. There were two books. One was a pre-revolutionary army-issue Bible. The other was the Comrade's Guide to Civic Duty. Leo took both. The doppelgänger was tearing up floorboards and stacking them under Yevgeny's chair. Leo got out. He was two hundred metres away before he turned and saw flames flickering in Yevgeny's apartment.

*

'Leo, you work wonders. You really are a saint. Where do you get all this? I've never eaten so well in months. Where do you get it from?'

'I made lots of contacts. People know me.'

Leo had moved Natasha and her baby out of the unsavoury Haymarket hovel and into the family home. In turn she cleaned the place thoroughly, made it more like the dwelling house it used to be. It was superior to anywhere she'd ever experienced, and she said so. He showed her his mother's best linen, and the silverware, and the samovar. 'You're too trusting,' she told him. 'Most whores would steal everything you've got.'

'So? Steal it. I've learned that I don't need any of it. Anyway, you're not like most whores.'

'What do you know, you little runt? Don't look at me that way! When I call you names it's a joke. Try to see it as a sign of affection. What exactly is in this broth we're eating?'

'Best steak.'

'So you keep telling me. Far be it from me to complain, Leo, you work miracles, but I think this time it's on the turn.'

'Shall I pour it away?'

'Are you crazy? We might not see the like for another six months. I only make the observation. And now my milk has come in properly Isaac is thriving. It's just that I can't help being curious about where you go.'

'All right. There are rumours around that the ice road is proving more successful every week. The occasional truck gets through. I think I've noticed an improvement, but it's more than I dare to speak about.'

'The ice-road!'

The ice-road was almost mythical. A perilous fog-bound sheet of glass, forming, breaking, re-forming to allow the sporadic relief convoy to squeeze between the blockade, a finger of relief prised between the windpipe and the frigid Nazi death grip. Some doubted its existence; most believed, and in their minds the ice-road was supernatural in its manifestations, a plumed serpent dipping from between the stars of the galaxy, or an iridescent leviathan sinking beneath the ice and rising again. The need to believe in the supernatural was strong, a survival reflex deep in the group mind. Useless rationality itself was rotting, ready to fall away like the spare inch of umbilical cord days after a delivery.

'The ice-road!' Natasha whispered to suckling Isaac.

Leo shivered. If he was going to give her hope like this he was going to have to make the ice-road more successful.

Natasha turned to him. 'Do you know what day it is tomorrow?'

He shrugged. 'Wednesday maybe. Or Saturday.'

'I'm going to show you something. We'll go out.'

'You're not well enough to go out!'

'Yes I am. My strength is returning.'

The following evening Natasha wrapped Isaac against the cold. She insisted they go out during a bombardment. 'No one must see us. Let's go now the shelling is at its heaviest.' The guns pounded from the lines and the shells whistled softly as they pummelled the town. Natasha led Leo to a place near the Summer Palace.

She led him to a library he recognised, though without her revealing a downward flight of steps, he would never have known of the cellar beneath. She pushed open a door to reveal an untidy circle of people, each of whom held a lighted candle against the dank and dark of the cellar. They looked up instantly, and with frightened eyes.

'Natasha,' one of them breathed. 'It is Natasha! We thought you were dead!'

The group instantly relaxed, embracing Natasha in turn. There were four elderly men and seven or eight women of different ages. 'So few of us now!' Natasha said.

One of the elderly men spoke up. 'We don't know who is dead, or in whom the spirit has died,' he said, hugging her fondly, 'but it warms my heart to see you tonight.'

Leo hung back, holding little Isaac, until Natasha beckoned him forward to be introduced. They shook his hand or kissed him and fussed the baby as if it were the last infant on earth. 'He's one of us,' Natasha said of Leo proudly. 'He doesn't know it yet, but he's one of us.'

'What's that?' Leo wanted to know.

The oldest man, a patriarch called Nikoli with a forked, iron-grey beard said, 'I'm sorry but we don't have a lot of time. We would like to be through before the bombardment ends.' A lighted candle was thrust into Leo's hand and he found himself drawn into the circle. 'On this special night,' Nikoli intoned, 'we thank you for bringing your daughter Natasha back to us, for her son Isaac, and for our new brother Leo. Each new or refound soul is a grain of light in this dark place, added to the general store. We ask for strength in the coming trials.'

The group murmured an answer to this appeal and began to sing. For fear of being discovered they sang in very soft, muted tones, and words that Leo had never heard before, but which Natasha knew by heart. Then Leo noticed something strange happening. During the singing, one of the group put down her candle, leaving it to burn on the floor, and she left without a word. A few moments later another member of the group did the same, then another. Soon there was only Nikoli and Natasha singing, with Leo gazing dumbly on. When they'd finished, Nikoli said, 'You go now and I'll follow in a few minutes.' He began to extinguish the flickering candles with his thumb and forefinger.

'Tomorrow?' Natasha said.

'But of course tomorrow!' Nikoli answered with a grin, but in the orange candlelight Leo could see that his leathery face was lined beyond all care. Then Natasha was tugging his sleeve. They left silently and were halfway home before the bombardment ended.

'Fuck the saints, I'm freezing!' said Natasha when they got home, 'but wasn't it worth it?'

'What are they?' Leo asked. 'Some kind of devil-worshippers?'

Natasha's face fell. 'Are you joking?'

'Of course I'm joking. They're Christians, aren't they? As you are. I knew. Even though you said you were a whore.' A light died in her eye when he said that, so rather quickly he asked, 'How did you know they were going to be there?'

She smiled again. 'It's Christmas Eve, of course! You didn't know that. Why should you? It's a special day for us.'

'But I did know, in a way. Here, I brought something for you.'

Leo had wrapped Yevgeny's army-issue Bible in a silk scarf of his mother's. Natasha accepted the gift, but before unwrapping it she stared hard at Leo and then flung her arms around him, smothering him in kisses.

'Stop it! Stop it! You haven't opened it yet!'

'But it's Christmas, Leo; it's what people used to do at Christmas. They gave each other gifts, and I have nothing for you!'

'You already gave me Isaac! Open it!'

She unwrapped the silk and her jaw dropped. She stroked the cheap binding, turned the Bible over and over, as if it were hot to hold. 'You know the trouble you could get into for having this?'

'I can't see why. I had a quick look at it, and it didn't seem to make much sense.'

'Where did you get it?'

Leo didn't have time to answer because there came a hammering on the door. Leo was paralysed. It had been so long since anyone had knocked upon his door that he didn't know what to do. Then Natasha lifted up her skirts and, almost by sleight of hand, spirited the small Bible away.

Leo moved to answer the door, opening it just a crack. Outside was a military man in a greatcoat. He wore a seaman's cap. 'Are you Leo Shapoval?'

'Yes.'

'I heard you've got a caul.'

He led the sailor inside and introduced him to Natasha. Leo spotted a movement in Natasha's eyes when she saw the man, but thought little of it. The sailor had overheard that a young boy had been trying to sell a caul in the Haymarket. He'd traced Leo here.

'We never see sailors these days,' Leo said.

'I got sick leave. Got a ride in a truck that came through the ice-road,' said the sailor.

'The ice-road,' Natasha murmured to Isaac. 'So it is true.' She seemed to bury her head in her baby's clothes.

'It's getting easier to break through,' said the sailor. 'Look, I don't have much money, but I can offer a few things.' He produced from his duffle-bag two apples, a tin of corned beef, a packet of dried figs and a bar of chocolate. What do you say?'

'Wow!' said Leo. 'I'd say we accept. Natasha?'

Natasha turned her face to the sailor for the first time. 'Of course we accept,' she said boldly.

Leo got the caul and gave it to the sailor, who held it in his hand as if it were a crystal in which he could see a dry future. Then he prepared to go, but before doing so he turned to Natasha. 'Have we met before?'

'No,' said Natasha, too firmly. 'We have never met before.'

The sailor coloured. 'My mistake. I'll be on my way. Thank you for the caul. May you all survive.'

Leo saw the sailor to the door. When he returned Natasha was strangely quiet. Her eyes carried the inward stare. 'God bless all the sailors,' she said. 'God bless the ships at sea. God bless all the men who have sailed in me.' Then she wept.

Leo, understanding none of this, said, 'Hey, sister! No need to cry! We've got all these good things the sailor brought. We've got each other. We've got Isaac!'

But that only caused great shuddering sobs to wrack her body. 'Are we in hell, Leo? Have we done bad things? I have been so wicked in my life.'

'We're all of us selfish, Natasha. All of us.'

Natasha sobs became hideously mixed up with laughter. 'You! You're a saint, Leo! A fucking angel! That's what upsets me so. I don't deserve you. If God has chosen to send me an angel then I must be so deep in hell that He is afraid I will never get out.'

'But I'm not an angel. And I don't believe in God.'

'But you're more of a Christian than any of them! If you have a coat, you give it away. You feed others before you feed yourself. You wander the scorched earth looking to do good. You go out of your way to help vile rubbish like myself.'

'Don't say that! I won't hear it!' Leo was on his feet. Now it was his eyes that were wet.

'I'm sorry. Come here, let me hold you.' Leo submitted his head to be cradled by her free arm. Isaac seemed to stare at him wide-eyed from his position at the other breast. 'Shall I tell you why I believe? The communists hate a whore. They said I was the worst kind, the original capitalist parasite. We won't mention that Lenin was a frequent punter at the Leningrad brothels; and I could tell you things I've heard about Uncle Joe Stalin that would make your skin crawl. And I spent two years in a re-education camp, with my head shaved, where my communist mentors called for my services in the night. One of my educators lectured us about the fetish-value of gold in a capitalist society during the day. At night he would make me wear a pair of golden high-heeled sandals. He always asked me how much I used to charge men in my old life. Then the pig would bend me over the table. Yes, it was quite a re-education. My arse would be so sore and he had me repeat over and over, "M-C-M" and "C+V+S" and all those things. Do you know what it means?'

'Not really.' Leo had become subdued. She stroked his hair.

'Something about surplus value and commodities. I never understood why they wanted us to know all that. But anyway it was at the camp that I met a woman, there to be re-educated because she was a Christian. She told me that Jesus loved whores and had a special place in his heart for a slut in the Bible called Mary Magdalene.

'She told me many things. She didn't need a Bible, it was all engraved word for word in her heart. We used to say "JC+MM=L". Love. We had private communion where she showed me how to eat the body and the blood of Jesus.'

Leo's ears pricked up. 'You did what?'

'We ate the body of Jesus. It's called Holy Communion. Tomorrow I will take you back to that place and we will all take the communion together. What's the matter, Leo, you look strange.'

Leo got up and filled the samovar with water. He had a hundred questions, but he couldn't ask any of them. 'Nothing. My stomach hurts. I'm going to make some special tea.'

'I thought you never would.'

The next day, being Christmas Day, there was no shelling. The haphazard deity of The Whistling Shell gave way to the discriminating God of The Middle-Eastern Shepherd Cult, but it gave the citizens of Leningrad no peace, because all day long they assumed it was a German trick, a ruse, a feint. The Hun, they were certain, would be sure to punish the communists for their atheism by slipping in a few mortars at the exact moment of the putative saviour's birth. Though even this was problematic since the despised and deposed Eastern Orthodoxy decreed that the saviour had sprung from his mother's virgin loins at precisely twenty minutes before six in the morning, whereas the Catholic or Calvinist Germans were rather more vague about the exact moment in which an unending ray of light entered this world.

They didn't seem to think it might have been twenty to six, Leo considered, since he was awake at that hour, and all was quiet. He'd been unable to sleep since Natasha had told him that they were to spend the day gorging on the cadaver of the saviour, if he had understood things right. But Natasha had also told him that the Germans, being not of Eastern Orthodox persuasion in these matters, had a looser idea about the exact moment of the nativity. That, it seemed, was more in line with his notion of the random dispensations of The Whistling Shell. Lying awake in bed that Christmas morning, his mind was already turning on a synthesis of the two creeds, one in which The Whistling Shell was sucked into the bosom of the suffering servant in an act of supreme sacrifice.

As he understood things from Natasha, there was the Father, the Son and the Holy Ghost. The first of these two were pretty damned clear, but the last figure in the trinity was a much more shadowy identity. Could this have been another name for the Kruppsteel God of The Whistling Shell? The point about the indiscriminate proclivities of The Whistling Shell was that in its dispensations it also triggered the random acts of kindness which motivated Leo in his wanderings throughout the city. Perhaps this could be rendered as a Marxist-style formula: F+S+WS. He was unsure. He would have to ask Natasha, who knew more about these things.

He became aware that Natasha, lying next to him, was awake and looking at him. Isaac, snug and warm between the two of them, slept on. 'What are you thinking?' Natasha asked. 'You are always thinking!'

Leo was about to answer, but she placed a finger on his lips. 'Never mind. I want to say something. In the night I woke and I cried because I had no gift to give you on Christmas Day. You, who have given me life, and my son's life, and your constant care and love. Why, you even troubled in all of this to find me a precious Bible. And I have nothing to return.'

'It doesn't matter.'

'Shhh! Let me speak. It was then, in the night, that I remembered I do have something very special to give you after all.'

She lifted Isaac, still sleeping, from between their bodies and laid him at the foot of the bed. Then she turned to him, her grey eyes like woodsmoke.

'What?' Leo said. 'Why are you looking at me like that?'

She kissed him. 'You're so sweet, Leo. You don't even know what it's for.' She reached down under the blankets and gently closed her fingers around his cock. He flinched immediately, but she held on to him. His breath came short as his cock started to fatten in her hand. 'See, Leo? You only need a little help.'

He was speechless as she teased him to full erection. 'I'm too sore and damaged from giving birth to Isaac,' she whispered, 'but there is some other thing I can do for you.'

Natasha planted a row of kisses down his chest. There was a cloying perfume that made him think, inexplicably, of dark orchids in the glasshouses of the State Horticultural Institute. He yelped when she slipped his cock into her mouth, thinking she must surely be planning to bite it off; perhaps as part of her perverse communions and body-eating rituals. But she stopped what she was doing, reassured him, stroked his cheek tenderly before resuming. It was while he shuddered, wide-eyed with pleasure and terror, that across the room he saw the doppelgänger, a shivering, ice-clung, hoar-crusted boy gazing back at him, astonished, incredulous.

Ignoring the doppelgänger he closed his eyes, abandoning himself to her. She was like an orange flame burning on a landscape of snow as she worked away; her mouth like a hot wind around an ice-fountain. And then he heard it. Or perhaps he only thought he heard it. One solitary whistling shell, falling softly from the sky, slow and drawn-out as it tumbled from the vortex of heaven, trilling and piping in the cold air until, in a sudden, tumultuous acceleration, it exploded in the street outside. Leo opened his eyes momentarily, to see the blast suck the doppelgänger clean out of the window.

The congregation had one or two less for the Christmas Day service than had been present for the previous evening's ceremony. The sense of disappointment was palpable. The patriarchal Nikoli referred to it in his informal talk. 'What can we do? They're starving, they're sick. Just to find the energy to move around consumes all their reserves. We'll pray for them.'

And after a prayer Nikoli said, 'Perhaps we are, all of us, being tested. Perhaps all of our suffering is a test, just as our Saviour was tested with suffering. Perhaps God wants to know how many of us will fall when so tested. And how tempting it is, under the burden of our suffering, to take the easy way, to want to steal, to cheat, to lie if it advantages us in some small way. Perhaps God needs to know what we are made of, deep down; to see who can still walk in the narrow beam of light our Saviour introduced into this dark world.

'But only think of this, brothers and sisters! How God will remember; and how we will remember for all our lives, the ones who, having so little, give freely of what little they have. Because he who can come through this test without falling, he will banquet for ever at the table of the Lord.'

Then Nikoli produced a silver chalice in which there was a spot of sour cloudberry wine, and a silver salver bearing few crumbs of bread. 'The body and the blood,' said Nikoli. 'Come forward those of you who will take communion.'

On their way home Leo had to point out that it wasn't really the blood and body of Christ which they had consumed.

'But it was!' Natasha explained. 'That is the miracle of communion. That horrible old cloudberry vinegar, and those stale scraps of bread, Leo, they were transformed into the real thing by our faith and by our love. The miracle is called transubstantiation.'

'It certainly didn't taste like the real thing.'

'What?'

'And tell me something else, Natasha,' Leo said quite seriously. 'What you did to me this morning. Was that transubstantiation?'

Natasha shrieked. 'That was a Natasha special. And it was our secret, okay? I don't think you should mention it to Nikoli and the others.'

Leo looked baffled. 'If you insist.'

'I do. I do insist. If you want me to do it to you again.'

'I do. I do quite want you to do it again.'

And that evening, that Christmas evening after she had indeed done it to him again, she stroked his hair and said, 'It upset me today, to see so few people gathered together to celebrate the birth of our saviour. I know I shouldn't ask you, Leo. I've noticed that food has been a little scarcer these last few days, and it seems to me you already perform miracles. But those people stayed away today only because they are suffering so badly. I just wondered if there was any way we could help them.'

Leo lay with his eyes closed, glistening with sweat, recovering, considering Natasha's request. Truth was he had already decided upon a course of action. 'Tomorrow,' he said decisively, 'I will go out, and I will see what I can get.'

Natasha kissed him.

Fortified by some of Yevgeny's tea he went out the next day, to the Haymarket. The same unsavoury tangle of spivs were gathered there, dealing in patties and onions and wizened beetroots. Leo walked past the sparse stalls a few times. The fat spivs eyed him sourly, stamping their feet against the cold, snuggling into their furs.

Leo retreated from the scene, finding a bombed-out shell of a bakery where he could sit and gather his thoughts. An open oven gaped, as if in surprise and dismay at its sudden superannuation. The opium was strong and the umber-coloured Leningrad of mid-morning was filling up with antic staircases, along which dead boys ran and flitted from stairway to stairway like small birds in a gigantic aviary. Then the doppelgänger came clambering down one of the ghost staircases, wielding a spade.

'Where have you been? Haven't seen you in a while.'

The doppelgänger wasn't looking too good. He was suffering from scurvy, and his mouth was pustuled with a fresh outbreak of cold sores. His coat hung from his limbs in rags, and he had about him a gamy odour. 'What do you care? Are you going to wait about here all day or are you going to earn us a patty or two?'

Leo didn't answer. He felt nauseous.

'Well?'

'Don't rush me. I'll go in my own time.'

'Don't wait too long,' said the doppelgänger, disappearing further into the bombed-out building with his spade. 'I'll get started.'

Dispirited, Leo returned to the small circle of stall-holders. He sought out the furs-and-beetroot trader, who seemed to recognise him, and who thrust out that fat blue slug of a tongue. 'Looking for a sweet pattie, pretty rose?'

'No. I just want a few beetroots. And an onion if you've got any.'

The trader levitated his eyebrows in surprise, waggling them suggestively before nodding in the direction of a dark alley a few metres away.

'No,' Leo said. 'I don't want these others to see me go off with you. See that bombed-out bakery? Meet me up there in a few minutes.'

'If you insist, pretty rose.'

'And please bring my onion.'

Leo dragged himself to the appointed place. It was a long walk, and the dirty compacted snow squeaked under his feet. He had to pass a burned-out tram car, its twisted, rusting frame like the skeleton of some fantastic beast. He took up position in the shadows of the bakery. Hiding in the oven, the doppelgänger flashed a shard of mirror at him in signal of readiness.

'It's not that they're not grateful,' Natasha cooed in his ear. 'It's just that they keep asking me how you do it. None of them have seen a beetroot or an onion in months, let alone all this. And such a wonderful stew! They keep asking me and what should I tell them?'

Leo had instructed Nikoli to gather together the underground faithful, particularly those who were hungry and suffering. He'd specified that they should bring a vessel, and that he would feed them. A congregation larger than usual turned out and Nikoli had conducted his candlelit service, after which Leo produced a vat of stew, dispensing equal and generous measures to everyone. He was disappointed that Nikoli hadn't incorporated this apportionment into the service, but he said nothing.

Natasha was insistent. 'They're all saying you work miracles, Leo.'

'It's not miracles.'

'But what shall I say to them when they ask what it is they're eating?'

'Say, "Best steak!" and don't wink.'

'I can't keep doing that! It's wearing thin.'

Leo dragged her aside and whispered harshly, 'What do you want to tell them? That what they're stuffing into their mouths is a putrid and decomposing rat chopped up with one of last year's beetroots? Tell them. Go on. See how that salts it for them.'

But Natasha had savoured rattus norvegicus more than once in the days before Leo stumbled into her life. She knew all its culinary limitations. 'Don't be angry, Leo. You work wonders. Everybody says so.'

But Natasha couldn't let the matter drop. The problem was that she was a true economist. It wasn't the Communist Party re-education camps who had imparted to her the universal laws governing the distribution, exchange and consumption of goods or the principles of surplus value; it was her career as a prostitute. Whoredom was a schooling based not on the classical laws of Diminishing Returns, but on the neoclassical tradition of Marginal Utility. Put another way, she knew the price of a fuck, and from that principle, asserted the neoclassical school of Whoring Economics, it was possible to calculate the price of everything.

Watching Leo dose himself with the dwindling resource of Uncle Yevgeny's tea made her think of her sisters of commerce fortifying themselves with vodka before an evening's work. It had crossed her mind several times that Leo was going out and whoring himself, but she knew that even the Tsar's courtesans couldn't have done this well in such conditions. So, swathing Isaac in blankets, she resolved one day to follow Leo.

The uncertain hour of The Whistling Shell was always Leo's favourite time for a foray, and at whatever time it came. Just like the underground Christian circle, his activities were protected by enemy fire. The sound of the first soft hooting of shells was to him like a peal of bells or the call of the adhan, and on this day the German bombardiers wound their timepieces for a noon invocation of the Kruppsteel God. With shells detonating about the city he went out, evidently without fear. She followed his slightly unsteady gait as he trudged the blackened snow along the street in the direction of the Haymarket.

He had no idea she was following him. He never looked back. Indeed, he seemed oblivious even to the bombardment going on, and instead of turning his head in the direction of this or that explosion, his eyes seemed to move up and down the vertical structures of the tallest Leningrad buildings, as if tracking someone moving among the parapets and the rooftops. Natasha's heart squeezed for him, this tender, distracted boy. At that point she almost went home, knowing from experience and intuition that she might find something here that would destroy their precarious and singular time together. He'd already delivered her from a world where no one asked another's business, where one learned to look the other way, where one remembered to forget instantly; and not because the truth couldn't be guessed at, but because it could. But she didn't turn back. He was too much of an enigma, this Leo, and she had to find out where he went.

Squeezing Isaac tight to her chest, Natasha followed him across the city for half an hour, until he reached the Haymarket. She had to duck into a doorway when, for the first time, he glanced around furtively. He didn't see her, she was certain, and she was more careful when she followed him into the charred wood and twisted steel wreckage of an old bakery.

Loitering behind a blackened pillar she watched him uncover a spade. He began scraping at the snow, but what puzzled Natasha was the argument he conducted with some unseen person. The dispute was acrimonious, and Natasha peered round her charred pillar to look for Leo's adversary, but she could see no one. Her heart quickened when she realised Leo was in dispute with none other than himself.

Leo remonstrated bitterly, working all the while, chipping with his spade at the hard-packed ice. After a while he tossed away the spade and produced a small hacksaw from his pocket, applying it energetically to some object buried in the ground. Leo cut a leathery slice free of the packed snow and rammed it into his coat pocket before returning to his hacksawing with renewed frenzy. Natasha crept up slowly behind him.

At first Natasha couldn't identify the object in the ground. Even when it became plain that it was a man, buried on his side in the snow, she wasn't able to reconcile the evidence of her eyes. The hacksaw was digging into the cadaver for a choice cut of rump. Natasha could see that the partially uncovered head wore, at the throat, a frayed ruff of dark and dirty ice.

At that moment Isaac chose to sneeze, and to let out a bleat of protest. Leo stopped sawing, and turned slowly. He tried to smile at Natasha, looking like a guilty child, wanting but failing to ingratiate.

Natasha sank to her knees. 'Is this how you saved us? Isaac and me? Is this how?'

Leo flicked his fringe from his eye. Natasha fell forward, her elbows in the snow, gagging without vomiting. She let Isaac slip from her grasp, as if he was befouled. Leo went to collect him up.

'Don't touch him!' Natasha screamed. 'Don't you lay a finger on him!' She gathered up her child and staggered away, slipping on the ice, falling on one knee, scrambling to put a distance between herself and the abominable Leo. 'Don't come near us again! Don't you ever!'

The shellburst had ended. Leo slumped in the burned-out bakery, staring into the black maw of the brick oven. A slack line of dead electric cable hung over his head, suspended between the broken walls, and the doppelgänger lay stretched comfortably along its length, hands clasped lightly behind his head. 'That's torn it,' said the doppelgänger.

'She hates me now.'

'You can do no good,' the doppelgänger said in Uncle Yevgeny's voice. 'Don't try to do good.'

'What will I do?'

'Survive. You must survive.'

'Go to hell,' Leo said, and the doppelgänger faded very slowly in the freezing air.

Leo stayed for a long time in the bombed-out bakery, amidst the charred wood and twisted metal, trying to puzzle things out. Perhaps Uncle Yevgeny and the doppelgänger were right, perhaps he should never have tried to do good. In doing good on a purely random basis, with no expectation of returned favour, he had attempted to act as an antidote to the random dispensations of The Whistling Shell. And for a while that had worked, and he was happy. But then selfishness had crept in, along with vanity and pride. When he had saved Natasha and Isaac from certain extinction, he had been too quick to gather up the rewards available in Natasha's love and respect, and within the boundless joys nesting in the cries and the gurgles of baby Isaac. From those two, and in the potential happiness of those two, he had taken his own happiness, and that, he knew, was where he had made his mistake.

For he had stolen Natasha and Isaac from the hungry God of The Whistling Shell. He had saved souls he had no right to save. The Kruppsteel God of The Whistling Shell was an indifferent God, and had forgiven him once, for the soul of Natasha, and twice, for the soul of Isaac. And The Whistling Shell had even fed him and those around him, had it not? But what The Whistling Shell could not forgive was desertion into the arms of another God, the jealous and cannibalistic God of the Christians. The feeding of the followers of this other God had made the God of The Whistling Shell angry. How could Leo ever make things right again? How could he ever restore faith?

As Leo brooded in that dark and icy place, the German gunners slipped in one of their random bursts of fire. Leo heard the single shell whistling softly, so softly it seemed to describe an illumined arc on its long trajectory through the freezing sky. Leo heard the whistle falter, waiting for the crump of explosion. But the shell, having landed, had failed to detonate. Instead it left an eerie silence, almost a vacuum, which was filled with whispered words. 'Give me Isaac,' it said. 'Your only son.'

Leo returned to his house. Natasha and Isaac were not there. The house echoed in their absence. Natasha had taken nothing which did not belong to her. All of the gifts of his mother's clothes and jewellery which Leo had made to her remained in the house. So too did Yevgeny's army-issue Bible, bookmarked by Natasha no deeper than a page of Genesis.

Leo waited three days for Natasha to come home. On the third night, dithering until the hour before dawn, he went back to look in the hideous apartment where he'd first found her. Silently he ascended the broken stairway, creeping into the room. She was there, lying on the bed under rank, coarse blankets, sleeping heavily. A muscular figure lay next to her, snoring. A sailor's cap hung on a nail on the wall. In a crib made in a chest of drawers, Isaac was awake. The baby seemed content, kicking his arms and legs. He gurgled happily as Leo lifted him out of the improvised crib.

Careful not to disturb the sleepers, Leo crossed the room without a sound, taking the baby with him.

Dawn was breaking, pearly-grey and tea-brown, as he walked through the streets clutching Isaac to his chest. Before he'd walked a quarter mile, he heard the first salvo of a German wake-up call. The shell was still whistling, this morning with a slight trill as its fins baffled the air currents, as Leo looked up saying, 'O thank you. I knew you would come.'

The first shell exploded somewhere near the Admiralty tower, followed by a series of muffled reports in the same vicinity. Leo made his way to Uprising Square and along Nevsky Prospect, hurrying towards the thick of the bombardment. A pale winter sun was climbing to the east of the Admiralty tower, flaring on the debris kicked up by the shell blasts, making dust fountains and ragged sculptures of floating ash. One building that had already taken a hit in a previous bombardment was on fire. Shells rained down ahead, some exploding, others failing to detonate in the deserted street. It seemed to him that more and more of the German shells were failing the longer the campaign went on. Leo saw another three shells blast the front house of the old cinema. That being the place where the shells rained thickest, he crossed the street and carefully placed Isaac on the icy pavement outside the burning cinema. He himself sat cross-legged on the dirty ice, and waited.

The barrage abated for a while, before resuming with increased ferocity, raining shells around them. Two buildings took direct hits; shards of scorching shrapnel went smoking and skidding across the icy road, but the main bombardment moved across Nevsky Prospect and settled at a distance of forty or fifty metres removed. Leo swept up Isaac and scurried towards the new target of the shells. One round came whistling in, thumping the elevation ten feet above his head, embedding itself in the concrete without detonating, the fins of the shell protruding from the wall like a cathedral gargoyle.

Neither he nor Isaac received so much as a scratch.

Again the locus of the barrage shifted, moving back across the road and up Nevsky Prospect towards the tower. Leo was furious. With buildings burning around him he ran into the smoke and dust fountains, his face blackened with soot, screaming at the metal storm, 'Here we are! Take him back! You can take him back!' His tears smudged on the soot of his face. 'Why don't you take the both of us?' he raged. 'Why won't you take us?'

But the bombardment shifted several degrees west of their position, and then the volleys ceased, quite suddenly. The only sound was of fires crackling and smouldering about him, and of dust and ash resettling on the ice pavements. He stood in the middle of Nevsky Prospect, hanging his head, and he knew it was over.

He knew it was over for everything: for God; for Communism; and for the smooth deity of The Whistling Shell. He knew now that The Whistling Shell in all its savage indifference didn't want Isaac back. Neither Isaac, nor Natasha, nor him in place of any of them. The Whistling Shell wasn't counting the corpses. It wasn't in the business of claiming souls, or balancing endless figures in infinite ledgers. The truth in this was quite horrendous. It meant that you could do good, and you could do bad, and even that you could try to do good by doing bad; but that nothing and no one could praise you or forgive you, but yourself.

It meant only this: that the purpose of a good life was a good life, and nothing more, nor less.

And as the smoke of bombardment cleared he looked about him and the innumerable staircases and ladders and flights of steps and platforms were diminishing, fading, closing down. The old Leningrad, the one from which he'd emerged, was reasserting itself.

It was a long walk back. People emerged from their houses to survey the latest damage. Men and women who would not be surprised by anything to be witnessed in the streets of Leningrad stopped to look at the ragged boy, tears streaming along his blackened cheeks, bearing in his arms a small baby.

He found Natasha in the streets near her hovel, who with Nikoli and some of the underground worshippers had come out to look for Leo. Natasha ran up and snatched Isaac from his arms, breathing a prayer of thanks that the child was unharmed. Nikoli stretched out a hand and touched Leo on the shoulder. The boy seemed not to see the old man.

'Does anyone know,' Leo said, 'the way to the front line?'

Natasha stepped forward, more than a little afraid of him. He didn't seem to recognise her. 'Leo, come back to us. I forgive you.'

'But can I forgive myself?'

'Whatever you have done,' said Nikoli, 'it can be addressed in Heaven.'

'You're wrong,' Leo said.

'Where are you going?' Natasha asked. 'What will you do?'

'It's time I got myself a gun. It's time I did the manly thing, and killed some Germans.'

They merely stared after Leo as he made his way out of the city, a small huddle of them watching in silence, with the sun turning a pallid yellow in the winter sky over Leningrad.

The fate of Leo Shapoval from that moment on is uncertain, though three stories circulate. One claims that he fought heroically in the lines, quickly becoming a young captain and from there, after changing his name, developed a career in the Communist Party. Another version suggested that he lasted mere days on the lines, and it was while recklessly leading a charge on the German lines that he was cut into a million pieces by the enemy machine guns. A third version insists that he survived the campaign and left the country in the confusion of the immediate post-war years, returning as a dissident, and that he was one of the architects of the overthrow of the Iron Curtain regime, dedicated to the renaming of his old city under a new administration.

I like to think the last version is true. Perhaps I want to think well of him, because, not knowing who my real father was, I think of him, Leo Shapoval, as my true father. He did after all give me life. And I only have the version of him told to me by my mother, his lover, Natasha. That and a photograph of Leo, taken before he had even met my mother, in which a young boy, perhaps a little too fat for his own good, smiles shyly into the camera, with no knowledge of the horrors foreshadowing him; and in which a strange and somewhat poetic curl of the lip seems to say to me across the years, 'What must you do? You must survive.'

james lovegrove

how the other half lives

One

It was another merely magnificent Monday in the life of William Ian North.

The chauffeur picked him up from the mansion punctually at seven fifteen a.m. and ferried him into the heart of London within a purring Daimler cocoon. In the back seat, North scanned the *FT* and checked the Nikkei Dow closing figures on the in-car terminal. The stereo played Wagner – operatic *Sturm und Drang* to get the heart pumping, the blood racing.

Arriving at the NorthStar International Building at eight thirty, North crossed the marble atrium and acknowledged the salutes of the uniformed guards at the security desk with a brisk nod. A private lift whisked him up twenty floors to an office the size of a ballroom, where a glass wall gave him a panoramic view of the City, its domes and dominions, edifices and empires all agleam in the new day's sun.

At his desk, whose calfskin-topped surface could have easily accommodated a kingsize mattress, North officiated all morning. He contacted various associates around the world via audiovisual telelink. For some of the people he was talking to, it was early evening; for others, the wee small hours of the morning. The time difference bothered neither him nor them. When William Ian North called you, it was at his convenience, not yours.

He brokered deals. He bought. He sold. He transferred from liquid to certificate and vice versa. He shifted between currencies. He invested. He disposed of. He topsliced and undercut. He creamed off and shored up. Across the planet, companies, industries, nations prospered or declined according to his dispensation. On a widescreen TV near his desk, tracker software registered the progress of the London market, describing the earth tremors of loss and gain as a wavering red line on a graph. The line seemed to respond to every one of North's decisions, every flex or contraction of his fiscal muscles.

He took lunch in the boardroom with a dozen of his immediate underlings. Business was not discussed, but every word North said, every nuance of every sentence he uttered, was listened to with the utmost attentiveness and later dissected and analysed, divined for hidden significance. As soon as the five-course meal concluded, one of the underlings was summoned to North's office and sacked for failing to meet her quotas. In truth, the woman had missed her mark by only the narrowest margin, but the occasional summary dismissal of an upper-echelon employee did wonders for the productivity of the rest of the workforce. 'It is thought well to kill an admiral from time to time,' as Voltaire said, 'to encourage the others.'

For half an hour North then rested, reclining supine on a velvet-upholstered chaise longue in a side-chamber of his office. Eyes closed, he sensed the thrum of activity emanating up from the building below. Beneath his back were a thousand people, each of them electronically connected to a thousand more, and all of them dedicated to a single task: that of augmenting the worldly wealth of William Ian North, inflating his already obscene capital value to yet greater heights of obscenity. He could feel them through layer upon layer of concrete and steel girder as they telephoned, tapped keyboards, made choices and calculations. For the most part he did not know their names; had no idea what they looked like. They were termites in a termitary, toiling frantically and anonymously on his behalf.

At three p.m. precisely, a staggeringly beautiful woman dressed in a crisp, short-skirted business suit was brought up to North's office by the chauffeur. This event occurred at the same hour every weekday. The woman was not always the same woman each time, but she was always unspeakably, apocalyptically gorgeous – in her field, the very best that money could afford. After the chauffeur made a discreet exit, the woman stripped bare and pleasured North on his desk. Then she dressed and departed, and North showered in his private bathroom, put on his suit again, along with a fresh shirt straight from the tailor's box, and resumed work.

By five, with the London market closed, North was ready to go home. Electronic memos had been squirted off to various foreign subsidiaries, giving advice on which holdings to keep an eye on, which to get rid of if they fell below a certain threshold, which to acquire if they rose above. There had been a small blip with a Latin American asset, nothing major, a depreciation of a few million, a drop in the ocean. Nevertheless, North demanded that an investigation be made into the loss and the person responsible disciplined. Apart from this, he left his office content that everything was running smoothly with NorthStar International and would continue to run smoothly overnight until he returned the following morning to pick up the reins once more.

The chauffeur drove him out of the darkening city, through the streams of red taillights, westwards into the sunset and the dusk-cloaked countryside. North thumbed through the *Evening Standard* and listened to Elgar. The music stirred nothing more in him than a vague sense of yearning, a knee-jerk nostalgia for a pastoral, idyllic England that never was. The newspaper was gossipy, simply written, undemanding.

By six thirty he was back at the mansion again. The chauffeur bade him goodnight and steered the Daimler back down the driveway to the lodge, where he would wash, wax and vacuum the car in readiness for tomorrow, then have supper with his wife and go out to the pub.

The domestic staff were long gone. A gourmet supper awaited North in the kitchen refrigerator, needing only to be heated up in the oven. North stood in his mansion, alone.

No, not quite alone.

In his study, he took a key from a hook attached to the mantelshelf above the fireplace. The key was long, black, iron, old-fashioned, solid. Clenched in North's fist, its teeth poked out one side of his fingers, its oval turnplate the other.

With the key, North went over to one of the bookcases that lined the study walls and tweaked a leather-bound volume of Dumas. The bookcase swung inwards to reveal a short, dusty passageway. North entered.

The bookcase automatically eased itself shut behind him as he strode the length of the passageway. He could reopen it by pressing a lever mounted on the wall beside its hinge mechanism. Arriving at a heavy wooden door at the far end of the passageway, he flicked a light switch. No light came on in the passageway, but from the other side of the door there was a muffled cry. Inserting the key into the lock, North turned it. A tumbler clunked chunkily. North grasped the door handle and rotated it. The door opened.

A vile stench gushed out through the doorway to greet him – an almost-visible miasma of awful odours. Faeces. Urine. Unwashed body. Stale, overbreathed air. Damp. Mildew. Blood. Despair. North recoiled involuntarily. Though he encountered the smell every day, he had never grown accustomed to it. He probably never would.

Breathing through his mouth, he passed through the door, closed and locked it behind him, then ventured down a flight of stone steps.

The room was fifteen feet by fifteen feet by fifteen feet, a windowless subterranean cube. The walls were whitewashed brick, the floor just plain brick. Illumination came from a single unshaded lightbulb wreathed in cobwebs and controlled solely by the switch outside.

Once upon a time this cellar had been used for cold storage. Now, in one corner there was a thin mattress, little more than a pallet really, its ticking patterned with countless stains, stains overlaying stains like jumbled continents on a map of a destroyed world. Beside the mattress there was a chamberpot draped with a square of teacloth. Next to that there was a half-used candle in a saucer, a water canteen, and an empty enamelware dish.

In the opposite corner someone crouched.

He was still just recognisably a human being. Tattered clothing hung on him like castoffs on a scarecrow. Bare, blackened feet protruded from the cuffs of what had once been a pair of designer jeans; a filthy Armani shirt clad a torso as bony as a dishrack. He was covering his eyes and snivelling. His fingernails, like those of his toes, were long, splintered and brown. The dark, straggly, matted hair on his head meshed with his dark, straggly, matted beard in such a way that it was impossible to tell where one ended and the other began. Rocking to and fro, the man huddled in the corner, trying to make himself as small as possible.

'Well, good evening again,' said North.

The man moaned and pressed his hands more tightly over his eyes.

'Look at me.'

Slowly, with reluctant obedience, the man parted his fingers slightly to form a lattice, through which he squinted up at North.

'Please,' he croaked.

'"Please"?' said North, tapping the door key up and down in his palm like a Victorian teacher with a ruler, sizing up a wayward pupil.

'Please don't,' said the man.

'Would that I had a choice,' said North, and, pocketing the key, stepped forwards.

The beating lasted five minutes. With the same imperious ruthlessness with which he pursued his financial affairs, North punched and kicked, slapped and struck, pounded and thumped. The man put up no resistance. The blows rained down, and he endured, crying out only when he was hit in a particularly tender spot, perhaps where an old contusion from a previous beating had not quite subsided or an old abrasion had not quite healed. He let the force of each impact knock him around wherever it would, rolling now this way, now that, making no effort to protect himself, for he knew that, whatever he did, North would always find a vulnerable area. If he tried to cover his belly, North would aim for his back; if he tried to shield his back, North would aim for his belly.

Eventually it ended, and North stepped away again, panting. There was blood on his knuckles, blood flecking his shoes. The man was coughing and gagging on the floor, writhing, fingers clawing at the slimy bricks.

'There we go,' said North, when he had got his breath back. He brushed his palms against each other. 'That's *that* over with for another day.' Tugging on his trousers creases, he squatted down so that his face was just a yard or so from the man's. 'You do understand how necessary all this is, don't you?'

Pink saliva bubbled between swollen lips.

'Look at me.'

North had been careful to stay clear of the man's eyes. They were the only part of him that he never hit.

The man's eyelids parted. Wincingly he peered up at his jailer and abuser.

North looked deep into his ice-blue irises. 'You *do* understand?' he insisted.

Painfully the man nodded.

North continued to gaze down on the man with his own ice-blue eyes. There was a long silence during which each beheld the other – the sharp, clean, expensively coiffed, smooth-shaven magnate and the unkempt, squalid, tangle-haired, mad-bearded prisoner. The face of one was tanned and flawless, the planes of its cheeks and chin well-delineated, its skin showing the evidence of weekly massaging and moisturising by a beautician; the face of the other was pallid, bruised, covered with sores, seamed with grime.

The moment of contact between the two men's matching eyes seemed to last for ever. Something passed between them, as it always did. Something that was like loathing but also like empathy.

Then North rose, and the man turned his head away.

North went to pick up the dish, canteen, and slopping chamberpot, and carried all three items up the steps. He unlocked and opened the door and went out, closing and locking the door behind him. A short while later he unlocked the door again and came back down with the chamberpot emptied out and wiped clean, the canteen refilled with water, and the dish laden with chunks of brown bread and cheese. The prisoner had not changed position in the interim. He was still sprawled on the floor, whimpering every now and then as various aches and agonies spasmed through him.

North set down the chamberpot, canteen and dish beside the mattress. Then he delved into his trouser pocket and produced a crimson-tipped universal match, which he placed in the candle's saucer.

'There,' he said. His voice was almost tender now. It was as if the violence of a few minutes earlier had drained him, purged him.

The man neither spoke nor moved. Quietly North withdrew from the room, closing the door one last time. Again, the key turned in the lock. A moment later the light clicked out and all was dark.

Two

An hour passed before the man stirred himself. Laboriously, hissing with pain, he levered himself up onto all-fours and began shuffling across the floor. When he reached the wall, he followed it round, groping, until he came to the food and water. He ate and drank in darkness. He was permitted only one candle a week, so he used it sparingly. He didn't need its light to be able to put bread into his mouth or lift the canteen to his lips.

Mr North had loosened a tooth again, so the man was obliged to chew on one side of his mouth. He finished almost all of the bread, leaving some for later, and ate about half the cheese. Sated, he crawled onto the mattress, curled up and fell asleep.

He was awoken some immeasurable period of time later by a brief, feathery tickling on the tip of his nose. His injured body had stiffened up while he slept. To straighten out his limbs and sit up was exquisite, rusty torture.

Carefully he reached out for the candle, and when his fingers found it, he ran them down its length until they encountered the match. Noises, from the same origin as the tickling on his nose, had started nearby – tiny claws tick-tacking on the enamelware dish, and a soft nibbling. Taking the match, he touched its head to the wall and scraped downwards.

On the third attempt, the match ignited.

In the flare of its flame, a pair of small black eyes glinted briefly, vanishing as their owner scuttled away into the dark. The man brought the match across to the candle. At first the candle refused to catch, and he held the rapidly depleting match to the wick with mounting anxiety. Then, just as his fingertips were starting to singe, the flame suddenly doubled in size, and he snatched the match away and extinguished it with a shake. The candle guttered indecisively for a few seconds, then began to burn with a strong, steady glow.

He scanned the room.

The rat was hunkered at the foot of the steps, just its nose and eyes showing. The man whistled softly, and with slow, tentative steps the rat came out from its hiding place and crossed towards him. Reaching the edge of the dish, where one of the smaller pieces of cheese already showed the marks of gnawing, the rat hesitated, as though awaiting permission.

'Not so bold now I can see you, eh?' said the man. 'Go on, help yourself.'

The rat snatched up the partially eaten piece of cheese in its forepaws, then settled back on its haunches and whittled the cheese down with its teeth until there was nothing left.

The man broke off another piece of cheese and held it out. The rat took the morsel from his hand and ate it under his approving gaze.

A third piece of cheese went the same way, and a fourth, and then the rat, evidently having eaten its fill, began washing itself, running its forepaws back and forth over its face and whiskers, licking and preening its dark-grey fur industriously.

Smiling, the man watched the rat at its ablutions. When it was done, he reached towards it very slowly, so as not to startle it, and stroked its back. The rat submitted to the attention happily. The man rejoiced in the sleek, velvety feel of the creature's fur and the warmth of its skinny body, remembering the first time the rat had let him touch it. How many months ago that had been, he could not recall, but he could remember vividly the sense of triumph he had felt – and the sense of relief, for on several of his previous attempts to stroke the rat he had received a bitten finger. Now the rat, though still timid, trusted him. It was his friend.

The man petted the rat until the ache of keeping his bruised, battered arm extended became too great to bear. He sat back on the mattress and rested for a while, and the rat crouched patiently on the floor, waiting for the next ritual of their regular candlelit meetings to commence. After the feeding came the drawing.

The man picked up the spent match and broke off its head, then revolved the curved, carbonised stem between thumb and forefinger until he had sharpened it to a point. Holding his makeshift pencil in his right hand, he turned to the rat.

'What'll it be today?'

The rat bristled its eyebrows and whiskers, regarding the man inquisitively with its bright black eyes.

'How about a tree? Haven't attempted one of those in a while.'

The rat did not demur, so the man set to sketching a tree with the match on the whitewashed brickwork of the wall.

The man did not know a time when he had not been a prisoner in this underground cell. As far as he was aware, he had always been here. For innumerable, interminable years he had lived in darkness – darkness interrupted once every twenty-four hours by the sudden blinding glare of light that presaged a visit from Mr North and a beating. The limits of his existence were this room, and continually renewed pain, and permanent misery.

But there were memories . . .

The man knew of things he had never seen. He dreamed of them sometimes. He could summon images of them into his head whenever he wanted.

Things like a man and a woman who could only be his father and mother. Like a house where he had been born and which he had called home. Like a school, and parks, and a town, and townspeople. Like books and television and radio. Like cars and buses and trains. Like hills – green, deep, and undulating. Like seas – green, deep, and undulating. Like winter and summer, autumn and spring. Like the sun and the moon. Like clouds and stars.

All these he could remember, could conjure up in his mind's eye – their colours, their textures, their smells. He knew what it was like to go on holiday and have picnics on the beach. He knew what it was like to sit indoors on a rainy day and listen to a piano being played. He knew what it was like to endure lessons in a classroom while outdoors was heat and sunshine, boundless freedom just a pane of glass away. He knew what it was like to attend college and partake of the hedonistic, last-gasp pleasures of student life. He knew what it was like to travel to work on a commuter express, jammed in a rickety, racketing carriage alongside dozens of men and women dressed, like him, in business suits. He knew what it was like to play squash and golf and tennis with workplace superiors, observing all the tactful laws of intra-hierarchy sports, defeating his opponents if he could, but stopping short of humiliating them. He knew what it was like to sink into the arms and loins of a sexual partner. He knew what it was like to work at a desk alongside other desk-workers and harbour ambition, nurture powerful dreams of success. He knew all these things as though they were parts of his own life.

Yet how could that be? How could he have these recollections, these impressions, these sensations lodged in his mind when he had never once set foot outside this room? The paradox troubled him, and sometimes he wished he did not have the memories at all, could just flush them clean out of his brain. For without them he would have no idea what he had been deprived of. Would not have the extra torment of knowing there was an existence beyond this harsh, wretched existence.

The tree he had decided to draw was an oak. With quick, deft strokes he etched its outline, thinking of an afternoon spent lying in an oak's shade, staring up into the radial splendour of its branches and seeing the sun dazzling through a complexity of rippled-edged leaves, casting shadows upon shadows, a myriad flickering shades of green. He did his best to capture the memory and majesty of the tree on the wall, but the match-pencil had a limited lifespan. Its charcoal was soon worn away and he had to abandon the drawing before he could complete it to his full satisfaction. Perhaps a tree had been a little ambitious. Hitherto he had usually confined himself to simpler objects, man-made ones more often than not – a car, a house, a chair. He had had a go at a willow once, but the drooping fronds had proved to be too much detail for his finite artistic materials.

Still, he was pleased with his effort. The drawn tree was inarguably oak-like, even if it was plainer and cruder than he would have wished.

He turned to the rat.

It was on the rat's behalf that the man had started doing the drawings in the first place. Had the rat never entered the cellar and his life, he would probably have never devised this form of entertainment. It was for the rat's benefit that he had originally taken a dead match and, in a spirit of light-hearted experimentation, dashed off a quick sketch on the wall – a rough, cartoonish representation of a rat. And he would probably have never repeated the experiment if the rat had not appeared so fascinated both by the act of drawing and by the finished product. The diversion had thereafter become a habit. Indeed, now, if ever the man for some reason failed to provide the rat with a daily picture – if, for instance, he could not get the candle to light, or Mr North had hurt his drawing hand so badly that he could not hold the match – then the rat would become agitated and register an angry protest, either by squeaking vociferously and scurrying around the cellar for several hours so that the man was prevented from getting to sleep, or by depositing a turd prominently in the middle of his food dish. The drawings, it seemed, were a source of solace to both of them. The man took pleasure in realising on the wall one of the intangible images that crowded his brain, while the rat took pleasure in –

In what, exactly?

It was unclear. It was obvious, though, that the rat did take pleasure in the drawings. Perhaps it derived its pleasure from the man's pleasure, through a sort of interspecies emotional osmosis. The man was unwilling to question the phenomenon too closely in case the act of querying robbed it of its magic. He was content to accept that he and the rat shared some kind of unspoken bond, and leave it at that.

The rat was eyeing the oak with all the beady attentiveness of a professional rodent art-critic. All at once, it dashed over to the wall and reared up, supporting itself with its forelegs, to sniff the picture all over, from the apex of the tree to the base of its trunk. Then it leaned round to look at the man. Its whiskers were fibrillating madly, reflecting the candle's flame as a golden shimmer.

The man stared back, curious. The rat showed more keenness about some of his pictures than others, but usually it was depictions of smaller objects that excited it. The man assumed this to be because the rat lived in a rat-proportioned world, where things that were small to humans loomed large in its perception and things that were large to humans were altogether too massive for its mind to encompass. In this instance, however, the rat had become worked up about something that was, by its standards, unfathomably immense. The rat never sniffed a picture unless it liked it. If it was unenthusiastic or indifferent, it would merely sit still, perhaps nod its head up and down contemplatively, perhaps twitch its whiskers once or twice. Today's offering, it seemed, had earned its artist full marks, ten out of ten, a big Double Gloucester on the cheese scale.

'Well, thank you,' the man said to the rat, genuinely gratified.

The rat sat back on its haunches, forepaws crossed, as if to say the man was welcome.

The man rewarded the rat with an extra chunk of cheese. Securing the chunk behind its incisors, the rat departed. It scampered to a corner of the room where there was a hole in the wall, a triangular fissure that looked too small for anything bigger than a mouse to crawl through. The rat glanced over its shoulder at the man, then dived into the hole. It squeezed and squirmed its way in until only its hindquarters remained visible. Then, with a scramble and scurry of its back legs, it shoved the last of itself through. A flicker of pink scaly tail, and it was gone.

For several minutes the man stared at the hole, feeling, as ever, a pang of parting-sorrow. He consoled himself with the thought that the rat would be back tomorrow. So, of course, would Mr North, but he preferred not to think about that. He preferred to think about just the rat.

Wearily he turned back to the drawing of the oak tree. He looked at it one final time, wondering what the rat had thought so special about it, then took hold of the cuff of his grimy shirt and wiped the picture off the wall with his sleeve, rubbing and rubbing at the spot until every last trace of charcoal had been smeared away. He had known instinctively, from the day he drew that very first picture for the rat, that Mr North would not approve of finding drawings on the wall. Mr North would consider such a thing a dangerous indulgence and, in order to compensate for it, would have to beat him harder. He might even take the candle away, in punishment. Thus the drawings, like the rat, had to remain a secret from Mr North.

The man ate the rest of the bread, then licked the tips of his thumb and forefinger and pinched the candle out.

In the darkness, he stretched himself out on the mattress once more, gritting his teeth and gasping at the twinges and the throbs and the dull, dolorous aches that inhabited his body.

Soon, despite his pains, he was asleep again.

Three

It began as another typically titanic Tuesday in the life of William Ian North.

The journey into London was mostly unproblematic. Owing to roadworks and a faulty set of traffic lights, North arrived at the NorthStar International Building a few minutes later than usual, but the delay was negligible, and he was soon ensconced in his office and working as normal, issuing edicts and directives left, right and centre to associates and subordinates both within the building and overseas. The London market was having an unsettled morning, fluctuating a little more violently than was desirable, but with North's assistance its trend remained upward.

Lunch was enjoyable, apart from one minor mishap. Smoked salmon was served as one of the starter courses, and North had expressly stipulated that this should never happen. He did not dislike the taste of smoked salmon, but it was a food the poor ate when they were pretending to be rich, and North wanted no part of common, cheap extravagances. A sous-chef was given his papers and shown the door.

North rested well after lunch, and was serviced admirably by his three o'clock prostitute. The woman was not perhaps his favourite among the professionals who regularly visited him, but by any objective standards of pulchritude she was still indisputably, outstandingly ravishing. An élite-class woman, one far beyond the reach of ordinary men – or ordinary millionaires, for that matter. A billionaires-only babe.

Following his shower, North took his seat again at his desk and assessed how his assets had been faring over the past couple of hours.

He was shocked to discover that yesterday's Latin American loss turned out to be far more severe than had originally been estimated. It wasn't simply a matter of a few million any more. It was a matter of a few *hundred* million. As a consequence, several local lending banks had collapsed, a number of major corporations had gone under, and the ensuing economic devastation had led to the military overthrow of at least two recently established and precariously balanced democratic governments.

All in the space of a few hours.

North demanded explanations. They were hesitantly forthcoming. From apologetic and sometimes trembling directors, vice-presidents, chairmen and chief executive officers he learned that the economic situation in the region had been unstable for some while now – more unstable than certain individuals had been prepared to admit. Balance-of-payment deficits had skyrocketed. Bad loans had been called in, and the debtors found incapable of repaying. Minor problems that had been brewing for a while had suddenly come to a head at once. It was as if several snowballs rolling downhill, slowly gathering speed and size, had unexpectedly converged and started an avalanche. Things had happened too fast. The problem had developed into a crisis too rapidly to be averted.

North listened, fired the appropriate people, promoted others, and spent the rest of the afternoon in a flurry of fund-transfers, sell-outs and buy-ins, moving around sums of money as vast as tectonic plates. By close of business in London, he had the situation back under control. Clicking the widescreen TV to a satellite news channel, he saw that the military juntas that had deposed the democratic governments had themselves been deposed and the originally elected officials – those who had not been shot – reinstated. Order had been restored. NorthStar International itself had sustained a severe financial blow, but North was confident that the loss would be recouped within a few days.

He left the office in a grim mood that neither Elgar nor the *Evening Standard* could alleviate.

The beating he delivered to the man in his cellar was twice as brutal as usual and lasted twice as long. This was not solely because North needed an outlet for his frustration, although that played a part. Principally it was because the increased viciousness would ensure that a day like today would not be repeated. It seemed that he had been going soft on his prisoner. He was not sure how this was possible, since he was not aware of treating the man any more kindly than usual over the past few weeks. Perhaps he had been slackening off with the beatings – pulling his punches, terminating the punishment after an increasingly short period of time – without realising it. And perhaps, incrementally and imperceptibly, he had begun putting more food on the man's dish. He would have to be more careful in future. It was vital that the man's sufferings were constant and unrelenting. Dr Totleben had been quite insistent about that. North must give the man no quarter, show him no mercy. To exhibit – even to feel – compassion towards him was to invite negative repercussions. The man must know no happiness, no delight, no joy. Ever.

North left the man with half as much food as yesterday. It was a very long time before the man was able even to think about crawling towards the dish, and when he did manage to reach it he found that his jaw was so pummelled and swollen that it would scarcely move. He was forced to eat the bread and cheese crumb by crumb, poking each piece between his lips and pushing it to the back of his mouth with his tongue. His body hurt too much to sleep, so he lit the candle straight after his meal and waited for the rat to come.

When it arrived, the rat was carrying something in its mouth. It approached the man in a gingerly fashion, like a religious supplicant bringing an offering before his god. It dropped the object at the man's feet and took a few hurried steps backward.

The man, puzzled by this unexpected development, struggled to bend towards to the object and then bring it into focus with his pain-wracked vision.

It was small and ovoid, composed of two distinct sections, the one yellow-green and smooth, the other light brown and rough-textured, culminating in a short stem.

The rat helped itself to some cheese while the man strove to recall what the object was and what it was called.

At last the answer came to him.
An acorn.

Four

The man studied the acorn for several minutes, turning it over and over with trembling fingers. He was no longer aware of his pain. His attention was fixed on the acorn to the exclusion of all else. He stroked it; sniffed it; even stuck out the tip of his tongue and tasted it. He thought he could detect warmth within it – a lingering trace of absorbed sunshine? Was it summer outside? The temperature in the cellar never varied. Down here, it was always damp January.

He marvelled at the glossiness of the acorn itself, and at the dimpled surface of its cup, and at the tight precision with which the one fitted into the other. It was quite the most beautiful thing he had ever set eyes on. In it, he saw the outside world encapsulated in miniature. He thought of all that the acorn had experienced in its short, budding life. The elements had touched it. Rain had drenched it, wind had buffeted it, sun had beaten down on it. And people. People had looked at it. People who were not confined as he was. Fortunate, free-roaming people. They might not have actually noticed the acorn, but it had fallen within the scope of their gazes. Perhaps some of them had lain within the shade of the tree from which it had come. Perhaps children had climbed that tree, shinning their way up its trunk, straddling its branches, clambering –

His imagination, in full flow, suddenly froze.

The tree from which it had come.

He turned to peer at the rat, which, having gorged itself, was now enjoying its customary post-prandial clean-up. Sensing his scrutiny, the rat threw a brief glance his way, then resumed washing.

The man's head hurt to shake, but he shook it nonetheless. No, it wasn't possible. It was a coincidence, that was all. The rat was intelligent, but not *that* intelligent. No, this was what had happened: for reasons of its own, the rat had decided to bring him a gift. The acorn was a tribute, the rat's way of thanking him for all the cheese and the drawings. He should infer nothing more from the event than that. The fact that the gift was directly related to the picture he had drawn yesterday was of no consequence. None whatsoever.

And yet . . .

He remembered how the picture of the oak had excited the rat, despite the fact that the rat traditionally showed little appreciation for drawings of large things. Was it conceivable that the rat had brought him the acorn in order to show that it knew that he had drawn an oak? Was it trying to demonstrate that it was even smarter than he already thought?

If that was the case, why had it not done so before? Why had it waited till now?

Perhaps because, before now, he had not drawn anything that the rat could easily fetch evidence of. After all, there was a limit to what the rat was capable of bringing into the cellar. Anything that could not fit through the fissure in the corner was excluded. Perhaps the oak was the first picture he had drawn that the rat had been able to act on in this way.

He tried to recall what else he had sketched for the rat over the past few months. He had done so many pictures for it, a couple of hundred at least. He could barely remember a tenth of them. He knew he had drawn a sailing ship once; the rat hadn't liked it. He had drawn a book; that, the rat had seemed mildly interested in. He had drawn a fanned hand of playing cards; that, the rat had given its full, close-sniffing approval. He had drawn a mountain; the rat had simply shrugged. He had drawn an apple – yes, now *there* was something the rat could have brought him a piece of. And, as he recalled, the picture of the apple *had* gone down well with the rat. And what about the willow? He had a feeling the rat had been reasonably intrigued by it. Surely, if the rat had wanted to show that it knew what a willow was, it could have presented him with a catkin the following day, or a leaf.

Yes. Maybe. But maybe the rat had not been able to locate an apple on that precise day. Perhaps the house above the cellar – the man knew that there was a house up there, and that it belonged to North – didn't contain any apples at that time. And perhaps the rat had not been able to find a willow, either, or had, but the timing had been wrong – when the man had drawn it, it had been winter and the trees had been bare.

So, all along, the rat had been waiting for a chance to prove himself. Each picture it had regarded as a kind of challenge. The man was asking it to retrieve these things from beyond the cellar, but until now it had been unable to comply successfully.

Was that it?

This would at least explain the correlation between the drawings and the degree of approval the rat accorded to each of them. The man had thought the rat preferred smaller things because it was familiar with them and had no understanding of objects over a certain size. But what if he had been looking at the situation the wrong way? What if the rat was gauging his pictures according to how easily it could obtain the item depicted (or a recognisable part thereof)?

It was incredible. Was a rat – a mere rodent – *really* capable of such complex mental processes? Could such reasoning and logic *really* be contained within that tiny, fur-capped skull? Surely not. Surely –

A sharp pricking on his left little toe interrupted the man's train of thought. He looked down to find that the rat sitting beside his foot, peering up expectantly. It had nipped him. It was waiting for him to do another drawing and had got bored and had nipped him!

'Cheeky little bugger,' the man mumbled with his barely mobile mouth. The words came out as *eegie igga ugga*. Had his damaged face allowed, he would have added a smile to the remark.

He picked up this evening's spent match and set about turning it into a drawing implement in the usual manner. Mr North had stamped on his right hand a couple of times during the beating, so the fingers were beginning to swell and weren't as dextrous as they might have been. Nevertheless, the man was determined not to be hampered by them. He was anxious to put his theory about the rat to the test.

What to draw? What to draw? Several times the match-pencil hovered over the wall, only to be snatched away before a mark could be made. What could he illustrate that the rat would be able to find? What was plentiful, perennial, common-or-garden, and could fit through the hole in the corner? He racked his brains. It was clear that the rat could come and go freely between the cellar and outdoors. Perhaps he should use this opportunity to find out whether it had the run of the house as well. Something domestic, then. Domestic and easily portable. Easily accessible, too. He didn't think the rat, clever though it was, was up to opening cupboards or drawers or undoing lids. A paper tissue, maybe? No, he doubted he had the draughtsmanship skills to represent one so that it was recognisable. A screw? No, people did not normally leave loose screws lying around. A paperclip? For the same reason, no. A flower? As a possibility, not without its merits. All the rat had to do was bring back a petal, after all. But really the man wanted something that was indisputably from inside the house. The rat might find flowers indoors, but it might equally venture outside for them. What about something from the kitchen, then? A teaspoon? No, a teaspoon was an awkward shape and not easily appropriated.

What about something of Mr North's? Some small personal item such as a wristwatch. No, smaller than that. Something Mr North removed every night when he went to bed. Like a tie-pin or a cufflink.

A cufflink.

The man had had enough close-up experience of Mr North's fists to know that Mr North always wore cufflinks. The pair he most commonly wore consisted of flat hexagons of gold engraved with the initials W.I.N. More often than he care to think, the man had glimpsed a flash of these cufflinks a millisecond before a punch connected.

What did you do with cufflinks when you undressed for bed? The man knew the answer to this question in the same way that he knew about everything else beyond the cellar walls – it was in his memories. He could see himself standing before a dressing-table, unpicking cufflinks from his shirtcuff buttonholes and laying them side-by-side in a small tortoiseshell tray. He was looking at himself in a mirror as he did this, admiring the immaculately maintained face and ice-blue eyes of his reflection, grinning serenely at himself.

Like all the man's other memories the image seemed to belong to someone else, yet at the same time he felt as though this *could* have been something he had done. It was as though he had fabricated a whole imaginary past for himself, and had somehow, over time, come to believe it might be real.

At any rate, he now had his subject-matter.

He roughed out one of the cufflinks, first the two hexagons, then the slender chain that joined them. He made the drawing large-scale – the cufflink as it might appear proportionate to him were he a rat. He suggested the shine of gold as best he could, using the cartoonist's shorthand of a small circle on each surface, denoting reflected light. Finally, he added the W.I.N. monogram to one of the hexagons, then leaned back to observe the rat's reaction.

The rat seemed unimpressed at first. Then – and the man was convinced he actually saw the light of recognition come on in its eyes – it sprang towards the picture and subjected it to a thorough, comprehensive, all-over sniffing. The creature was quivering from nose-tip to tail when it finally turned away from the drawing. It was almost as if it knew there had been a breakthrough; that at last the man had grasped what it had been trying to convey to him all these months. It darted off without a backward glance, plunging into the corner hole, a rat with a mission.

Candle snuffed, the man lay in the dark and counted all the many reasons why he should not expect the rat to return with the cufflink.

The cufflink had been an ambitious choice of object to be retrieved. Perhaps he should have thought of something simpler (although nothing simpler had sprung to mind). And then there was the possibility that the rat might not be able to gain access to Mr North's bedroom. And even if it could, it might not be able to reach the top of the dressing-table. And even if it managed that, the cufflink might not be there.

A whole series of even-ifs, each reducing the percentage chance of success that bit further.

And then, of course, there was the likelihood that the whole phenomenon was something he had invented. The rat was not some devastatingly brilliant master-rat but just an averagely intelligent rodent that could perform a couple of neat tricks.

But the rat had left the cellar with such apparent confidence . . .

Lying with the acorn clasped in his hand, staring into utter blackness, the man envisaged his little friend scurrying beneath the floorboards, behind wainscoting, up ladders of lath-and-plaster, through all the musty interstices of the house, searching for Mr North's bedroom.

Aloud, he wished it good luck.

'Oo uh,' was what he said.

Five

It was another wildly wonderful Wednesday in the life of William Ian North – for about the first five minutes of it.

Because five minutes was how long it took North to shave and start to get dressed, and it was as he started to get dressed that he noticed that one of his pair of gold monogrammed cufflinks was missing.

He rooted around in the tortoiseshell tray, stirring through all the other pairs of cufflinks there. The platinum pair. The ivory pair. The diamond-encrusted pair. The pair adorned with lapis lazuli Buddhas carved to a fantastically fine degree of intricacy. The pair made (allegedly) from the knucklebones of Howard Hughes. The pair fashioned from polished lunar olivine, so rare and irreplaceable that no insurance company would provide coverage for them.

The gold cufflink was definitely not there.

Had he been wearing the gold pair yesterday? No, yesterday it had been the turn of the platinum pair. He had worn the gold the day before, though, and remembered taking them off that evening. He could have dropped one then, he supposed. He checked beneath the dressing-table and, for good measure, under the bed. The cufflink was nowhere to be seen.

That left two options. Either the cufflink had been accidentally vacuumed up by a member of the domestic staff yesterday, or it had been stolen.

He discounted the latter possibility straight away. None of the domestic staff would dream of stealing something from the mansion of William Ian North, least of all an item as intimate and as readily missed as one of his cufflinks. None of them would be that stupid.

They knew that not only would the culprit inevitably be found, but he or she would be *destroyed.*

North would phone his major domo once he got to the office and order a thorough search to be made for the cufflink. The household rubbish would have to be sifted. The whole building would have to be checked from top to bottom. If, after that, the cufflink still did not turn up, then measures would be taken. Inadvertent negligence was still negligence, after all. Someone's head would have to roll, and it would probably be the major domo's.

North was not a sentimental man. The gold cufflinks were significant to him insofar as they were the first decent pair he ever bought himself, back at the very beginning of his rise to moguldom. Nowadays, though, they were the most modest and least expensive pair he possessed. If one of them was lost for good, that was disappointing but no reason to get upset.

Still, the cufflink's disappearance annoyed him. Coming on the heels of yesterday's business traumas, it made him feel edgy and paranoid. Nothing was meant to go wrong. That was the bargain, wasn't it? That was what he had paid Dr Totleben all that money for. A life free from failure. Continued material success in everything he did.

Then he remembered Dr Totleben's words. He could see Totleben speaking them, see the little German as clearly as though he were standing in front of him right now – those quick, pecking nods of his bald head, his fingers plucking out trills on an invisible piano keyboard. 'But you understand, Herr North, it can never be always perfection, *ja*? The man for whom nothing bad ever happens, he is not a man at all, but God. You understand? And you, Herr North, are many things, but you will never be God.'

North was proud of his reply. 'Maybe not,' he had said, 'but will God ever be William Ian North?'

He donned the diamond-encrusted cufflinks, finished dressing, ate his breakfast, and by seven twelve was standing on the front doorstep, ready for the Daimler.

They encountered the first delay shortly after turning out of the driveway. For some reason – it never became clear why – a tailback had formed leading up to a normally unbusy junction. Still, there was the *FT* and the overture to *Die Meistersinger* to occupy North's mind, and the Daimler was soon past the hold-up and sweeping towards London at a fair lick.

The journey ground to a halt again on the motorway. A container lorry had jack-knifed across two lanes, and the rush-hour traffic was backed up for three and a half miles. As the car inched forwards, North resolutely ignored the gawping stares from drivers and passengers in vehicles alongside. You would think none of these people had seen an internationally famous tycoon in his Daimler before. He focused his attention on the Nikkei Dow figures as they scrolled across the screen of the in-car terminal.

Hang on a moment . . .

He pulled the terminal's keyboard towards him on its swivel-arm and tapped in a series of commands. Onscreen, certain holdings were highlighted, charts of their day's performance appearing alongside in inset windows.

What the . . .?

A rattling flurry of keystrokes.

'Quick, the phone.'

The chauffeur removed the car-phone handset from its dash-mounted recharger and passed it over his shoulder to his boss.

North keyed a speed-dial preset number and held the phone to his ear.

No response.

He tried the number again.

Still no response.

'Bloody thing! Are you sure it's fully charged?'

Looking at North in the rearview mirror, the chauffeur nodded.

'Well, it's not bloody working!'

The chauffeur intimated that the signal might be blocked. Perhaps the exchange was overburdened – all the other businessmen in the cars around them trying to make phone-calls, too.

'But their calls aren't a tenth as important as mine!' North exclaimed, with perfect solipsistic logic.

He hurled the handset onto the footwell carpet and seized the terminal keyboard again. If he could not contact anyone in Tokyo, he would just have to manage things by himself from here.

The Far East was on the verge of meltdown. Certain key stocks had plummeted, dragging others down with them. Though trading on the Pacific Rim stock exchanges had ceased for the day, North knew that if he didn't act right now, the losses would continue when the exchanges reopened. Preventative steps had to be taken immediately, or the consequences would be catastrophic for NorthStar International.

Barely had he began to enter the relevant commands in the computer, however, than the screen image stuttered and jumped. A moment later, text began to disappear, to be replaced by jumbled nonsense – meaningless strings of numerals, punctuation marks, dingbats. Finally, before North's gaping, appalled eyes, the screen went blank.

He entered the key-sequence for Restart.

Nothing.

He switched the computer off and then on again.

Nothing.

He tried the if-all-else-fails tactic of hitting the machine.

The screen stayed stubbornly dead.

North screamed so loudly that the startled chauffeur nearly veered into an adjacent Bedford van.

'This can't be! This is impossible! It's a nightmare! This cannot be happening to *me*!' North continued to rant in this vein until they were clear of the jack-knifed lorry and were cruising at a respectable speed once more. At that point, he calmed down a little. They were making good progress again, and barring further obstacles he would be at his office soon, where matters could be taken firmly in hand.

Further obstacles presented themselves in the shape of roadworks (not just one set of them, as yesterday, but three), faulty traffic lights (affecting a major five-way intersection), and a bomb scare at the Bank of England, which brought most of the Square Mile to a standstill as police cordoned off streets and all the available alternative routes rapidly became clogged. The chauffeur used every back alley, cut-through and rat-run he knew, and even, at North's urging, drove the wrong way down a one-way thoroughfare, but for all his best efforts he was unable to get North anywhere near the NorthStar International Building until well past nine thirty.

North leapt out of the car when it was still a good half-mile from the building and ran the rest of the way. Sprinting through the entrance and across the atrium, he skidded to a halt at the doors to his private lift and hammered the call-button.

Nothing happened. No whirr of mechanism. The lift would not come.

He didn't bother hammering the button again. Obviously technology was against him today.

'The stairs!' he yelled at the security guards. 'Where are the fucking stairs?'

A beefy index finger timorously pointed him in the right direction.

Twenty flights up, a gasping, sweat-drenched, green-gilled North staggered into his office and collapsed into his chair.

The widescreen TV was showing a downward line as steep as a ski-jump. His desktop telelink was, thank Christ, operational. As soon as the fire in his lungs had died down and he no longer felt he was going to vomit, North set about addressing the situation in the Far East.

Again, as with Latin America, it transpired that numerous mini-crises had simultaneously ballooned into a single maxi-crisis. Problems-in-waiting had developed together into fully fledged problems, all exacerbating one another – an exponentially cumulative concatenation of shortfalls, implosions, disasters and depressions. Already there had been eleven ritual suicides among the senior management of NorthStar International's Pacific Rim empire, and every face that appeared on North's screen was glazed with tears and contorted with agonies of contrition. But North did not want to hear regrets and excuses. He wanted to hear strategies. For two hours solid he and Asian underlings worked out a package of countermeasures that would limit the damage to NorthStar International's holdings in the region and ensure a swift bounce-back. During this time another three of his employees took their own lives, one of them while North had put him on hold in order to talk to someone else – the man simply got up from his desk, opened the window of his eighth-storey office, and stepped out.

By the time the countermeasures had been decided upon and

implemented, North was a haggard, febrile wreck. He began putting together a projected estimate of the total capital devaluation NorthStar International was going to incur as a result of everything that had gone wrong today and yesterday, and stopped when the figure exceeded the available space on his calculator's readout. At least London seemed to be recovering. The ski-jump now ended in an optimistic little upturn.

Bad news from Russia swept in like a chill wind from the Volga. A *putsch* had occurred in Moscow. All western-owned assets had been seized and declared property of the state by the Communist/ military axis that now held sway in the Kremlin. The country was in upheaval. Every one of his Russian employees North tried to contact either was not at his desk at all, or was lying under it, vodka bottle in hand, singing 'Kalinka'.

There was only one thing North could do. He called every western head of state currently on his payroll and decreed that political pressure be brought to bear on Russia. Embargoes, sanctions, blockades and even war should be threatened.

War *was* threatened. For half an hour the world teetered on the brink. Then, reluctantly and with much grumbling, the Communist-military axis backed down and agreed to return westerners' assets to their rightful owners. London surged back up to its start-of-day level, buoyed largely by relief that Armageddon had been avoided. Wall Street opened with a plunge, as if to indicate that it, too, had feelings, but then swiftly rallied.

Lunch? North barely had any appetite for lunch. Besides, not only was smoked salmon served *again*, but another proscribed dish somehow found its way onto the menu as well: roast pigeon, which North detested both because the meat was stringy, tough and tasteless, and because he could not disassociate the thing on his plate from a mental image of London pigeons with their frayed feathers and scrawny necks, gobbling up garbage and shitting all over the shop. North strode from the boardroom spitting with rage. The kitchen staff were subjected to a volcanic tirade. Inexcusable! Unforgivable! Unacceptable! Outrageous! Sackings were meted out indiscriminately, like sparks shooting from a fire.

Dizzy with his own anger, North returned to his office and paged his personal assistant.

'Get me Dr Totleben,' he told her.

Three minutes later his PA came back with the news that Dr Totleben was away from his office, attending some kind of convention in Düsseldorf as Guest of Honour.

'No, you misunderstood me,' said North. 'When I said, "Get me Dr Totleben", I didn't mean get him on the phone, I meant *get* him. Send over the Lear jet for him. I want him in my office as soon as is humanly possible.'

He tried to rest, but he couldn't rest. The chaise longue felt lumpy and unwelcoming. He paced and paced and paced. His stomach felt like a knot of eels. It was drizzling over the City. The overcast sky looked so heavy, he thought it might give way under its own weight.

I was promised I could not fail, he thought. Totleben all but guaranteed it. Never mind what he said about my not being God. He was just covering his own backside, allowing himself a get-out clause. He told me nothing could go wrong, and today *everything* has gone wrong. There'd better be a damned good explanation, that's all I can say. A *damned* good explanation.

When his three o'clock whore came, he was tempted to send her away, but then thought that he could do with the distraction. Right now, perhaps a spot of mindless carnal abandon would be just what the doctor ordered.

The woman – incandescently lovely, but wearing a perfume that North found eye-watering and bitter – took her clothes off and his, and straddled him on the desk. North lay there, waiting for the flood of heat to his groin. The woman began to ride and fondle and wriggle. Ah yes, North thought, *this* is what I need. She explored his body with an expert touch. Lips, hands, vulva. Any minute now, thought North, the stress and strain of the morning will be nothing but a memory. All anxieties will have disappeared, subsumed beneath a tsunami of sexual pleasure. Oh yes. Any minute now. Forget the Far East. Forget Russia. Become lost in unfurling lust . . .

Limp as a paraplegic's legs.

The woman did everything she could.

Limp as a lorry-flattened lugworm.

Tweaked, tickled, tongued, teased.

Limp as a lounge-lizard's languor.

Rimmed, fingered, palpated, throated.

Nothing doing.

At last North threw her off and stalked over to the windows. Stark naked, he gazed out over the City, his ice-blue eyes glassier and more glacial than they had been in a long time.

When he turned away from the windows again, the prostitute was no longer there. She had beaten a subtle and hasty retreat. North showered off and reclothed himself.

When he re-entered his office, Dr Totleben was standing by the desk.

North was overcome by an urge to go over and hug the little German, but settled for a brisk, forthright handshake.

'Dr Totleben, thank God you could come.'

Totleben pecked the air and ran off a little scale with his left hand. 'It was an order I had no choice but to obey,' he replied. 'When William Ian North summons, one either answers his call or forfeits all rights to be called sane.'

'Please, please, sit down.' North drew up a deep, buttoned-leather armchair. 'Would you like something to drink? Some refreshments?' Totleben, seating himself, declined. 'Nothing at all?'

'*Nein danke*. So, Herr North, what appears to be the problem? And why this urgency? Why was I dragged away from the Fifth Annual Metascientists' Symposium – in the middle of a most interesting lecture by the University of Chicago's Professor MacGruder on the topic of Infernal Thermodynamics – and rushed over to London with such haste?'

'What appears to be the problem?' North echoed. 'Dr Totleben, have you not been watching the news?'

Totleben executed a pair of contrapuntal arpeggios, one ascending, the other descending. 'If you are referring to the nuclear war that nearly occurred this morning, it so happened that word of the crisis reached us at the symposium during a practical demonstration of micromancy. Immediately we ran the runes through the randomising software and divined from the results that events would turn out well, and the symposium continued on as normal. Other than that . . . well, in common with most metascientists I am of a somewhat unworldly disposition. I do not really keep abreast of current affairs.'

'So you know nothing about the financial turmoil there's been all across the world these past couple of days? You haven't heard about the chaos in Latin America and Asia and Russia?'

'I'm afraid not.' Totleben jabbed his nose forwards three times in quick succession. 'But this turmoil you mention, this chaos – it has affected NorthStar International badly, *ja*?'

'Very badly. You see before you a man who has been robbed of nearly a quarter of his wealth in the space of thirty-six hours.'

'If that is so, then I also see before me a man who, even three-quarters as rich as he once was, still has more money than most people can even conceive of.' Totleben capped the remark by stabbing out the circumflex climb-and-fall of the opening phrase of the last movement of Beethoven's *Ninth*.

'That, Doctor, is not the point. The point is, you assured me I would have nothing but success.'

'Forgive me, Herr North, but I assured you – '

North interrupted him with a wave. 'Yes, yes, I remember what you said. The gist of it was, though, that as long as that thing in my cellar suffers, I would not suffer at all. And look at me.' He gestured at himself. 'Is this the face of a man who is not suffering?'

Totleben peered at North's face, and nodded. 'So what do you need from me, Herr North?'

'I need to know what's to be done. I need to know how I can prevent this shitstorm from getting any worse.'

'Very well. But before we go any further, I must remind you, Herr North, as I told you all those years ago when we first met: metascience is not an exact science. If you want testable hypotheses and systematically reproducible results, I am not the man to be talking to. My field is the fusion of the tangible and the intangible. I, and my colleagues, operate in the narrow margin where what is known and what is sensed overlap; where physics and fantasy, chemistry and alchemy, biology and belief collide. It is, in every respect, a grey area. Within it, nothing can be pinned down with absolute precision. Nothing can be stated empirically.'

'I understand that.'

'I hope, for both our sakes, Herr North, that you do. Now, tell me about the clone-golem. You have been regularly mistreating him?'

'Every day.'

'Starving him?'

'I feed him just enough so he doesn't die.'

'Beating him?'

'Religously.'

'Keeping from him all means of entertaining himself?'

'Unless he thinks bruises and bleeding are fun.'

'He has no hope of ever escaping his predicament?'

'He's given up even trying to try. In the early days he'd make the occasional bid for the door, but he's long since ceased to bother.'

'Hmmm,' said the doctor, running off some double-handed, triple-octave glissandos. His bald head gleamed like the six-point ball in snooker.

'"Hmmm"?' said North, his voice beginning to rise. 'That's it? That's the best you can offer? "Hmmm"? Dr Totleben, perhaps you are forgetting how much you owe me. You were an unknown dabbler when I first tracked you down all those years ago, working at various ill-paying odd jobs in order to finance your esoteric experiments. I'd heard about you and what you claimed you could do, and I funded you to the tune of Christ knows how much so that you could devote yourself full-time to your researches. You had nothing – *were* nothing – when I found you. You had no reputation, no respect, no renown. I created everything that you are now. I *made* you! If it wasn't for me, you wouldn't be junketing all over the world to conferences and conventions and symposia. Your textbooks would not be on the shelves of every university library. Your eccentric hobby wouldn't have become a world-wide, legitimate field of academic study. You'd still be a desperate little nonentity, festering away in a crumbling council high-rise in Baden-Baden!'

Totleben spread out some smooth major chords. 'Please, Herr

North, do not think me ungrateful for your generous patronage. Please also believe me, however, when I say that, even without you, the disciplines to which I adhere would still have gained respectability eventually. Science and mysticism are forever growing closer, are they not? As science progresses and becomes more complex, so our minds have to take greater and greater leaps of faith and imagination in order to keep with each new theory that scientists come up with. Ultimately science and arcane belief will become indistinguishable from each other. There are those, indeed, who already consider science an occult art. I, then, have invented nothing new. All I have done is taken a step before the rest of mankind takes it. I will not deny that the worldly benefits have been welcome, but when all is said and done it is the pursuit of achievement that spurs me on, the furtherance of my researches. In that regard, your difficulties with the clone-golem concern me because they present me with a professional and intellectual challenge. So, allow me to think for a moment. Could there have been a contamination of the tissue sample I took from you?'

'Is that the answer?' North asked eagerly, surmising that if that was the case, then all Totleben had to do was take another tissue sample and manufacture another clone-golem.

'Please, Herr North. I am musing out loud, that is all.'

'Oh. Of course.'

'No,' said the doctor, in reply to his own question, 'the laboratory was purified and sealed to the highest clinical and magickal standards. Hermetic in both senses. Then the growing method itself? Perhaps a flaw in the incubation and incantation? No, not possible. The sigils were time-honoured, the protoplasmic growth-solution the very latest that biogenetics has to offer. I created the tetragrammata using only the very best and most reliable kabbalistic sources, working them around A, C, G and T, the initial letters of the four genetic nucleotide bases in DNA. The encoding was perfect. No, there is no way that the problem can lie within the creature himself. Then some outside influence, perhaps . . .?'

And so on and so forth in this manner the doctor ruminated, while his hands, seemingly of their own accord, executed variations on a theme, skirling through melodic permutations and changes of tempo and key. North knew he should leave Totleben to his musings and get back to work. NorthStar International desperately needed him at the helm. However, he could not bear to let Totleben out of his sight, and so he prowled the office in an agony of impotence, keeping an ear attuned to Totleben's voice in case its tone should suddenly alter to a triumphal note of *eureka*. His PA had put a hold on all incoming calls. Unguided, London wavered uncertainly, fluctuating within a ten-point band. Outside, the buildings and pavements of the City succumbed to a sudden sluice of rain.

At last the doctor seemed to come to a conclusion. He stopped talking, at any rate, and North snapped round, hoping for enlightenment, resolution, answers.

Totleben's expression was not encouraging.

'Well?'

'Ah, Herr North, as I told you at the beginning, metascience is not an exact science. We are dealing with forces that some might say have a mind of their own.'

'Meaning?'

'In metascience we are not immune for the laws of nature. Not only that but we believe that *nothing* is immune from the laws of nature. Even your stock markets reflect the system of checks and balances that operate within ecologies, *nein*? So, allowing for that, we must see that, in your case, a great pressure has been exerted in one direction – namely your tremendous, world-beating success. We must also see, therefore, that in the interests of natural equilibrium an equal and opposite counterpressure must be brought into play at some stage, in order to redress the imbalance.'

'What are you saying? Am I going to lose *everything*?'

'Bear with me. When I created the clone-golem for you, I invested him with every part of your genetic make-up that was predisposed to failure. In effect, I sucked all the potential fallibility out of you and transferred it into your twin organism. The creature in your basement is the absolute antithesis of all that you have become. He is, to his marrow, every dream of yours that will be dashed, every project that will not come to fruition, every prize you grasp at but cannot reach.'

'Yes, yes, you told me all this at the time.'

'I restate these facts so that you may understand clearly. You were already successful when I first met you, but now your success has exceeded all my expectations. This has put an undue strain on the capacity of the clone-golem. Sooner or later, Herr North, something must give. The wheel must turn. Not even you, with all the wealth you have at your disposal, all the power and influence you wield, can prevent that. Sooner or later, nature will find a way of evening things out – assuming she has not begun to do so already.'

'But why' – North clutched the air – 'why didn't you tell me this before? Why did I have to wait till now to find this out?'

'Because, Herr North, metascience is not an exact – '

North took two steps towards Totleben, fists raised. 'Say that one more time, Doctor, and so help me I'll throttle the life out of you.'

Totleben twitched all over, then calmed himself. 'If you would permit me, Herr North – this aggression is unwise. I say so, not for my personal benefit, but with regard to the clone-golem. It would be regrettable were you, for some reason, to visit such fatal violence on the creature. Killing me would do you little harm. Killing the clone-golem, on the other hand . . .'

North stared at the doctor, then nodded slowly to himself and lowered his hands. Totleben had emphasised, right from the start, that the clone-golem must always be kept alive. Physically the clone-golem was more resilient than most human beings, capable of enduring a level of hardship and abuse that would destroy an ordinary mortal man. There were limits, however, to what even that creature of metascientific origin could endure, and Totleben had warned North to be careful not to overstep them. Were North to do so, the consequences would be terrible for him. All the negative energy that had been stored up in the clone-golem over the years would be released at once. 'Such a torrent of misfortune,' Totleben had said, 'I do not believe even you, Herr North, would be able to withstand.'

'Maybe,' said Totleben now, 'you would do well simply to accept that there are some things beyond your control, Herr North.'

'I can bring this planet to the edge of annihilation and pull it back again,' North replied matter-of-factly. 'There is nothing, Doctor, that I cannot control.'

Totleben, unconvinced, prodded out a hesitant version of the Funeral March, then said, 'Well. If that will be all?' He raised himself from the chair as though hauling his body up a flight of stairs with his chin.

'Yes, that will be all.'

'Good. Professor Levi of Haifa University is chairing a debate on Fractal Demonology this evening that I would be loath to miss.'

'What about payment for your services, Doctor?'

'No need.'

'I insist that you should be paid.'

'If it will make you feel better that money changes hands, then by all means, go ahead. Whatever figure suits you. You have my bank account details.'

North extended his hand. 'Thank you, Dr Totleben.'

Totleben performed a curt bow as they shook hands. 'Not at all, Herr North. An honour to be of service.'

After Totleben was gone, North made a careful survey of the world economic situation, foresaw no further disturbances looming on the immediate horizon, and informed his PA that he would be taking the rest of the day off. The chauffeur was instructed to bring the car round, and North was soon wending his way homewards through the comparatively light mid-afternoon traffic.

At the mansion, he dismissed the domestic staff. It occurred to him, just as the last of them was leaving the building, that he had not discussed the cufflink with his major domo. It could wait till tomorrow, he decided. For now, there was something more important that needed to be done.

There were riding stables in the ground of the mansion. North had not actually ventured out on horseback in several years, but he kept a few mounts and paid for them to be groomed and exercised just in case the mood for a jaunt in the saddle should take him. In the same way, he paid for a private golf links in the grounds to be tended and maintained, and kept a golf pro on permanent retainer, just in case he should feel the urge for a quick round of eighteen holes.

Now, he went to the stables and fetched a riding crop. Armed with this, he headed for his study and the cellar.

Six

The man was in so much pain, he almost felt nothing at all. It was as if there was a level beyond which physical agony ceased to have any meaning. If he lay still, the pain at least remained at a constant. If he tried to move, it bloomed to indescribable proportions. He lost and regained consciousness so frequently that it became hard to grasp what consciousness *was* any more. In the end, he knew that he had been unconscious only because he knew that he had not been so aware of his pain for a while. Otherwise, he was simply exchanging one kind of disembodied blackness for another.

Time ebbed by. Dimly he remembered that the rat was due to visit at some point. He could not recall, with his pain-ravaged brain, why the arrival of the rat should be any more significant today than it had been on previous days. Something about gold? He could not reforge the connection between the rat and gold. Perhaps the rat had already been and gone, and he had missed it. Even if it came, Mr North had seen fit to provide him with neither food nor a match. So the rat might as well not come at all. There would be no meal today and no picture.

Spreadeagled prone on the floor, the man quietly wept. Tears poured from his eyes, mingling with the congealing blood on his face. Crying was something that did not figure in his memories at all – or at least, in his memories of adulthood. Childhood tears he could recall, the natural response to a barked shin or a parental ticking-off or a moment of intolerable frustration. But grown-up tears? There had been no excuse for them, no reason good enough to warrant them. He had cried in this cellar, many times, but in the life contained in his memories – that false life he had never lived – he had managed to develop such a control over his emotions that nothing, not even grief at his parents' funerals, could irrigate his eyes. He must be a hard man, he thought, this man whose past he shared. A hard and un-self-forgiving man. And for all his terribly agony he found himself pitying him. As salt-water spilled down his cheeks and onto the floor, he felt a strange sense of relief that at least *he* was able to feel sorry for himself.

The rat did come, eventually. He heard it skittering and scuttering about. He heard it clamber all over the enamelware dish, as if unable to believe that it was empty. Finally, he heard the rat come bounding over to him. Something small and metallic clinked to the floor in front of his face. He tried to move his right hand to grope for the offering, and groaned as fresh pain blasted through the muscles, sinews and fibres of his arm. The arm remained static, as though welded to the floor. The rat chittered irritably, but there was nothing the man could do. Mr North had beaten him for – how long? Half an hour? Longer? Fists, feet and that riding crop, striking him again and again until the blows had merged into a single thudding drumbeat without end. He could not recall when he had last endured an assault so severe.

The rat became increasingly peeved by the man's unresponsiveness and immobility. It scurried all over the man's body. It stood on his head and shrilled in his ear. It even nipped him on the toe again, although, of course, the man barely noticed – it was just one more source of pain amidst a myriad. Finally, after defecating right by the man's nose, the rat departed in high dudgeon, and the man was alone again in the cellar, a mind trapped inside a body in torment.

Imperceptibly the hours passed and the pain began to abate, receding from all over his body to a few keys areas – a hand, a knee, the ribs, the kidneys, the testicles. A snapped tooth drilled relentlessly into his skull. Two of the fingers of his right hand felt bent and broken. His back and shoulders were covered with lacerations, Mr North having pulled up his shirt and whipped him fiercely enough to break the skin. Now, it was no longer impossible for the man to move, merely sheer hell. He was able – though he nearly passed out several times during the procedure – to bring his hand up and feel the floor in front of his face for the object the rat had deposited there. He found the rat's turd first, and arduously wiped off his fingers on the bricks before resuming the painstaking (and pains-giving) search for the rat's other offering.

He found it. Two hard, smooth hexagons of metal linked by a short, delicate length of chain. Slowly it came back to him what this was, what he had drawn for the rat to fetch.

He laughed as best as his throbbing ribs and flayed back would allow. He laughed, and then he cried again, and then he cried and laughed together until the sobs and the chuckles were one and the same.

In the cold confines of his brick-walled world, the noise echoed and reverberated. It sounded as though there were a dozen prisoners present, all racked with tragic joy.

Seven

It was another thoroughly thunderous Thursday in the life of William Ian North. At least, so he hoped, as he woke to it at six thirty a.m., brought forth from slumber by his alarm clock's sleep-censoring bleep.

Nothing went awry during his washing, shaving and dressing. He performed each task with the air of a man expecting calamity to occur at any moment, but the basin did not collapse, the mirror did not fall on top of him, and none of his clothes ripped as he put them on. The cufflink was still absent, but then he had not thought it would just miraculously reappear on the dressing-table overnight. Shirtcuffs secured with Howard Hughes's knucklebones (allegedly), he ate his breakfast. The toaster did not explode, the milk had not gone off, the handle of the cafetère did not come loose as he poured it, the marmalade did not contain broken glass.

The chauffeur made his scheduled appearance at seven fifteen. No problems with the car. Engine running smoothly, phone fully operational, terminal online and reporting promising signs of a turnaround in the Far East. The journey was somewhat stop-start, but there was no repeat of yesterday's tailbacks and other traffic tribulations. Arrival at the NorthStar International Building was achieved in reasonably good time. The lift was functioning again.

The London market slowly rose, and so did the value of North's vast portfolio. Every gain, it seemed, was earned only with the greatest of effort. North felt as if he were swimming against a strong current, walking into a powerful wind. But he made headway, that was the main thing. Effortful though it was, he was going forward once more, not back.

His shoulder ached from using the riding crop yesterday. His knuckles hurt, too, so much so that he could barely straighten out his fingers. As the morning wore on, however, and no mishaps occurred, he became confident that these minor physical inconveniences were worthwhile. His tactic had paid off. All it had taken was one particularly intensive beating for the status quo to be restored. Dr Totleben had been proved wrong, and North thought he knew why. The doctor had bleated on about forces of nature, but had neglected to take into account the fact that William Ian North was himself a force of nature – a great, sweeping hurricane of drive and ambition and will.

Lunch was delicious, the menu error-free. North's underlings observed their boss's upbeat, confident demeanour and inferred that all was right again with the world. Their relief communicated itself to the workforce. Productivity in the NorthStar International Building leapt.

North enjoyed the post-lunch rest he deserved, and his three o'clock prostitute brought him – after a few tentative false starts – to tumescence and thence to bucking, howling orgasm. The rest of the afternoon passed as though in a dream, and before he realised it North was heading home again, at a comfortable pace, with a crisp tabloid and Elgar to reassure him that everything was back in its rightful place.

The clone-golem submitted to his daily beating with scarcely a murmur. In a way, the man's abject passivity was disappointing. North had not realised how essential a part of the ritual the groans and cries and flinches of his victim were. It wasn't that North enjoyed inflicting pain. Rather, it was that the audible and visible responses to his efforts indicated that he was doing his job properly. He assumed that the close-golem was not fully recuperated from the previous day's drubbing. He was doubtless also weak from lack of food. North swilled out the blood-pinkened urine from his chamberpot, put bread and cheese on his dish, and gave him – why not? – a match.

North went to bed and fell into a deep, just, contented and dreamless sleep.

Eight

His broken-fingered right hand was incapable of holding anything. With his left, he clumsily swept the match down the wall. Once. Twice. Three times. The match did not even spark. In his mind's eye he saw its crimson head crumbling with each downstroke, dextrin-bonded sulphur wearing away to raw wood. A fourth time. Still the match would not ignite. He mumbled a prayer through his mangled lips. Please. Please let there be light.

And, on the fifth attempt, there was light.

The candle illumined the cellar. The man did not pause to inspect his injuries. A glimpse of bulbously bent middle and index fingers was enough for him. He turned his attention elsewhere.

The rat was sitting beside the food dish. It hadn't touched the cheese. Its bright eyes seemed to be demanding one thing from the man. A picture.

And have I got a picture for you, my little friend, the man thought.

He made a pencil out of the match and held it up to the wall in his left hand. The pose felt ungainly. The distance from hand to wall seemed hard to judge. With his first stroke he accidentally snapped off a couple of precious millimetres of the carbonised wood. Carefully, slowly, he persevered, etching out a shape. He kept it simple, and though the end-product was shakily rendered, it was also immediately identifiable. The rat seemed to think so, at any rate. No sooner had it looked at the finished drawing than it was off.

The man scrubbed the picture from the wall. Then, by the light of the candle, he took from his pocket the two items the rat had so far brought him and visually examined them, one of them for the first time. He couldn't decide which was the lovelier, the acorn or the cufflink. In the acorn, nature had created something of marvellously deceptive simplicity, the blueprint for an oak compressed into a nut no bigger than a thumb-tip. As for the cufflink, mankind had used its ingenuity and know-how to take a raw material like gold ore and refine something from it as beautiful as gold, and then transform that gold into an efficient and elegant sartorial accessory. There was an interchange there, of sorts, embodied in these two seemingly unconnected objects – a transfer of complexity. One was condensed potential, the other potential condensed.

He returned the acorn and the cufflink to his pocket and snuffed out the candle.

That night he barely felt his injuries at all.

Nine

It was another frankly fabulous Friday in the life of William Ian North. Throughout, however, North could not escape the feeling that its fabulousness was a sham, a charade, a convenient façade for something altogether more unwholesome. Everything went according to plan, everything fell out to his advantage as it was meant to, yet everything seemed to be happening too easily. The morning traffic seemed too clear, the reports from his subordinates seemed too positive, the lunch seemed too well planned and presented, his rest seemed somehow too relaxing, the prostitute seemed too enthusiastic and accommodating, the stock market seemed too obligingly responsive to his financial manoeuvres. It felt constantly as though someone was doing him a favour. A card-dealer was taking from the bottom of the deck to give him useful hands. A teacher was supplying him with all the answers to an upcoming exam. A tennis coach was going easy on him, lobbing him nothing but slow drop-shots. The day was not without its challenges, and he worked hard, but all along he could not shake the conviction that someone, somewhere, was stringing him along. That behind its mask of impartiality, fate was slyly smirking.

He put this impression down to fatigue. It had, by anyone's

standards, been a traumatic week. Little wonder that he should be feeling underwhelmed and exhausted by its end. He would have a completely idle weekend, he decided. Lie in bed. Finally make time to watch the laserdiscs that had been sent to him by the various movie companies he owned. Take long baths, long walks. Generally have a break for a couple of days from the pressures and responsibilities of being William Ian North.

Outside the mansion, the chauffeur wished him goodnight. North told him that his services would not be required this weekend, and the chauffeur tipped his cap gratefully.

North entered the house. He was tired, and was looking forward to pouring himself a glass of brandy and starting to unwind. But there was, of course, one last duty to be done.

In his study, he took the key from the hook on the mantelshelf, not noticing that one of the brass fire-implements on the hearth below was absent. He tugged on the Dumas and the bookcase swung inwards. With a yawn, he entered the short passageway, rolling his shoulders like a boxer limbering up on his way to the ring. At the far end of the passageway, he flipped the cellar light-switch and brought the key down to unlock the door.

He heard footsteps behind him – bare feet, running. He half turned in time to glimpse a shaggy, bestial-looking silhouette bearing down on him. Something throbbed through the air and struck him on the side of the head. He heard himself cry out, felt himself fall. As pain exploded through his skull, consciousness closed on itself like a flower at evening.

Ten

The man stood over the prone form of Mr North, panting. With the brass poker still aloft in his left hand, ready to deliver another blow if necessary, he nudged Mr North in the ribs with his toes. There was no response. He nudged him again, harder. Mr North was out cold. As planned.

Bending down, the man laid the poker aside and wrested the key from Mr North's fingers. He unlocked the door and opened it, then, stowing the key in the frayed breast pocket of his grubby shirt, he grabbed Mr North by the armpits and set to hauling him through the doorway.

Mr North was by no means heavy, but to the man, debilitated by years of confinement and malnourishment, he weighed a ton. The pain from his broken fingers didn't help, either. He managed to get him to the top of the steps but nearly fainted from the exertion. Sick and dizzy, he viewed the prospect of lugging Mr North all the way down the steps with dismay. There was nothing else for it. Summoning up one last burst of energy, he launched Mr North off the top steps with a grunting shove. Gravity did the rest. Mr North banged, bounced and barrel-rolled down the steps, fetching up at their foot in a gangling, insensible heap.

The man, on his knees, waited for his head to clear and his heart to stop thumping. Eventually, he was able to stand up and close and lock the door. He made his way back along the passageway to the bookcase, tugged the lever, and emerged, on unsteady legs, into Mr North's study.

There he found the rat. It was squatting on the mantelshelf, just above the hook for the cellar key, as if it wanted to show the man how clever it had been to scale the mantelshelf and detach the key from the hook. The man scratched its head for a while, the rat half-closing its eyes in pleasure.

'You're pretty much finished here, aren't you?' he said to it. 'Your work's done. You're back off to where you came from, wherever that is.' He forced his inflamed, lumpen lips into a smile. 'Thanks, little friend. I'm going to miss you.'

The rat gave the man's fingertip a playful, affectionate little nip, as though for old times' sake, then raced off along the mantelshelf, dangled over the end, dropped to the floor, and vanished between two bookcases.

The man hung the key back on the hook, remembering how the rat had brought it to him earlier that day. He had been surprised at first that the rat had not waited till their usual rendezvous time, but then, running his fingertips over the contours of the key in the dark, he had realised that the break from routine made sense. The rat could not have brought the key any later. Otherwise Mr North would have come home, discovered it missing, and then the game would have been up.

When he had sufficiently recovered his strength, he set about exploring the mansion. That afternoon he had ventured no further than the study, for there had been domestic staff everywhere else. Now, alone, he roamed the vastness of the building, wandering through its numerous bedrooms, its winding corridors, its majestic halls and spiralling staircases, its recreation rooms, its luxuriously appointed bathrooms, the whole gilt and splendour of the place. He gazed out at the night views: a clear moon and intermittent, silver-edged clouds, lawns patterned with slanting lozenges of window-glow, dark trees – oaks among them, no doubt – and, far off, a row of hills, black against the deep starry blue of the sky. He found a well-stocked first aid kit and constructed a splint for his fingers using bandages and tongue depressors, then fixed himself a meal in the kitchen. When he had eaten, he gathered up armfuls of dry goods and bottled water from the pantry and carried them to the cellar door. Having first established that Mr North was still unconscious, he piled up the supplies next to the mattress. Even in the dark, Mr North would find them soon enough.

He ran a deep bath, filled it with scents and oils, and soaked in it for an hour. He scrubbed himself clean and washed the dirty, tangled mass of his hair half a dozen times, using up an entire bottle of shampoo. With a pair of scissors, he stood before the bathroom mirror and hacked off his damp, straggling locks, cropping close to his scalp. He chopped off most of his beard as well, and shaved the rest with a razor. Then he presented himself before the mirror again.

The man who stared back at him was gaunt and pale and battered and haggard, but still unmistakably, undeniably, William Ian North.

He spent the most comfortable night of his life in Mr North's double-divan, beneath Mr North's eiderdown duvet, wearing Mr North's silk pyjamas. Come dawn, he was up and about. It wouldn't do to waste the day.

He dressed in a set of Mr North's casual clothes and went around the house again and also the grounds, familiarising himself with every aspect of Mr North's domestic existence. He revelled in the taste and smell of outdoor air, the glitter of dew on the grass, the twitter of bird-song. He wandered, sometimes giggling to himself. The liberty to move unconstrained seemed a gift of incalculable value. The sky was immense and infinite. There was almost more brightness and detail than his eyes could cope with.

And inside the mansion, too, there were delights to be cherished. Television, stereos, an indoor swimming pool, a collection of fine wines. Such things were familiar to the man from his memories, but he also felt as if he was experiencing them for the first time. He luxuriated and self-indulged, and went to bed as gorged and giddy as a child after a birthday party.

Sunday was a day of rest, a day of retrenchment. The man soberly contemplated his next move. He was growing comfortable within the skin of Mr North. He was beginning to regard himself as William Ian North. Things he did not know about Mr North's existence he was able to intuit. For instance, he could not have known that Mr North was able to call on the services of an expert beautician twenty-four hours a day, seven days a week, but somehow he assumed this would be the case, and having looked up the beautician's phone number in Mr North's electronic personal organiser (which again, intuitively, he knew how to operate) he summoned her to the mansion.

She did not hide her shock at his appearance, but when he explained that he had been thrown from a horse yesterday – for he knew that Mr North had stables – she took his injuries in her stride and set about tidying him up. She manicured his nails, wondering aloud how he had managed to let them fall into such a state of disrepair in a little over a week. She showed him how to touch up his facial bruises with foundation so that they would be less noticeable. She called a friend of hers, a hairstylist, who came round and tidied up his hair. He apologised for its condition, saying he had thought he might be able to trim it himself and save himself some money. The beautician and the hairstylist – assuming, as most people do, that eccentricity is innate in the incredibly wealthy – accepted this excuse without batting an eyelid.

When they were gone, he examined himself in a mirror.

No one would be able to tell.

Eleven

It was another merely magnificent Monday in the life of William Ian North.

On the way into London, he chatted with the chauffeur, while Wagner played and the Tokyo index scrolled by all but ignored. The chauffeur was initially startled to have his opinion consulted on matters as diverse as bond options and the correct choice of sock-colour, but he soon got into the swing of things, and even dared to share with his uncharacteristically jolly employer a mildly blue joke he had been told in the pub on Saturday night. He assumed that the riding accident with which his boss accounted for his injuries had also knocked a few braincells loose. North, he was sure, would be back to his usual intense, taciturn self within a day or so.

The security guards at the NorthStar International Building saluted their boss as he walked in, and were informed that in future there would be no need for such formalities. In his office, North reclined in his desk chair and simply admired the view of the City for a while. Then, with an eye on the red line on the widescreen TV, he set about dismantling NorthStar International assest by asset.

By morning's end, he was worth about half as much as he had been when he started. Worried calls were coming in over the telelink. What was going on? Underlings were knocking at his door but none was invited to come in.

Lunch was a silent, perplexed affair. The other diners at the boardroom table did not broach the subject, but you could see it in their eyes: bewilderment bordering on fear. Had the boss gone mad? He was selling off holdings at a small fraction of their worth, incurring unthinkable quantities of Capital Gains Tax in the process. Management consortia were forming and making ridiculously low bids for ownership of his companies, and he was accepting them. Subsidiary parts of NorthStar International were being entrusted solely to their administrative boards. North had, it seemed, let go of the steering wheel, and the car wasn't simply careering out of control, it was falling to bits as well.

North ate lavishly. His subordinates barely touched their food.

He rested well, and the woman who came to see him at three was bemused, and perhaps a little flattered, by the hymns to her beauty that North sang before, during and after coitus. He seemed somehow less mature and less experienced than she remembered. Like the chauffeur, she ascribed the change in personality to a knock on the head, and thought no more of it.

Markets across the world seesawed dramatically as the piecemeal disintegration of NorthStar International went on. The structure that had been built, to a large extent, on the clone-golem's pain, was coming apart, brick by brick. The process continued over the next few days. By the end of the week, there was barely a NorthStar International left. The company was still trading, but ninety per cent of its workforce had moved across into other jobs or were now running smaller, independent outfits, answerable only to themselves, responsible for their own successes and failures.

In Latin America, the Far East, Europe, the United States, everywhere, people – even people who had no direct connection with NorthStar International – were left wondering what had happened. Without knowing quite why, they sensed that, somewhere, some huge, obstructing blockage had been cleared. There was chaos, but within the chaos new shapes could be discerned like figures in mist. World-wide, there was a sense of trepidation and, at the same time, jubilation.

Twelve

North had no idea how long the door had been open. His captor must have unlocked it while he had been asleep.

He climbed the steps and tottered into the passageway. He opened the bookcase and walked, blinking, into his study. What day was it? How long had he been a prisoner? He had tried to keep track of time by rationing out the food and water that the clone-golem had left him, using the circadian rhythms of hunger as his guide, but the method did not work because he had no idea how long he had been unconscious to begin with and because the trauma of captivity destroyed his appetite. In a timeless, benighted limbo he had alternately screamed with panic, pecked at food, stood at the door pounding and begging for release, curled up on the floor whimpering, and fleetingly and sporadically slept. For how many days had he existed in this wretched state? Three, he estimated. Four at the most.

He was shocked to discover, via the television, that it was a Friday. A week. He had been down in the cellar for a whole week.

Where was the clone-golem? Where had he got to? What had he done while he had been keeping North in the cellar?

North found out soon enough by accessing his accounts from the computer in his study. And as he surveyed the ruin of his empire, he felt a solitary, humiliating kind of grief. The loss gutted him. At the same time, however, he felt a peculiar sensation of lightness. It was as though, having had so much gouged out of him financially, he actually weighed less.

The clone-golem had left him with enough to live on in reasonable comfort. The mansion was still his. The chauffeur would not have to go, although the stables and the golf course were now under public proprietorship. Things were not *so* bad.

In examining the state of his finances, North also found that monies had been diverted to an anonymous Swiss bank account. The sum was exactly the same amount as the clone-golem had left him for his own use.

At midnight, he went to the window and peered out into the darkness.

He was out there somewhere. The man who had his face, his DNA, his memories. Out there, roaming the world. Exploring. Discovering. Exulting in his freedom.

North's instinctive urge was to have him tracked down. Set the very best and most expensive private detectives he could find on the clone-golem's trail. It wouldn't take long. Whatever steps the clone-golem took to disguise his appearance, people would always note someone who bore a marked resemblance to William Ian North. He would be found and brought back to England to face North's full wrath. Money would be no object . . .

But of course, money *was* an object, now that North had comparatively little of it. And besides, for some strange reason North could not bring himself to hate the clone-golem. It seemed incomprehensible to him, after what the clone-golem had done to him, but he could find in himself no great desire to recapture the creature and begin the whole cycle of achievement and beatings all over again. Down in the cellar he had had a taste of what he had put the clone-golem through. He had suffered nowhere near as grievously as the clone-golem had suffered . . . but the experience had been bad enough. He now knew the true price at which his success had been bought.

The clone-golem had, under the circumstances, treated him with undeserved mercy. The least he could do was return the favour.

Solemnly staring out into the night, William Ian North – in what was probably the first genuinely charitable act of his life – wished the creature happiness.

kim newman

andy warhol's dracula

For Sara and Randy

Kim Newman

As Nancy snuffed, her blood curdled. The taste of the vile scabs flooded his mouth. He pushed her away, detaching fangs from her worn wounds. Ropes of bloody spittle hung from her neck to his maw. He wiped his mouth on his wrist, breaking their liquid link. A last electric thrill shuddered, arcing between them. Her heart stopped.

He had pulled her backward onto the bed, holding her down on him as he worked at her throat, her hands feebly scrabbling his sides. Empty, she was deadweight on top of him. He was uncomfortably aware of the other garbage in the bed: magazines, bent spoons, hypodermic needles, used Kleenex, ripped and safety-pinned clothes, banknotes, congealed sandwiches, weeks of uneaten complimentary mints. A package of singles – Sid's 'My Way' – had broken under them, turning the much-stained mattress into a fakir's bed of nails. Vinyl shards stabbed his unbroken skin.

Johnny Pop was naked but for leopard-pattern briefs and socks, and the jewellery. Prizing his new clothes too much to get them gory, he had neatly folded and placed the suit and shirt on a chair well away from the bed. His face and chest were sticky with blood and other discharges.

As the red rush burst in his eyes and ears, his senses flared, more acute by a dozenfold. Outside, in iced velvet October night, police sirens sounded like the wailings of the bereaved mothers of Europe. Distant shots burst as if they were fired in the room, stabs of noise inside his skull. Blobby TV light painted neon a cityscape across ugly wallpaper, populated by psychedelic cockroaches.

He tasted the ghosts of the Chelsea Hotel: drag queens and vampire killers, junkies and pornographers, artists and freaks, visionaries and wasters, Pressing into his mind, they tried to make of his undead body a channel through which they could claw their way back to this plane of existence. Their voices shrieked, clamouring for attention. Cast out of Manhattan, they lusted for restoration to their paved paradise.

Though his throat protested, Johnny forced himself to swallow. Nancy's living blood had scarcely been of better quality than this dead filth. Americans fouled their bodies. Her habits would have killed her soon, even if she hadn't invited a vampire into Room 100. He didn't trouble himself with guilt. Some people were looking for their vampires, begging all their lives for death. His *nosferatu* hold upon the world was tenuous. He could only remain on sufferance. Without the willing warm, he would starve and die. They fed him. They were to blame for him.

Dead blood, heavy with Tuinol and Dilaudid, smote his brain, washing away the ghosts. He had to be careful; this city was thronged with the truly dead, loitering beyond the ken of the warm, desperate for attention from those who could perceive them. When he was feeding, they crowded around. Having been dead, however briefly, he was a beacon for them.

He yowled and threw the meat-sack off him. He sat up in the bed, nerves drawn taut, and looked at the dead girl. She was ghost-white flesh in black underwear. The flowering neck wound was the least of the marks on her. Scarifications criss-crossed her concave tummy. Pulsing slits opened like gills in her sides, leaking the last of her. The marks of his talons, they were dead mouths, beseeching more kisses from him.

Since arriving in America, he'd been careful to take only those who asked for it, who were already living like ghosts. They had few vampires here. Drained corpses attracted attention. Already, he knew, he'd been noticed. To prosper, he must practise the skills of his father-in-darkness. First, to hide; then, to master.

The Father was always with him, first among the ghosts. He watched over Johnny and kept him from real harm.

Sid, Belsen-thin but for his Biafra-bloat belly, was slumped in a ratty chair in front of blurry early early television. He looked at Johnny and at Nancy, incapable of focusing. Earlier, he'd shot up through his eyeball. Colours slid and flashed across his bare, scarred-and-scabbed chest and arms. His head was a skull in a spiky fright-wig, huge eyes swarming as *Jose and the Pussycats* reflected on the screen of his face. The boy tried to laugh but could only shake. A silly little knife, not even silver, was loosely held in his left hand.

Johnny pressed the heels of his fists to his forehead, and jammed his eyes shut. Bloodred light shone through the skin curtains of his eyelids. He had felt this before. It wouldn't last more than a few seconds. Hell raged in his brain. Then, as if a black fist had struck him in the gullet, peristaltic movement forced fluid up through his throat. He opened his mouth, and a thin squirt of black liquid spattered across the carpet and against the wall.

'Magic spew,' said Sid, in amazement.

The impurities were gone. Johnny was on a pure blood-high now. He contained all of Nancy's short life. She had been an all-American girl. She had given him everything.

He considered the boy in the chair and the girl on the bed, the punks. Their tribes were at war, his and theirs. Clothes were their colours, Italian suits versus safety-pinned PVC pants. This session at the Chelsea had been a truce that turned into a betrayal, a rout, a massacre. The Father was proud of Johnny's strategy.

Sid looked at Nancy's face. Her eyes were open, showing only veined white. He gestured with his knife, realising something had happened. At some point in the evening, Sid had stuck his knife into himself a few times. The tang of his rotten blood filled the room. Johnny's fangs slid from their gum-sheaths, but he had no more hunger yet. He was too full.

He thought of the punks as Americans, but Sid was English. A musician, though he couldn't really play his guitar. A singer, though he could only shout.

America was a strange new land. Stranger than Johnny had imagined in the Old Country, stranger than he could have imagined. If he drank more blood, he would soon be an American. Then he would be beyond fear, untouchable. It was what the Father wanted for him.

He rolled the corpse off his shins, and cleaned himself like a cat, contorting his supple back and neck, extending his foot-long tongue to lick off the last of the bloodstains. He unglued triangles of vinyl from his body and threw them away. Satisfied, he got off the bed and pulled on crusader white pants, immodestly tight around crotch and rump, loose as a sailor's below the knee. The dark purple shirt settled on his back and chest, sticking to him where his saliva was still wet. He rattled the cluster of gold chains and medallions – Transylvanian charms, badges of honour and conquest – that hung in the gap between his hand-sized collar-points.

With the white jacket, lined in blood-red silk, Johnny was a blinding apparition. He didn't need a strobe to shine in the dark. Sid raised his knife-hand, to cover his eyes. The boy's reaction was better than any mirror.

'Punk sucks,' said Johnny, inviting a response.

'Disco's stupid,' Sid sneered back.

Sid was going to get in trouble. Johnny had to make a slave of the boy, to keep himself out of the story.

He found an unused needle on the bed. Pinching the nipple-like bulb, he stuck the needle into his wrist, spearing the vein perfectly. He let the bulb go and a measure of his blood – of Nancy's? – filled the glass phial. He unstuck himself. The tiny wound was invisibly healed by the time he'd smeared away the bead of blood and licked his thumbprint. He tossed the syrette to Sid, who knew exactly what to do with it, jabbing it into an old arm-track and squirting. Vampire blood slid into Sid's system, something between a virus and a drug. Johnny felt the hook going into Sid's brain, and fed him some line.

Sid stood, momentarily invincible, teeth sharpening, eyes reddened, ears bat-flarred, movements swifter. Johnny shared his sense of power, almost paternally. The vampire buzz wouldn't last long, but Sid would be a slave as long as he lived, which was unlikely to be forever. To become *nosferatu*, you had to give and receive blood; for centuries, most mortals had merely been giving; here, a fresh compact between the warm and the undead was being invented.

Johnny nodded towards the empty thing on the bed. Nobody's blood was any good to her now. He willed the command through the line, through the hook, into Sid's brain. The boy, briefly possessed, leaped across the room, landing on his knees on the bed, and stuck his knife into the already dead girl, messing up the wounds on her throat, tearing open her skin in dozens of places. As he slashed, Sid snarled, black fangs splitting his gums.

Johnny let himself out of the room.

They were calling him a vampire long before he turned.

At the Silver Dream Factory, the Mole People, amphetamine-swift dusk-til-dawners eternally out for blood, nicknamed him 'Drella': half-Dracula, half-Cinderella. The coven often talked of Andy's 'victims': first, cast-offs whose lives were appropriated for Art, rarely given money to go with their limited fame (a great number of them now truly dead); later, wealthy portrait subjects or **Inter/VIEW** *advertisers, courted as assiduously as any Renaissance art patron (a great number of them ought to be truly dead). Andy leached off them all, left them drained or transformed, using them without letting them touch him, never distinguishing between the commodities he could only coax from other people: money, love, blood, inspiration, devotion, death. Those who rated him a genius and those who ranked him a fraud reached eagerly, too eagerly, for the metaphor. It was so persistent, it must eventually become truth.*

In Swimming Underground: My Years in the Warhol Factory *(1995), supervamp Mary Woronov (**Hedy/The Shoplifter,** 1965;* **The Chelsea Girls,** *1966) writes: 'People were calling us the undead, vampires, me and my little brothers of the night, with our lips pressed against the neck of the city, sucking the energy out of scene after scene. We left each party behind like a wasted corpse, raped and carelessly tossed aside . . . Andy was the worst, taking on five and six parties a night. He even looked like a vampire: white, empty, waiting to be filled, incapable of satisfaction. He was the white worm – always hungry, always cold, never still, always twisting.' When told that the artist had actually turned vampire, Lou Reed arched a ragged eyebrow and quizzed, 'Andy was* **alive**?' *In the multitude of memoirs and word or song portraits that try to define Andy Warhol, there is no instance of anyone ever using the adjective 'warm' about him.*

Valerie Solanas, who prompted Andy's actual turning, took superstitious care to shoot him with homemade silver bullets. She tried wrapping .32 ammunition in foil, which clogged the chambers, before resorting to spray-paint in the style of Billy Name (Linich), the silver-happy decorator of the Factory who coffined himself in a tiny back-room for two years, coming out only at dead of night to forage. The names are just consonants short of anagrams: Andy Warhola, Wlad Draculya; Valerie Solanas, Van Helsing. Valerie's statement, the slogan of a fearless vampire killer: 'he had too much control over my life.' On the operating table – 4.51 pm, Monday, June 3, 1968 – Andy Warhol's heart stopped. He was declared clinically dead but came back and lived on, his vision of death and disaster fulfilled and survived. The stringmeat ghost of the latter years was sometimes a parody of his living self, a walking Diane Arbus exhibit, belly scars like zippers, Ray-Ban eyes and dead skin.

Warhola the Vampyre sloped **nosferatu**-*taloned through the seventies, a fashion-setter as always, as – after nearly a century in the open in Europe – vampirism (of a sort) at last established itself in America. He had no get, but was the fountainhead of a bloodline. You can still see them, in galleries or* **People**, *on the streets after dark, in the clubs and cellars. Andy's kids: cloned creatures, like the endless replications of his silkscreen celebrity portraits, faces repeated until they become meaningless patterns of colour dots. When alive, Andy had said he wanted to become a machine and that everybody should be alike. How did he feel when his wishes were coming true? How did he feel about anything? Did he feel? Ever? If you spend any amount of time trying to understand the man and his work, you can't help but worry that he's reaching from beyond the grave and forcing you to become Valerie.*

Consider the signs, the symptoms, the symbols: that pale, almost-albino face, simultaneously babyish and ancient, shrinking like a bucket of salted slugs when exposed to the sun; the sharp or battered black clothes, stiff from the grave; the goggle-like dark glasses, hypnotic black holes where eyes should be; the slavic monotone of the whispery voice and the pared-down, kindergarten vocabulary; the covert religiosity, the prizing of sacred or silver objects; the squirrelling-away of money and possessions in a centuried lair; even the artificial shocks of grey-white-silver hair. Are these not the attributes of a classical vampire, Dracula himself? Look at photographs taken before or after June 1968, and you can't tell whether he is or isn't. Like the murgatroyds of the 1890s, Andy was a disciple before he became a vampire. For him, turning was dropping the seventh veil, the last chitinous scrap of chrysalis, a final stage in becoming what he had always meant to be, an admittal that this was indeed what was inside him.

His whole life had revolved around the dead.

Kathleen Conklin,

'Destroying Drella'*, paper delivered at 'Warhol's Worlds', inaugural conference of The Andy Warhol Museum (April 21–23, 1995); revised for publication as 'Warhola the Vampyre' in* ***Who is Andy Warhol?****, edited by Colin MacCabe with Mark Francis and Peter Wollen (The British Film Institute and The Andy Warhol Museum, 1997).*

He stepped out of the Chelsea Hotel onto the sidewalk of West 23rd Street, and tasted New York. It was the dead time, the thick hours before dawn, when all but the most committed night owls were home abed, or at least crashed out on a floor, blood sluggish with coffee, cigarettes or drugs. This was the vampire afternoon, and Johnny understood how alone he was. There were other vampires in this city, and he was almost ready to seek them out, but none like him, of his line.

America was vast, bloated with rich, fatty blood. The fresh country supported only a few ticks that tentatively poked probosces through thick hide, sampling without gorging. By comparison, Johnny was a hungry monster. Minutes after taking Nancy, he could have fed again, and again. He had to take more than he needed. He could handle dozens of warm bodies a night without bursting, without choking on the ghosts. Eventually, he would make children-in-darkness, slaves to serve him, to shield him. He must pass on the bloodline of the Father. But not yet.

He hadn't intended to come to this city of towers, with its moat of running water. His plan was to stick to the film people he had hooked up with in the Old Country, and go to fabled Hollywood on the Pacific. But there was a mix-up at JFK and he was detained in Immigration while the rest of the company, American passports brandished like protective banners, were waved on to catch connecting flights to Los Angeles or San Francisco. He was stuck at the airport in a crowd of overeager petitioners, dark-skinned and warm, as dawn edged threateningly closer. The Father was with him then, as he slipped into a Men's Room and bled a Canadian flight attendant who gave him a come-on, invigorating himself with something new and wild. Buzzing with fresh blood, first catch of this new land, he concentrated his powers of fascination to face down the officials who barred his way. It was beneath him to bribe those who could be overpowered by force of will.

America was disorienting. To survive, he must adapt swiftly. The pace of change in this century was far more rapid than the glacial shifts of the long years the Father had in his Carpathian fastness. Johnny would have to surpass the Father to keep ahead, but bloodline would tell. Though of an ancient line, he was a 20th Century creature, turned only thirty-five years earlier, taken into the dark before he was formed as a living man. In Europe, he had been a boy, hiding in the shadows, waiting. Here, in this bright America, he could fulfil his potential. People took him for a young man, not a child.

Johnny Pop had arrived.

He knew he had been noticed. He was working hard to fit in, but recognised how gauche he had been a few short weeks ago. On his first nights in New York, he had made mistakes. Blood in the water excited the sharks.

Someone stood on the corner, watching him. Two black men, in long leather coats. One wore dark glasses despite the hour, the other had a slim-brimmed hat with a tiny feather in the band. Not vampires, there was something of the predator about them. They were well-armed. Silver shoe-buckles and buttons, coats loose over guns. And their bodies were weapons, a finished blade, an arrow shaft. From inside his coat, the black man in sunglasses produced a dark knife. Not silver, but polished hardwood.

Johnny tensed, ready to fight and kill. He had just fed. He was at his strongest.

The knifeman smiled. He balanced his weapon by its point, and tapped his forehead with its hilt, a warrior salute. He would not attack yet. His presence was an announcement, a warning. He was showing himself. This man had seen Johnny before he was seen. His night-skills were sharp.

Then, the knifeman and his partner were gone. They had seemed to disappear, to step into a shadow even Johnny's night eyes could not penetrate.

He suppressed a shudder. This city was not yet his jungle, and he was exposed here – out on the street in a white suit that shone like a beacon – as he had not been in the Old Country.

The black men should have destroyed him now. When they had a chance. Johnny would do his best to see they did not get another.

It was time to move on, to join the crowd.

A mustard-yellow taxi cruised along the street, emerging like a dragon from an orange-pink groundswell of steam. Johnny hailed the cab, and slid into its cage-like interior. The seat was criss-crossed with duct tape, battlefield dressings on a fatal wound. The driver, a gaunt white man with a baggy military jacket, looked instinctively at the rear-view mirror, expecting to lock eyes with his fare. Johnny saw surprise in the young man's face as he took in the reflection of an empty hack. He twisted to look into the dark behind him and saw Johnny there, understanding at once what he had picked up.

'You have a problem?' Johnny asked.

After a moment, the taxi driver shrugged.

'Hell, no. A lot of guys won't even take spooks, but I'll take anyone. They all come out at night.'

Behind the driver's gunsight eyes, Johnny saw jungle twilight, purpled by napalm blossoms. He heard the reports of shots fired years ago. His nostrils stung with dead cordite.

Uncomfortable, he broke the connection.

Johnny told the driver to take him to Studio 54.

*

Even now, this late in the night, a desperate line lingered outside the club. Their breaths frosted in a cloud, and they stamped unfashionably-shoed feet against the cold. Losers with no chance, they would cajole and plead with Burns and Stu, the hard-faced bouncers, but never see the velvet rope lifted. An invisible sign was on their foreheads. Worse than dead, they were boring.

Johnny paid off the cab with sticky bills lifted from Nancy's purse, and stood on the sidewalk, listening to the throb of the music from inside. 'Pretty Baby', Blondie. Debbie Harry's living dead voice called to him.

The taxi did not move off. Was the driver hoping for another fare from among these damned? No, he was fixing Johnny in his mind. A man without a reflection should be remembered.

'See you again soon, Jack,' said the white man.

Like the black men outside the Chelsea, the taxi driver was a danger. Johnny had marked him. It was good to know who would come for you, to be prepared. The white man's name was written on his licence just as his purpose was stamped on his face. It was Travis. In Vietnam, he had learned to look monsters in the face, even in the mirror.

The cab snarled to life and prowled off.

Moving with the music, Johnny crossed the sidewalk towards the infernal doorway, reaching out with his mind to reconnect with the bouncers, muscular guys with Tom of Finland leather caps and jackets. Burns was a moonlighting cop with sad eyes and bruises, Stu a trust fund kid with his own monster father in his head; Johnny's hooks were in both of them, played out on the thinnest of threads. They were not, would never be, his get, but they were his. First, he would have warm chattels; get would come later.

He enjoyed the wails and complaints from losers as he breezed past the line, radiating an 'open sesame' they could never manage. Stu clicked the studded heels of his motorcycle boots and saluted, fingers aligned with the peak of his black leather forage cap with Austro-Hungarian precision. Burns smartly lifted the rope, the little sound of the hook being detached from the eye exciting envious sighs, and stood aside. To savour the moment, Johnny paused in the doorway, knowing the spill of light from inside made his suit shine like an angelic raiment, and surveyed those who would never get in. Their eyes showed such desperation that he almost pitied them.

Two weeks ago, he had been among them, drawn to the light but kept away from the flame. Like some older creatures of his kind, he could not force his way into a place until he had been invited across the threshold. Then, his clothes – found in a suitcase chosen at random from the carousel at the airport – had not been good. Being *nosferatu* was unusual enough to get him attention. Steve Rubell was passing the door, and took note of Johnny's sharp, beautiful face. Possessed of the knack of seeing himself as others saw him, Johnny understood the owner-manager was intrigued by the vampire boy on his doorstep. But Shining Lucifer himself couldn't get into 54 with a Bicentennial shirt, cowboy boots and black hair flattened like wet sealskin to his skull.

When he came back, the next night, he wore clothes that fit: a Halston suit – black outside in the dark, with a violet weave that showed under the lights – and a Ralph Lauren shirt with fresh bloodstains across the polo player. They still smelled faintly of their previous owner, Tony from Brooklyn. The bouncers didn't even need to check with Steve to let Johnny in, and he took the opportunity, later that night in the back rooms, to lay a tiny smear of his blood on them both, apparently a token of gratitude, actually a sigil of ownership. Johnny was saving them for later, knowing they would be needed.

As he ducked past the curtains and slid into 54, Johnny felt Tony's ghost in his limbs. He had taken much from Tony Manero, whom he had exsanguinated on the Brooklyn Bridge. From the boy, he had caught the blood rhythms that matched the music of the month. Tony had been a dancer; Johnny had inherited that from him, along with his fluffed-up but flared-back hairstyle and clothes that were not just a protective cover but a style, a display.

Tony was with him most nights now, a ghost. The kid had never made it to 54, but he'd been better than Brooklyn, good enough for Manhattan. Johnny thought Tony, whose empty carcass he had weighted and tossed off the Bridge, would be happy that some of him at least had made it in the real city. When the blood was still fresh in him, Johnny had followed its track, back to Tony's apartment, and slipped in – unnoticed by the kid's family, even the fallen priest – to take away his wardrobe, the night-clothes that were now his armour.

He let the music take him, responding to it with all his blood. Nancy's ghost protested, making puking motions at the sound of the disco despised by all true punks. By taking her, Johnny had won a great victory in the style wars. He liked killing punks. No one noticed when they were gone. They were all committing slow suicide anyway; that was the point, for there was no future. To love disco was to want to live forever, to aspire to an immortality of consumption. Punks didn't believe in anything beyond death, and loved nothing, not even themselves.

He wondered what would happen to Sid.

A man in the moon puppet, spooning coke up his nose, beamed down from the wall, blessing the throng with a 1978 benediction. As Johnny stepped onto the illuminated floor and strutted through the dancers, his suit shone like white flame. He had the beat with his every movement. Even his heart pulsed in time to the music. He smiled as he recognised the song, fangs bright as neons under the strobe, eyes red glitterballs. This was the music he had made his own, the song that meant the most of all the songs.

'Staying Alive', The Bee Gees.

In its chorus, he heard the wail of the warm as they died under his kisses, ah-ah-ah-ah, staying alive. In its lyric, he recognised himself, a woman's man with no time to talk.

His dancing cleared a circle.

It was like feeding. Without even taking blood, he drew in the blood of the crowd to himself, loosening the ghosts of those who danced with him from their bodies. Tulpa spirits stretched out through mouths and noses and attached to him like ectoplasmic straws. As he danced, he sucked with his whole body, tasting minds and hearts, outshining them all. No one came near, to challenge him. The Father was proud of him.

For the length of the song, he *was* alive.

*

Andrew Warhola was an American – born in Pittsburgh on August 6th, 1928 – but his family were not. In ***The Life and Death of Andy Warhol*** *(1989), Victor Bockris quotes his statement 'I am from nowhere', but gives it the lie: 'The Warholas were Rusyns who had emigrated to America from the Ruthenian village of Mikova in the Carpathian Mountains near the borders of Russia and Poland in territory that was, at the turn of the century, part of the Austro-Hungarian Empire'. Bockris takes care, introducing early the theme that comes to dominate his biography, to note 'The Carpathian Mountains are popularly known as the home of Dracula, and the peasants in Jonathan Harker's description kneeling before roadside shrines, crossing themselves at the mention of Dracula's name, resemble Andy Warhol's distant relatives.'*

The third son of Ondrej and Julia Warhola grew up in Soho, an ethnic enclave that was almost a ghetto. From an early age, he seemed a changeling, paler and slighter than his family, laughably unfit for a future in the steel mills, displaying talent as soon as his hand could properly hold a pencil. Others in his situation might fantasise that they were orphaned princes, raised by peasant woodcutters, but the Warholas had emigrated – escaped? – from the land of the vampires. Not fifty years before, Count Dracula had come out of Carpathia and established his short-lived empire in London. Dracula was still a powerful figure then, the most famous vampire in the world, and his name was spoken often in the Warhola household. Years later, in a film, Andy had an actress playing his mother claim to have been a victim, in childhood, of the Count, that Dracula's bloodline remained in her veins, passing in the womb to her last son. Like much else in Andy's evolving autobiography, there is no literal truth in this story but its hero spent years trying to wish it into reality and may even, at the last, have managed to pull off the trick. Before settling on 'Andy Warhol' as his eventual professional name, he experimented with the signature 'Andrew Alucard'.

Julia was horrified by her little Andrew's inclinations. For her, vampires were objects not of fascination but dread. A devout Byzantine Catholic, she would drag her children six miles to the wooden church of St John Chrystostom's on Saline Street and subject them to endless rituals of purification. Yet, among Andy's first drawings are bats and coffins. In the 1930s, as Dracula held court in one of his many exiles, the American illustrated press were as obsessed with vampires as movie stars. There were several successful periodicals – **Weird Tales, Spicy Vampire Stories** *– devoted almost entirely to their social activities. To look through these magazines, as the child Andy did, is to understand what it is to learn that a party is going on after your bedtime, to which you cannot possibly secure an invitation. Literally, you had to die to get in. In Vienna, Budapest, Constantinople, Monte Carlo and private estates and castles scattered in a crescent across Europe, vampire kings and queens held court.*

Young Andrew clipped photographs and portraits from the magazines and hoarded them for the rest of his life. He preferred photographs, especially the blurred or distorted traces of those who barely registered on cameras or in mirrors. He understood at once that creatures denied the sight of their own faces must prize portrait painters. He wrote what might be called 'fan letters' to the leaders of vampire fashion: de Lioncourt of Paris, Andrew Bennett of London, the White Russian Rozokov. His especial favourites among the undead, understandably, were the child-vampires, those frozen infant immortals Noel Coward sings about in 'Poor Little Dead Girl'. His prize possession as a boy was an autographed portrait of the martyred Claudia, ward of the stylish de Lioncourt, considered a paragon and an archetype among her kind. He would later use this image – a subscription gift sent out by **Night Life** *– in his silkscreen,* **Vampire Doll** *(1963).*

In his fascination with the undead, Andy was in the avant-garde. There were still very few vampires in America, and those American-born or -made tended to flee to a more congenial Europe. There was a vampire panic in the wake of the First World War, as returning veterans brought back the tainted bloodline that burned out in the epidemic of 1919. The lost generation new-borns, who all incubated within their bodies a burning disease that ate them up from the inside within months, were ghastly proof that vampires would never 'take' in the New World. Congress passed acts against the spread of vampirism save under impossibly regulated circum-

stances. J. Edgar Hoover ranked vampires just below communists and well above organised crime as a threat to the American way of life. In the 1930s, New York District Attorney Thomas Dewey led a crusade against an influx of Italian vampires, successfully deporting coven-leader Niccolo Cavalanti and his acolytes. In the South, a resurgence of the Ku Klux Klan viciously curbed a potential renaissance of interlocked vampire **hounforts** *in New Orleans and throughout the bayou country.*

America, like Julia Warhola, considered all vampires loathsome monsters. Yet, as Andy understood, there was a dreadful glamour. During the Depression, glimpses of the high life lived in another continent and by another species, seemed enticing. The Hungarian Paul Lukas was the first Hollywood actor to specialise in undead roles, from **Scarface** *(1932) to* **The House of Ruthven** *(1937). A few real vampires, even, made it in the movies: Garbo, Malakai, Chevalier Futaine. With the rise of fascism and the Second World War came a trickle of vampire refugees from the Old World. Laws were revised and certain practices tolerated 'for the duration', while Hoover's FBI – constantly nagged by America's witch-hunters Cardinal Spellman and Father Coughlin – compiled foot-thick dossiers on elders and new-borns alike. As Nazi eugenicists strived to cleanse his bloodline from the Reich, Dracula himself aligned with the Allies, and a vampire underground in occupied Europe co-operated with the liberating forces.*

When the War was over, the climate changed again and a round of blacklistings, arrests and show-trials – notably the prosecution for treason of American-born and -made vampire Benjamin Lathem by Robert F. Kennedy – drove all but those who could 'pass for warm' back to Europe. That was the era of the scare movies, with homburg-hatted government men taking crucifix and stake to swarthy, foreign infiltrators: **I Married a Vampire** *(1950),* **I was a Vampire for the FBI** *(1951),* **Blood of Dracula** *(1958). Warhol was in New York by now, sketching shoes for ad lay-outs or arranging window displays for Bonwit Teller's, making a hundred thousand dollars a year but fretting that he wasn't taken seriously. Money wasn't enough for him; he needed to be famous too, as if under the curse described by Fritz Leiber in 'The Casket Demon' (1963) –*

unless known of and talked about, he would fade to nothingness. Like America, he had not outgrown his vampire craze, just learned to keep quiet about it.

In 1956, the year **Around the World in 80 Days** *took the Best Picture Oscar, Andy took an extended trip with the frustratingly unforthcoming Charles Lisanby – Hawaii, Japan, India, Egypt, Rome, Paris, London. Throughout that itinerary, he saw vampires living openly, mingling with the warm, as adored as they were feared. Is it too much to suppose that, in a maharajah's palace or on a Nile paddle-wheeler, spurned by Charles and driven to abase himself before some exotic personage, he was bitten?*

Conklin, *ibid*

'Gee, who is that boy?' asked Andy, evenly. 'He is fantastic.'

Penelope was used to the expression. It was one of Andy's few adjectives. Everyone and everything was either 'fantastic' or 'a bore' or something similar, always with an elongated vowel early on. All television was 'fa-antastic'; World War II was 'a bo-ore'. Vintage cookie tins were 'si-imply wonderful'; income taxes were 'ra-ather old'. Famous people were 've-ery interesting'; living daylight was 'pra-ctically forgotten'.

She turned to look down on the dance floor. They were sitting up on the balcony, above the churning masses, glasses of chilled blood on the table between them, at once shadowed enough to be mysterious and visible enough to be recognisable. There was no point in coming to Studio 54 unless it was to be seen, to be noticed. At tomorrow's sunset, when they both rose from their day's sleep, it would be Penny's duty to go through the columns, reading out any mentions of their appearances, so Andy could cluck and crow over what was said about him, and lament that so much was left out.

It took her a moment to spot the object of Andy's attention.

For once, he was right. The dancer in the white suit was fantastic. Fa-antastic, even. She knew at once that the boy was like her, *nosferatu*. His look, his style, was American, but she scented a whiff of European grave-mould. This was no new-born, no *nouveau*, but an experienced creature, practised in his dark-skills. Only a vampire with many nights behind him could seem so *young*.

It had to happen. She was not the first to come here. She had known an invasion was inevitable. American could not hold out forever. She had not come here to be unique, but to be away from her kind, from her former lives. Though she had inevitably hooked up with Andy, she did not want to be sucked back into the world of the undead. But what she wanted meant very little any more, which was as it should be. Whatever came, she would accept. It was her duty, her burden.

She looked back at Andy. It took sharp senses indeed to distinguish his real enthusiasms from his feigned ones. He had worked hard – and it did not do to underestimate this languid scarecrow's capacity for hard work – to become as inexpressive as he was, to cultivate what passed in America for a lack of accent. His chalk-dusted cheeks and cold mouth gave nothing away. His wig was silver tonight, thick and stiff as a knot of fox-tails. His suit was quiet, dark and Italian, worn with a plain tie.

They both wore goggle-like black glasses to shield their eyes from the club's frequent strobes. But, unlike some of his earlier familiars, Penny made no real attempt to look like him.

She watched the dancer spin, hip-cocked, arm raised in a disco heil, white jacket flaring to show scarlet lining, a snarl of concentration on his cold lovely face.

How could Andy not be interested in another of the undead? Especially one like this.

At least the dancing boy meant the night wasn't a complete wash-out. It had been pretty standard, so far: two openings, three parties and a reception. One big disappointment: Andy had hoped to bring Miz Lillian, the President's mama, to the reception for Princess Ashraf, twin sister of the Shah of Iran, but the White House got wind and scuttled the plan. Andy's fall-back date, Lucie Arnaz, was hardly a substitute, and Penny was forced to make long conversation with the poor girl – whom she had never heard of – while Andy did the silent act most people thought of as deliberate mystification but which was actually simply sulking. The Princess, sharp ornament of one of the few surviving vampire ruling houses, was not exactly on her finest fettle, either – preoccupied by the troubles of her absolutist brother, who was currently back home surrounded by Mohammedan fanatics screaming for his impalement.

In the car between Bianca Jagger's party at the Tea Rooms and L. B. Jeffries's opening at the Photographers' Gallery, Paloma Picasso rather boringly went on about the tonic properties of human blood as face cream. Penny would have told the warm twit how stupid she was being about matters of which she plainly knew nothing, but Andy was frozen enough already without his faithful vampire conpanion teeing off someone so famous – Penny wasn't sure what exactly the painter's daughter was famous *for* – she was sure to get his name in *Vanity Fair*. At Bianca's, Andy thought he'd spotted Davie Bowie with Catherine Deneuve, but it turned out to be a far less interesting couple. Another disappointment.

Bob Colacello, editor of *Inter/VIEW* and Andy's connection with the Pahlavis, wittered on about how well the Princess was bearing up, and was trying to sell him on committing to an exhibition in the new museum of modern art the Shah had endowed in Teheran. Penny could tell Andy was chilling on the idea, sensing – quite rightly – that it would not do well to throw in with someone on the point of losing everything. Andy elaborately ignored Bob, and that meant everyone else did too. He had been delighted to learn from her what 'being sent to 'Coventry' meant and redoubled his use of that ancient schoolboy torture. There was a hurt desperation in Bob's chatter, but it was all his own fault and she didn't feel a bit sorry for him.

At the Photographers', surrounded by huge blow-ups of war orphans and devastated Asian villages, Andy got on one of his curiosity jags and started quizzing her, Penny, about Oscar Wilde. What had he been like, had he really been amusing all the time, had he been frightened when the wolves gathered, how much had he earned, how famous had he really been, would he have been recognised everywhere he went? After nearly a hundred years, she remembered Wilde less than many others she had known in the '80s. Like her, the poet was one of the first modern generation of new-born vampires. He was one of those who turned but didn't last more than a decade, eaten up by disease carried over from warm life. She didn't like to think of contemporaries she had outlived. But Andy insisted, nagging, and she dutifully coughed up anecdotes and aphorisms to keep him contented. She told Andy that he reminded her of Oscar, which was certainly true in some ways. Penny dreaded being recategorised from 'fascinating' to 'a bore', with the consequent casting into the outer darkness.

All her life, all her afterlife, had been spent by her own choice in the shadows cast by a succession of tyrants. She supposed she was punishing herself for her sins. Andy had noticed; in the Factory, she was called 'Penny Penance' or 'Penny Penitent'. However, besotted with titles and honours, he usually introduced her to outsiders as 'Penelope Churchward, Lady Godalming'. She had never been married to Lord Godalming (or, indeed, anyone), but Arthur Holmwood had been her father-in-darkness, and some vampire aristos did indeed pass on titles to their get.

She was not the first English rose in Andy's entourage. She had been told she looked like the model Jane Forth, who had been in Andy's movies. Penny knew she had only become Andy's Girl of the Year after Catherine Guinness left the Factory to become Lady Neidpath. She had an advantage over Andy's earlier debs, though: she was never going to get old. As Girl of the Year, it was her duty to be Andy's companion of the night and to handle much of the organisational and social business of the Factory, of Andy Warhol Enterprises, Incorporated. It was something she was used to, from her Victorian years as an 'Angel in the Home' to her nights as last governess of the House of Dracula. She could even keep track of the money.

She sipped her blood, decanted from some bar worker who was 'really' an actor or a model. Andy left his drink untouched, as usual. He didn't trust blood that showed up in a glass, and nobody ever saw him feeding. Penny wondered if he were an abstainer. Just now, the red pinpoints in his dark glasses were fixed. He was still watching the dancer.

The vampire in the white suit hooked her attention too.

For a moment, she was sure it was *him*, come back yet again, young and lethal, intent on murderous revenge.

She breathed the name, 'Dracula'.

Andy's sharp ears picked it up, even through the dreadful guff that passed for music these days. It was one of the few names guaranteed to provoke his interest.

Andy prized her for her connection to the late King Vampire. Penny had been at the Palazzo Otranto at the end. She was one of the few who knew the truth about the last hours of *il principe*, though she jealously kept that anecdote to herself. It was bad enough that the memories lingered.

'The boy looks like him,' she said. 'He might be the Count's get, or of his bloodline. Most vampires Dracula made came to look like him. He spread his doppelgängers throughout the world.'

Andy nodded, liking the idea.

The dancer had Dracula's red eyes, his aquiline nose, his full mouth. But he was clean-shaven and had a bouffant of teased black hair, like a Broadway actor or a teenage idol. His look was as much Roman as Romanian.

Penny had understood on their first meeting that Andy Warhol didn't want to be just a vampire. He wanted to be *the* vampire, Dracula. Even before his death and resurrection, his coven had called him 'Drella'. It was meant to be cruel: he was the Count of the night hours, but at dawn he changed back into the girl who cleared away the ashes.

'Find out who he is, Penny,' Andy said. 'We should meet him. He's going to be famous.'

She had no doubt of that.

Flushed from dancing and still buzzed with Nancy's blood, Johnny moved on to the commerce of the night. The first few times, he had set up his shop in men's rooms, like the dealers he was rapidly putting out of business. Spooked by all the mirrors, he shifted from striplit johns to the curtained back rooms where the other action was. All the clubs had such places.

In the dark room, he felt the heat of the busy bodies and tasted ghosts, expelled on yo-yo strings of ectoplasm during orgasm. He threaded his way through writhing limbs to take up his habitual spot in a leather armchair. He slipped off his jacket, draping it carefully over the back of the chair, and popped his cuff-links, rolling his sleeves up to his elbows. His white lower arms and hands shone in the dark.

Burns, on a break, came to him first. The hook throbbed in his brain, jones throbbing in his bones like a slow drumbeat. The first shot of drac had been free, but now it was a hundred dollars a pop. The bouncer handed Johnny a crisp C-note. With the nail of his little finger, Johnny jabbed a centimetre-long cut in the skin of his left arm. Burns knelt down in front of the chair and licked away the welling blood. He began to suckle the wound, and Johnny pushed him away.

There was a plea in the man's eyes. The drac jolt was in him, but it wasn't enough. He had the strength and the senses, but also the hunger.

'Go bite someone,' Johnny said, laughing.

The bouncer's hook was in deep. He loved Johnny and hated him, but he'd do what he said. For Burns, hell would be to be expelled, to be denied forever the taste.

A girl, in a shimmering fringed dress, replaced the bouncer. She had violent orange hair.

'Is it true?' she asked.

'Is what true?'

'That you can make people like you?'

He smiled, sharply. He could make people *love* him.

'A hundred dollars and you can find out,' he said.

'I'm game.'

She was very young, a child. She had to scrape together the notes, in singles and twenties. Usually, he had no patience for that, and pushed such small-timers out of the way to find someone with the right money, as curt as a bus driver. But he needed small bills too, for cabfare and tips.

As her mouth fixed on his fresh wound, he felt his barb sink into her. She was a virgin, in everything. Within seconds, she was his slave. Her eyes widened as she found she was able to see in the dark. She touched fingertips to her suddenly sharp teeth.

It would last such a pathetically short time, but for now she was a princess of the shadows. He named her Nocturna, and made her his daughter until dawn. She floated out of the room, to hunt.

He drew more cuts across his arm, accepted more money, gave more drac. A procession of strangers, all his slaves, passed through. Every night there were more.

After an hour, he had $8,500 in bills. Nancy's ghost was gone, stripped away from him in dribs and drabs, distributed among his children of the night. His veins were sunken and tingling. His mind was crowded with impressions that faded to nothing as fast as the scars on his milky skin. All around, in the dark, his temporary get bit each other. He relished the musical yelps of pain and pleasure.

Now, he thirsted again.

Vampires show up in the 1950s fashion drawings, if only through coded symbols: ragged-edged batwing cloaks, draped over angular figures; red lipstick mouths on sharp-cheeked, black and white faces; tiny, almost unnoticeable, fangs peeping from stretched smiles. These in-jokes are self-criticism, a nervous admission of what had to happen next. To become 'Andy Warhol', the illustrator and window-dresser must die and be reborn as an Artist. Those who accuse him of being concerned only with his earnings – which, to be fair, is what he told anyone who would listen – forget that he abandoned a considerable income to devote all his energies to work which initially lost a lot of money.

Shortly before the Coca-Cola Bottle and Campbell's Soup Can series made him famous, and in a period when he feared he had recovered from one 'nervous breakdown' only to be slipping into another, Warhol did a painting – synthetic polymer and crayon on canvas – of ***Batman*** *(1960), the only vampire ever really to be embraced by America. Though justifably eclipsed by Lichtenstein's appropriations from comic strip panels,* ***Batman*** *is an important work in its own right, an idea seized but abandoned half-finished, the first flash of what would soon come to be called Pop Art. Like much from the period before Warhol hit upon repetition and manufacture as modes of expression, it seems incomplete, childish crayon scribbles across the cowled Bob Kane outline of the classic* *vampire vigilante. Exhibited at the Castelli Gallery, the work was the first Warhol piece to command a serious price from a private collector – an anonymous buyer on behalf of the Wayne Foundation – which may have encouraged the artist to continue with his personal work.*

During an explosion of creativity that began in 1962 and lasted at least until he was shot, Warhol took a lease on a former hat works at 231 East 47th Street and turned the loft space into the Factory, with the intention of producing Art on a production line. At the suggestion of assistant Nathan Gluck, Warhol seized upon the silkscreen process and ('like a forger'), turned out series of dollar bills, soup cans and Marilyn Monroes. It seems that he didn't care what his subjects were, so long as they were famous. When Henry Geldzahler, Assistant Curator for 20th Century American Art at the Metropolitan Museum, told him he should apply himself to more 'serious' subjects, Warhol began his 'death and disaster' series, images of car crashes, suicides and the electric chair. Straddling the trivial and the serious are his vampire portraits: **Carmilla Karnstein** *(1962),* **Vampire Doll** *(1963),* **Lucy Westenra** *(1963). Red-eyed and jagged-mouthed undead faces, reproduced in sheets like unperforated stamps, vivid greens and oranges for skin-tones, the series reinvents the 19th Century genre of vampire portraiture. The vampire subjects Andy chose shared one thing: all had been famously destroyed. He produced parallel silkscreens of their true deaths: impalements, decapitations, disintegrations. These are perhaps the first great works, ruined corpses swimming in scarlet blood, untenanted bodies torn apart by grim puritans.*

In 1964, Andy delivered a twenty by twenty black and white mural called 'Thirteen Vampires' to the American pavilion at the New York World's Fair, where it was to be exhibited beside work by Robert Rauschenberg and Roy Lichtenstein. Among the thirteen, naturally, was Warhol's first Dracula portrait, though all the other undead notables represented were women. The architect Philip Johnson, who had commissioned the piece, informed Warhol that word had come from the Governor that it was to be removed because there was concern that it was offensive to the God-fearing. When Warhol's suggestion that the portraits all be defaced with burning crosses to symbolise the triumph of the godly was vetoed, he went out to the fair with Geldzahler and another of his assistants, Gerard Malanga, and painted the mural over with a thick layer of undead-banishing silver paint, declaring 'and that'll be my art'. We can only speculate about the lost Dracula portrait, which none of the few who saw it can describe in detail. Which of the many, many images of the King of the Vampires – then truly dead for only five years – did Warhol reproduce? The most tantalising suggestion, based on Malanga's later-retracted version, is that for the only time in his entire career as an Artist, Warhol drew on his own imagination rather than copied or reproduced from life. Andy lied constantly, but this is the only occasion when anyone has ever accused him of ***making something up****.*

Warhol's first experiments with film, conducted in real-time with the co-opted collaboration of whoever happened to be hanging about in the Factory, are steeped in the atmosphere of vampirism. The camera hovers over the exposed throat of John Giorno in ***Sleep*** *(1963) as if ready to pounce. The projection of film shot at twenty-four frames per second at the silent speed of sixteen frames per second gives Giorno's six-hour night a suggestion of vampire lassitude. The flashes of white leader that mark the change of shots turn dirty sheets into white coffin plush, and the death rattle of the projector is the only soundtrack (aside from the comical yawns and angry ticket-money-back demands of any audience members happening upon the film in a real theatre). That same year, Warhol shot more explicit studies of vampirism: in* ***Kiss****, a succession of couples osculate like insects unable to uncouple their complex mouth-parts; in* ***Eat****, Robert Indiana crams his mouth with unidentifiable meats; and* ***Suck-Job*** *is an extended (thirty minutes) close-up of the face of a young man who is being nibbled by beings who never intrude into the frame or register on film. For* ***Suck-Job****, Warhol had arranged with Alex Ford, a real vampire, to 'appear' but Ford didn't take him seriously and failed to show up at the Factory for the shoot, forcing the artist to substitute pasty-faced but warm hustlers dragged off the street.*

When Warhol turned his camera on the Empire State Building in ***Empire*** *(1964), it saw the edifice first as the largest coffin in the* *world, jutting out of the ground as if dislodged by some seismic activity. As night slowly falls and the floodlights come on, the building becomes a cloaked predator standing colossal over New York City, shoulders sloped by the years, head sprouting a dirigible-mast horn. After that, Warhol had fellow underground filmmaker Jack Smith swish a cape over Baby Jane Hudson in the now-lost* **Batman Dracula** *(1964). Only tantalising stills, of Smith with a mouthful of plastic teeth and staring Lon Chaney eyes, remain of his film, which – as with the silver-coated 'Thirteen Vampires' – is perhaps as Andy wanted it. As with* **Sleep** *and* **Empire**, *the idea is more important than the artefact. It is enough that the films exist; they are not meant actually to be seen all the way through. When Jonas Mekas scheduled* **Empire** *at the Filmmakers' Co-Op in 1965, he lured Warhol into the screening room and tied him securely to one of the seats with stout rope, intent on forcing the creator to sit through his creation. When he came back two hours later to check up, he found Warhol had chewed through his bonds – briefly, an incarnation of* **Batman Dracula** *– and escaped into the night. In the early sixties, Warhol had begun to file his teeth, sharpening them to piranha-like needle-points.*

Conklin, *ibid*

A red-headed vampire girl bumped into her and hissed, displaying pearly fangs. Penelope lowered her dark glasses and gave the chit a neon glare. Cowed, the creature backed away. Intrigued, Penny took the girl by the bare upper arm, and looked into her mouth, like a dentist. Her fangs were real, but shrank as she quivered in Penny's *nosferatu* grip. Red swirls dwindled in her eyes, and she was warm again, a frail thing.

Penny understood what the vampire boy was doing in the back room. At once, she was aghast and struck with admiration. She had heard of the warm temporarily taking on vampire attributes by drinking vampire blood without themselves being bitten. There was a story about Katie Reed and a flier in the First World War. But it was rare, and dangerous.

Well, it used to be rare.

All around her, mayfly vampires darted. A youth blundered into her arms and tried to bite her. She firmly pushed him away, breaking the fingers of his right hand to make a point. They would heal instantly, but ache like the Devil when he turned back into a real boy.

A worm of terror curled in her heart. To do such a thing meant having a vision. Vampires, made conservative by centuries, were rarely innovators. She was reminded, again, of Dracula, who had risen among the *nosferatu* by virtue of his willingness to venture into new, large-scale fields of conquest. Such vampires were always frightening.

Would it really be a good thing for Andy to meet this boy?

She saw the white jacket shining in the darkness. The vampire stood at the bar, with Steve Rubell, ringmaster of 54, and the movie actress Isabelle Adjani. Steve, as usual, was flying, hairstyle falling apart above his bald spot. His pockets bulged with petty cash, taken from the overstuffed tills.

Steve spotted her, understood her nod of interest, and signalled her to come over.

'Penny darling,' he said, 'look at me. I'm like you.'

He had fangs too. And red-smeared lips.

'I . . . am . . . a vampiah!'

For Steve, it was just a joke. There was a bitemark on Adjani's neck, which she dabbed with a bar napkin.

'This is just the biggest thing evah,' Steve said.

'Fabulous,' she agreed.

Her eyes fixed the vampire newcomer. He withstood her gaze. She judged him no longer a new-born but not yet an elder. He was definitely of the Dracula line.

'Introduce me,' she demanded, delicately.

Steve's red eyes focused.

'Andy is interested?'

Penny nodded. Whatever was swarming in his brain, Steve was sharp.

'Penelope, this is Johnny Pop. He's from Transylvania.'

'I am an American, now,' he said, with just a hint of accent.

'Johnny, my boy, this is the witch Penny Churchward.'

Penny extended her knuckles to be kissed. Johnny Pop took her fingers and bowed slightly, an old world habit.

'You cut quite a figure,' she said.

'You are an elder?'

'Good grief, no. I'm from the class of '88. One of the few survivors.'

'My compliments.'

He let her hand go. He had a tall drink on the bar, blood concentrate. He would need to get his blood count up, to judge by all his fluttering get.

Some fellow rose off the dance floor on ungainly, short-lived leather wings. He made it a few feet into the air, flapping furiously. Then there was a ripping and he collapsed onto the rest of the crowd, yelling and bleeding.

Johnny smiled and raised his glass to her.

She would have to think about this development.

'My friend Andy would like to meet you, Johnny.'

Steve was delighted, and slapped Johnny on the arm.

'Andy Warhol is the Vampire Queen of New York City,' he said. 'You have arrived, my deah!'

Johnny wasn't impressed. Or was trying hard not to be.

Politely, he said, 'Miss Churchward, I should like to meet your friend Mr Warhol.'

So, this ash-faced creature was coven master of New York. Johnny had seen Andy Warhol before, here and at the Mudd Club, and knew who he was, the man who painted soup cans and made the dirty movies. He hadn't known Warhol was a vampire, but now it was pointed out, it seemed obvious. What else could such a person be?

Warhol was not an elder but he was unreadable, beyond Johnny's experience. He would have to be careful, to pay proper homage to this master. It would not do to excite the enmity of the city's few other vampires: at least, not yet. Warhol's woman – consort? mistress? slave? – was intriguing, too. She danced on the edge of hostility, radiating prickly suspicion, but he had a hook of a kind in her too. Born to follow, she would trot after him as faithfully as she followed her artist master. He had met her kind before, stranded out of their time, trying to make a way in the world rather than reshape it to suit themselves. It would not do to underestimate her.

'Gee,' Warhol said, 'you must come to the Factory. There are things you could do.'

Johnny didn't doubt it.

Steve made a sign and a photographer appeared. Johnny noticed Penelope edging out of shot just before the flash went off. Andy, Steve and Johnny were caught in the bleached corner. Steve, grinning with his fresh teeth.

'Say, Johnny,' Steve said, 'we will show up, won't we? I mean, I've still got my image.'

Johnny shrugged. He had no idea whether the drac suck Steve had taken earlier would affect his reflection. That had as much to do with Nancy as him.

'Wait and see what develops,' Johnny said.

'If that's the way it has to be, that's the way it is.'

It didn't do to think too hard about what Americans said.

'Gee,' mused Andy, 'that's, uh, fa-antastic, that's a thought.'

Within months, Johnny would rule this city.

From 1964 to 1968, Andy abandoned painting – if silkscreen can be called that – in favour of film. Some have suggested that works like ***Couch*** *(1964) or* ***The Thirteen Most Beautiful Boys*** *(1965) are just portraits that move; certainly, more people caught them as an ambient backdrop to the Exploding Plastic Inevitable than endured them reverentially at the Co-Op.* ***Movies,*** *not films, they were supposed to play to audiences too busy dancing or speeding or covering their bleeding ears to pay the sort of attention required by Hollywood narrative.*

By now, 'Andy's vampire movies' had gone beyond standing joke – eight hours of the Empire State Building!! – and were taken seriously by genuine underground filmmakers like Stan Brakhage (who considered silent speed the stroke of genius). The Filmmakers' Co-Op regularly scheduled 'Warhol Festivals' and word got out that the films were, well, **dirty**, *which – of course – pulled in audiences.* **Suck-Job** *was about as close to vampirism as even the most extreme New York audiences had seen, even if it was silent, black-and-white and slightly out of focus. Isabelle Dufresne, later the supervamp Ultra Violet, saw* **Suck-Job** *projected on a sheet at the Factory, and understood at once the strategy of incompletion, whereby the meat of the matter was beyond the frame. In* **Dead for Fifteen Minutes: My Years With Andy Warhol** *(1988), Ultra Violet writes: 'Although my eyes remain focused on the face of the young man receiving the suck job, my attention is constantly drawn to the empty space on the sheet below the screen. I am being visually assaulted and insulted at the same time. It is unnerving. I want to get up and seize the camera and focus it downward to capture the action. But I can't, and that's where the frustration comes in.'*

Ultra Violet also reports that, during that screening, some Factory hangers-on present relieved the frustration by nibbling each other, drawing squeals of pain and streaks of quick-drying blood. Such tentative pretend-vampirism was common among the Mole People, the nighttime characters Andy gathered to help make 'his' movies and turned into his private coven in the back room of Max's Kansas City. With no genuine undead available, Andy made do with self-made supervamps, who showed up on film if not at rehearsals: Pope Ondine (who drew real blood), Brigid (Berlin) Polk, Baby Jane Hudson (who had once been a real-live movie star), Malanga's muse Mary Woronov, Carmillo Karnstein, Ingrid Supervamp. Brian Stableford would later coin the term 'lifestyle fantasists' for these people and their modern avatars, the goth murgatroyds. Like Andy, the Mole People already lived like vampires: shunning daylight, speeding all night, filing their teeth, developing pasty complexions, sampling each other's drug-laced blood.

The butcher's bill came in early. The dancer Freddie Herko, who appears in **Kiss** *(1963) and* **Dance Movie/Roller Skates** *(1963), read in Montague Summers'* **The Vampire: His Kith and Kin** *(1928) that those who committed suicide spectacularly enough 'without fear' were reborn as 'powerful vampires'. Just before Halloween 1964, Herko danced across a friend's Greenwich Village apartment, trailing a ten-foot Batman/Dracula cloak, and sailed elegantly out of a* *fifth-floor window. Having skim-read the Summers and not bothered to form a Pact with the Devil, an essential part of the immortality-through-self-slaughter gambit, Herko did not rise from the dead. When he heard of Herko's defenestration, Warhol was almost irritated. 'Gee,' he sighed, 'why didn't he tell me he was going to do it? We could have gone down there and filmed it.' Herko was just the first of the Warhol death cluster, his personal disaster series: Edie Sedgwick (1971), Tiger Morse (1972), Andrea Feldman (1972), Candy Darling (1974), Eric Emerson (1975), Gregory Battcock (1980), Tom Baker (1982), Jackie Curtis (1985), Valerie Solanas (1989), Ondine (1989). And Warhol himself (1968?). Only Andy made it back, of course. He had to be the vampire they all would have been, even Valerie.*

In 1965, the term 'vampire movies' took on another layer of meaning at the Factory, with the arrivals of Ronald Tavel, a playwright hired to contribute situations (if not scripts) for the films, and Edie Sedgwick, a blueblood blonde who was, in many ways, Andy's ultimate supervamp. Movies like ***The Death of Radu the Handsome*** *(1965), with Ondine as Vlad the Impaler's gay brother, and* ***Poor Little Dead Girl*** *(1965), with Edie as the Vampire Claudia, run seventy minutes (two uninterrupted thirty-five minute takes, the length of a film magazine, stuck together), have intermittently audible soundtracks and mimic Hollywood to the extent of having something approaching narrative. Were it not for the incandescent personalities of the supervamps, the beautiful and the damned, these efforts would be more like 'zombie movies', shambling gestures of mimesis, constantly tripping up as the immobile image (Andy had the most stoned Mole Person handle the camera) goes in and out of focus or the walk-on 'victims' run out of things to do and say. Ondine, Edie and a few others understand that the films are their own shot at vampire immortality. With dimestore plastic fangs and shrouds from the dress-up chest, these living beings cavort, preserved on film while their bodies are long in the grave, flickering in undeath. For Andy, the film camera, like the silkscreen or the polaroid, was a vampire machine, a process for turning life into frozen death, perfect and reproducible. Hurting* *people was always so interesting, and left the most fabulous Rorschach stain patterns on the sheets.*

Edie cut her hair to match Andy's wigs and took to wearing imitations of his outfits, especially for photographs and openings. They looked like asexual twins or clones, but were really trying to model themselves on that most terrifying denizen of the world of darkness, the old vampire couple. R. D. Laing's study **Helga and Heinrich** *(1970) suggests that, after centuries together, vampire couples mingle identities, sharing a consciousness between two frail-seeming bodies, finishing each other's sentences as the mind flickers between two skulls, moving in on their victims in an instinctive pincer movement. If one partner is destroyed, the other rots in sympathy. Edie would probably have gone that far – she did eventually commit suicide – but Andy was too self-contained to commit anything or commit to anything. He saw her as the mirror he didn't like to look in – his reflection reminded him that he was alive, after all – and would often play the mimic game, patterned after Harpo Marx, with her, triumphantly squirting milk from his mouth or producing a walnut from a fist to show he was the original and she the copy. When he said he wanted everyone to be alike, he was expressing a solipsist not an egalitarian ideal: everyone was to be like him, but he was still to be the mould.*

Conklin, *ibid*

He fed often now, less for sustenance than for business. This one, seized just before sunrise, was the last of three taken throughout a single April night. He had waylaid the Greek girl, a seamstress in the garment district, on her way to a long day's work. She was too terrified to make a sound as Johnny ripped into her throat. Blood poured into his gaping mouth, and he swallowed. He fed his lust, his need. It wasn't just blood, it was money.

The girl, dragged off the street into an alley, had huge, startled eyes. Her ghost was in him as he bled her. She was called Thana, Death. The name stuck in his craw, clogging the lizard stem of his brain that always came alive as he fed. She should have been called

Zoë, Life. Was something wrong with her blood? She had no drugs, no disease, no madness. She started to fight him, mentally. The girl knew about her ghost, could struggle with him on a plane beyond the physical. Her unexpected skill shocked him.

He broke the bloody communion and dropped her onto some cardboard boxes. He was exhilarated and terrified. Thana's ghost snapped out of his mind and fell back into her. She sobbed soundlessly, mouth agape.

'Death,' he said, exorcising her.

Her blood made him full to the point of bursting. The swollen veins around his mouth and neck throbbed like painful erections. Just after a big feed, he was unattractively jowly, turgid sacs under his jawline, purplish flush to his cheeks and chest. He couldn't completely close his mouth, crowded as it was with blocky, jagged fangs.

He thought about wasting Thana, fulfilling the prophecy of her name.

No. He must not kill while feeding. Johnny was taking more victims but drinking less from each, holding back from killing. If people had to be killed, he'd do it without taking blood, much as it went against the Father's warrior instinct that subjugation of the vanquished should be commemorated at least by a mouthful of hot blood. This was America and things were different.

Who'd have thought there'd be such a fuss about Nancy and Sid? He was surprised by the extensive news coverage of another drab death at the Chelsea. Sid, a slave who could never finger Johnny without burning out his brain completely, was charged with murder. Out on bail, he was remanded back to jail for bottling Patti Smith's brother. On Riker's Island, he found out 'punk' had another meaning in prison. Kicked loose again, he had turned up dead of an overdose, with a suntan that struck witnesses as being unusual for February. It was either down to the political situation in Iran or Johnny's own enterprise: in the weeks Sid was locked up and kicking, heroin had become infinitely purer, perhaps thanks to Persians getting their money out in drugs, perhaps dealers competing with drac. Because Sid was well-known, the ragged end of his life was picked apart by a continuing police investigation. Loose ends could turn up; someone like Rockets Redglare, who had dealt in Room 100, might remember seeing Sid and Nancy with a vampire on the night of the killing. Johnny had no idea a singer who couldn't sing would be so famous. Even Andy was impressed by the headlines, and wondered whether he should do a Sid picture to catch the moment.

He knelt by Thana, holding her scarf to her throat wound. He took her hand and put it up to the makeshift dressing, indicating where she should press. In her hating eyes, he had no reflection. To her, he was nothing.

Fine.

Johnny left the girl and looked for a cab.

He had a penthouse apartment now, rent paid in cash every month, at the Bramford, a Victorian brownstone of some reputation. A good address was important. He needed somewhere to keep his clothes, and a coffin lined with Transylvanian dirt. At heart, Johnny was a traditionalist. Andy was the same, prizing American antique furniture – American antique, hah! – and art deco bric-a-brac, filling his town house with the prizes of the past while throwing out the art of the future in his Factory.

Johnny had over $11,500,000 in several accounts, and cash stashes in safe deposit boxes all over the city. He intended to pay income taxes on some of it, quite soon. In a moment of candour, he had discussed his business with the Churchward woman. She was the only vampire of real experience in the city, besides Andy – who clammed up shut when asked about feeding, though Johnny knew he took nips from all his assistants. Johnny and Penelope couldn't decide whether what he did was against the law or not, but judged it best to keep quiet. Selling his own blood was a legal grey area, but assault and murder weren't. He was reluctant to relinquish those tools entirely, but accepted that standards of behaviour in America were ostensibly different from those of his European backwater homeland. It wasn't that assault and murder were less common here than in Romania, but the authorities made more noise about it.

Those like Thana, left alive after his caresses, might argue that his powers of fascination constituted coercion, that he had perpetrated upon them a form of rape or robbery. Statues against organ-snatching might even be applicable. Penelope said that soon it wouldn't be safe to pick up a Mr Goodbar and suck him silly without getting a signature on a consent form.

The first real attempt to destroy him had came not from the church or the law, but from criminals. He was cutting into their smack and coke action. A couple of oddly dressed black men came for him with silver razors. The iron of the Father rose up within him and he killed them both, shredding their clothes and faces to make a point. He found out their names from the *Daily Bugle*, Youngblood Priest and Tommy Gibbs. He wondered if the black men he had seen outside the Chelsea on the night he met Andy were in with that Harlem crowd. He had glimpsed them again, several times, singly and as a pair. They were virtual twins, though one was further into the dark then the other. The knifeman's partner packed a crossbow under his coat. They would not be so easy to face down.

The Mott Street Triads had found a vampire of their own – one of those hopping Mandarins, bound by prayers pasted to his forehead – and tried feeding and milking him, cooking their own drac. Markedly inferior, their product was exhausted within a month, an entire body gone to dust and sold on the street. Soon such *nosferatu* slaves, captured and used up fast, would be common. Other vampires would sell their own drac, in America or their homelands. If the craze could take off in New York, then it would eventually trickle down to everywhere.

Johnny had repeatedly turned down offers of 'partnership' from the established suppliers of drugs. A cash payment of $6,000,000 to the Prizzi Family eliminated most of the hassle his people had been getting on the street. The Harlem rogues were off his case. He could pass for Italian, which meant he was to be respected for the moment. Mafia elders like Corrado Prizzi and Michael Corleone were men of rough honour; younger wiseguys like John Gotti and Frank White, on the rise even as the dons were fading, were of a different stripe. Gotti, or someone like him, would eventually move into drac. By then, Johnny intended to be retired and in another city.

The cops were interested. He had spotted them at once, casually loitering around crime scenes, chatting with dazed witnesses, giving penetrating stares. He had them marked down: the bogus hippie with the woolly vest, the completely bald man with the good suit, the maniac driver in the battered porkpie hat. Like the Father, he knew when to be careful, when to be daring. The police meant nothing in this land. They didn't even have silver bullets, like *Securitate* in the Old Country.

His own children – the dhampires – were busy. With his blood in them, they changed for a while. The first few times, they just relished the new senses, the feel of fangs in their mouths, the quickening of reflexes. Then, red thirst pricked. They needed to assuage it, before the suck wore off.

Apparently, the biting had started in the semi-underground gay clubs, among the leather-and-chains community. Johnny guessed one of the Studio 54 bouncers was the fountainhead. Both Burns and Stu were denizens of those cruising places. Within a few months, the biting had got out of hand. Every week, there were deaths, as dhampires lost control during the red rush, took too much from their lovers of the moment.

The money, however, kept coming in.

In the lobby, already brightening with dawnlight, an unnerving twelve-year-old clacked together two pink perspex eggs on a string. Johnny understood he was trying to get into the *Guinness Book of Records*. The child was a holy terror, allowed to run loose by his indulgent parents and their adoring circle. More than one resident of the Bramford had expressed a desire to be around when little Adrian Woodhouse 'got his come-uppance', but Johnny knew it would not do to cross the boy. If you intend to live forever, do not make enemies of children.

He hurried towards the cage elevator, intent on getting out of ear-range of the aural water torture.

'Johnny, Johnny . . .'

As he spun around, excess blood dizzied him. He felt it sloshing around inside. Everything was full: his stomach, his heart, his veins, his bladder, his lungs. It was practically backing up to his eyeballs.

The dhampire was cringing in a shrinking shadow.

'Johnny,' she said, stepping into the light.

Her skin darkened and creased, but she ignored it. She had crumpled bills in her hand, dirty money. He could imagine what she had done to get it.

It was the girl he had once called Nocturna. The Virgin of 54. She wasn't fresh any more, in any way.

'Please,' she begged, mouth open and raw.

'Things have changed,' he said, stepping into the elevator, drawing the mesh across between them. He saw her red-rimmed eyes.

'Take it,' she said, rolling the bills into tubes and shoving them through the grille. They fell at his feet.

'Talk to Rudy or Elvira,' he said. 'They'll fix you up with a suck.'

She shook her head, desperately. Her hair was a mess, singed white in patches. She grabbed the grille, fingers sticking through like worms.

'I don't want a suck, I want *you*.'

'You don't want me, darling. You can't afford me. Now, pull in your claws or you'll lose them.'

She was crying rusty tears.

He wrenched the lever and the elevator began to rise. The girl pulled her hands free. Her face sank and disappeared. She had pestered him before. He would have to do something about her.

It wasn't that he didn't do business that way any more, but that he had to be more selective about the clientele. For the briefest of suckles from the vein, the price was now $10,000. He was choosy about the mouths he spurted into.

Everyone else could just buy a suck.

Rudy and Elvira were waiting in the foyer of the apartment, red-eyed from the night, coming down slowly. They were dhampires themselves, of course. The Father had known the worth of warm slaves, his gypsies and madmen, and Johnny had taken some care in selecting the vassals he needed. As Johnny entered the apartment, peeling off his floor-length turquoise swede coat and tossing away his black-feathered white Stetson hat, Rudy leaped up from the couch almost to attention. Elvira, constricted inside a black sheath dress low-necked enough to show her navel, raised a welcoming eyebrow and tossed aside *The Sensuous Woman*. Rudy took his coat and hat and hung them up. Elvira rose like a snake from a basket and air-kissed his cheeks. She touched black nails to his face, feeling the bloat of the blood.

They proceeded to the dining room.

Rudy Pasko, a hustler Johnny had picked up on the A-train, dreamed of turning, becoming like his master. Jittery, nakedly ambitious, *American*, he would be a real monster, paying everybody back for ignoring him in life. Johnny wasn't comfortable with Rudy's focused needs, but, for the moment, he had his uses.

Elvira, this year's compleat Drac Hag, was a better bet for immortality. She knew when to run cool or hot, and took care to keep a part of herself back, even while snuffing mountains of drac and chewing on any youth who happened to be passing. She liked to snack on gay men, claiming – with her usual dreadful wordplay – that they had better taste than straights. Andy had passed her on, from the Factory.

The money was on the polished oak dining table, in attaché cases. It had already been counted, but Johnny sat down and did it again. Rudy called him 'the Count', almost mockingly. The boy didn't understand, the money wasn't Johnny's until it was counted. The obsessive-compulsive thing was a trick of the Dracula bloodline. Some degenerate, mountain-dwelling distant cousins could be distracted from their prey by a handful of pumpkin seeds, unable to pass by without counting every one. That was absurd, this was important. Andy understood about money, why it was essential, not for what it could buy, but in itself. Numbers were beautiful.

Johnny's fingers were so sensitive that he could make the count just by riffling the bundles, by caressing the cash. He picked out the dirty bills, the torn or taped or stained notes, and tossed them to Rudy.

There was $158,591 on the table, a fair night's taking. His personal rake would be an even $100,000.

'Where does the ninety-one dollars come from, Rudy?'

The shrugged. The non-negotiable price of a suck was $500. There shouldn't be looser change floating around.

'Boys and girls have expenses,' Rudy said.

'They are not to dip into the till,' Johnny said, using an expression he had recently learned. 'They are to hand over the taking. If they have expenses, they must ask you to cover them. You have enough for all eventualities, have you not?'

Rudy looked at the heap of messy bills and nodded. He had to be reminded of his hook sometimes.

'Now, things must be taken care of.'

Rudy followed him into the reception room. The heart of the penthouse, the reception room was windowless but with an expanse of glass ceiling. Just now, with the sun rising, the skylight was curtained by a rolling metal blind drawn by a hand-cranked winch.

There was no furniture, and the hardwood floor was protected by a plastic sheet. It was Rudy's duty to get the room ready for Johnny by dawn. He had laid out shallow metal trays in rows, like seed-beds in a nursery.

Johnny undid his fly and carefully pissed blood onto the first tray. The pool spread, until it lapped against the sides. He paused his flow, and proceeded to the next tray, and the next. In all, he filled thirty-seven trays to a depth of about a quarter of an inch. He lost his bloat, face smoothing and tightening, clothes hanging properly again.

Johnny watched from the doorway as Rudy worked the winch, rolling the blind. Rays of light speared down through the glass ceiling, falling heavily on the trays. Morning sun was the best, the purest. The trays smoked slightly, like vats of tomato soup on griddles. There was a smell he found offensive, but which the warm – even dhampires – could not distinguish. Like an elder exposed to merciless daylight, the blood was turning to granulated material. Within a few hours, it would all be red dust, like the sands of Mars. Drac.

*

In the afternoon, as he slept in his white satin-lined coffin, a troop of good Catholic boys whose fear of Johnny was stronger than the bloodhooks in their brains came to the apartment and, under Elvira's supervision, worked on the trays, scooping up and measuring out the powdered blood into foil twists ('sucks' or 'jabs') that retailed for $500 each. After sunset, the boys (and a few girls) took care of the distribution, spreading out to the clubs and parties and street corners and park nooks where the dhampires hung out.

Known on the street as drac or bat's blood, the powder could be snuffed, swallowed, smoked or heated to liquid and injected. With a fresh user, the effect lasted the hours of the night and was burned out of the system at sunrise. After a few weeks, the customer was properly hooked, a dhampire, and needed three or four sucks a night to keep sharp. No one knew about long-term effects yet, though serious dhampires like Nocturna were prone to severe sunburn and even showed signs of being susceptible to spontaneous combustion. Besides a red thirst for a gulp or two of blood, the dhampire also had a need, of course, to raise cash to feed the habit. Johnny didn't care much about that side of the business, but the *Daily Bugle* had run editorials about the rise in mugging, small burglary, car crime and other petty fund-raising activities.

Thus far, Johnny was sole supplier of the quality stuff. During their short-lived venture, the Triads had cut their dwindling drac with cayenne pepper, tomato paste and powdered catshit. The Good Catholics were all dhampires themselves, though he kicked them out and cut them off if they exceeded their prescribed dosage – which kept them scrupulously honest about cash. His major expenses were kickbacks to the Families, club owners, bouncers, street cops and other mildly interested parties.

Johnny Pop would be out of the business soon. He was greedy for more than money. Andy had impressed on him the importance of being famous.

Warhol and Tavel made ***Veneer*** *(1965), the first film version of Bram Stoker's* ***Dracula*** *(1897). In* ***Stargazer: Ady Warhol's World and His Films*** *(1973), Stephen Kock reports: 'Warhol handed Tavel* *a copy of the novel with the remark that it might be easier to compose a scenario based on fiction than one spun out of pure fantasy. He had acquired the rights to the Stoker book for $3,000, he said; it ought to make a good movie. And so it did. It's not hard to guess why Warhol was impressed by* **Dracula**. *(I should mention in passing that, contrary to the myth he propagates, Warhol is quite widely read.) The book is filled with the sexuality of violence; it features a tough, erotic vampire dandy joyously dominating a gang of freaks; its theme is humiliation within a world that is simultaneously sordid and unreal; it is a history which at once did and did not happen, a purposeful lie. Finally, there is the question of class . . . I think Warhol participates very deeply in America's best-kept secret – the painful, deeply denied intensity with which we experience our class structure. We should not forget that we are speaking of the son of semiliterate immigrants, whose father was a steelworker in Pittsburgh. Within the terms of his own intensely specialised mentality, Warhol has lived through American class humiliation and American poverty. And* **Dracula**, *although British, is very much about the sexuality of social class as it merges with spiritual domination.'*

Casting Edie as an ephebic silver-haired Dracula (Drella, indeed), Gerard Malanga as a whip-wielding but humiliated Harker and Ondine as a sly Van Helsing, Warhol populated the Factory's Transylvania and Carfax Abbey (the same 'set', black sheets hung with silver cobwebs) with lost souls. Well before Francis Ford Coppola, Warhol saw that the problems in filming the novel could be side-stepped by force of will. Indeed, he approached the enterprise with a deliberate diffidence that all but ensured this would not be a 'proper' film. Ronnie Tavel at least read half the book before getting bored and typing out a script in his usual three days. Since shooting consisted of a complete run-through of the script as a performance, with breaks only when the magazine ran out, Tavel considered that there ought to be actual rehearsals and that the actors should stoop to learning their lines. Too fearful of confrontation to disagree, Warhol simply sabotaged the rehearsals Tavel organised and even the shooting of the film by inviting the Press and various parasites to the Factory to observe and interfere, and sending Malanga off on trivial errands or keeping him up until dawn at parties to prevent him from even reading the script (as in the book, Harker has the most to say). Koch, again: 'The sense that making a film was work – that it should involve the concentrated attention of work – was utterly banished, and on shooting day the Factory merely played host to another "Scene", another party.'

Stoker's intricate plot is reduced to situations. Harker, in black leather pants and Victorian deerstalker, visits Castle Dracula, carrying a crucifix loaned to the production by Andy's mother, and is entertained, seduced and assaulted by the Count (Edie's enormous fangs keep slipping out of her mouth) and his three gesticulating vampire brides (Marie Mencken, Carmillo Karnstein, International Velvet). Later, in Carfax Abbey, Harker – roped to the Factory Couch – watches as Dracula fascinates and vampirises Mina (Mary Woronov) in a tango that climaxes with Mina drinking Campbell's Tomato Soup from a can Dracula has opened with a thumb-talon and which he declares is his vampire blood. Van Helsing appears, with his fearless vampire hunters – Lord Godalming (Chuck Wein), Quincey Morris (Joe Dallesandro), Dr Seward (Paul America) – dragged by Renfield (a young, ravaged Lou Reed), who is leashed like a bloodhound.

Crucifixes, stakes, whips and communion wafers are tossed back and forth in a bit of knockabout that makes some of the cast giggle uncontrollably and drives others – notably, the still-tethered Malanga – to furious distraction. In Tavel's script, as in Stoker's novel, Van Helsing's band corner and destroy Dracula, who was to be spray-painted silver and suffocated, but Ondine is distracted when a girl who happens to be on the couch for no real reason – she seems to be a set-visitor straying into frame – calls him a 'phony', and Ondine ignores the King Vampire to lash out at this impertinent chit, going for her face with his false fingernails. Ondine's methadrine rant rises in a crescendo, peaks and fades: 'May God forgive you, you're a phony, Little Miss Phony, you're a disgusting phony, get off this set, you're a disgrace to humanity, you're a disgrace to yourself, you're a loathsome fool, your husband's a loathsome fool . . . I'm sorry, I just can't go on, this is just too much, I don't want to go on.' The camera, handled this time by

Bud Wirtschafter, tries to follow the unexpected action, and for a few brief frames catches the ghost-white face of Andy himself hanging shocked in the gloom; the removal of this slip is perhaps the only proper edit in any Warhol film made before the arrival of Paul Morrissey. Van Helsing, inconsolable, stands alone and the film runs on and on, as he reassembles himself.

Edie, fangs spat out but still regally and perfectly Dracula, gets Wirtschafter's attention by tossing the soup can at him, spattering the lens, and commands the frame, hands on hips, for a few seconds before the film runs out. 'I am Dracula,' she insists, the only line of dialogue taken directly (if unintentionally) from the book. 'I **am** *Dracula,' she repeats, sure of herself for the last time in her life. Stoker had intended to inflict upon Dracula the defeat he eluded in reality, but Edie has dragged Warhol's Dracula movie back to the truth. In the Factory, Drella bests the squabbling Vampire Slayers and reigns forever.*

Conklin, *ibid*

Johnny Pop was certainly the social success of the Summer. He had just showed up at Trader Vic's with *Margaret Trudeau* on his elegant arm. Penelope was not surprised, and Andy was silently ecstatic. An inveterate collector of people, he delighted in the idea of the Transylvanian hustler and the Prime Minister's ex getting together. Margaux Hemingway would be furious; she had confided in Andy and Penny that she thought it was serious with Johnny. Penny could have told her what was serious with Johnny, but she didn't think any warm woman would understand.

From across the room, as everyone turned to look at the couple, Penny observed Johnny, realising why no one else saw him as she did. He had Olde Worlde charm by the bucketful, and that thirsty edge that had made him seem a rough beast was gone. His hair was an improbable construction, teased and puffed every which way, and his lips were a girl's. But his eyes were Dracula's. It had taken her a while to notice, for she had really known *il principe* only after his fire had dwindled. This was what the *young* Dracula, freshly *nosferatu*, must have been like. This was the bat-cloaked creature of velvet night who with sheer smoking magnetism had overwhelmed flighty Lucy, virtuous Mina and stately Victoria, who had bested Van Helsing and stolen an empire. He didn't dance so often now that he had the city's attention, but all his moves were like dancing, his gestures so considered, his looks so perfect.

He had told several versions of the story, but always insisted he was Dracula's get, perhaps the last to be turned personally by the King Vampire in his five-hundred-year reign. Johnny didn't like to give dates, but Penny put his conversion at somewhere before the Last War. Who he had been when warm was another matter. He claimed to be a lineal descendant as well as get, the last modern son of some byblow of the Impaler, which was why the dying bloodline had fired in him, making him the true Son of Dracula. She could almost believe it. Though he was proud to name his Father-in-Darkness, he didn't like to talk about the Old Country and what had brought him to America. There were stories there, she would wager. Eventually, it would all come out. He had probably drained a commissar's daughter and got out one step ahead of red vampire killers.

There was trouble in the Carpathians now. The Transylvania Movement, wanting to claim Dracula's ancient fiefdom as a homeland for all the displaced vampires of the world, were in open conflict with Ceausescu's army. The only thing Johnny had said about that mess was that he would prefer to be in America than Romania. After all, the modern history of vampirism – so despised by the Transylvanians – had begun when Dracula left his homelands for what was in 1885 the most exciting, modern city in the world. She conceded the point: Johnny Pop was displaying the real Dracula spirit, not TM reactionaries like Baron Meinster and Anton Crainic who wanted to retreat to their castles and pretend it was still the Middle Ages.

Andy got fidgety as Johnny worked the room, greeting poor Truman Capote or venerable Paulette Goddard, sharp Ivan Boesky or needy Liza Minnelli. He was deliberately delaying his inevitable path to Andy's table. It was like a Renaissance court, Penny realised. Eternal shifts of power and privilege, of favour and slight. Three months ago, Johnny had needed to be in with Andy; now, Johnny had risen to such a position that he could afford to hold himself apart, to declare independence. She had never seen Andy on the hook this badly, and was willing to admit she took some delight in it. At last, the master was mastered.

Eventually, Johnny arrived and displayed his prize.

Penny shook Mrs Trudeau's hand and felt the chill coming from her. Her scarlet choker didn't quite match her crimson evening dress. Penny could smell the musk of her scabs.

Johnny was drinking well, these nights.

Andy and Johnny sat together, close. Neither had anything interesting to say, which was perhaps why they needed so many people around them.

Mrs Trudeau frowned, showing her own streak of jealousy. Penny wouldn't be able to explain to her what Andy and Johnny had, why everyone else was superfluous when they were together. Despite the fluctuations in their relationship, they were one being with two bodies. Without saying much, Johnny made Andy choke with laughter he could never let out. There was a reddish flush to Andy's albino face.

'Don't mind them,' Penny told Mrs Trudeau. 'They're bats.'

'I don't suppose this'd do anything for you,' said the girl from *Star Wars* whose real name Penny had forgotten, cutting a line of red powder on the coffee table with a silver razorblade.

Penny shrugged.

Vampires did bite each other. If one were wounded almost to death, an infusion of another's *nosferatu* blood could have restorative powers. Blood would be offered by an inferior undead to a coven master to demonstrate loyalty. Penny had no idea what, if any, effect drac would have on her and wasn't especially keen on finding out. The scene was pretty much a bore.

Princess Leia was evidently a practised dhampire. She snorted through a tubed $100 bill and held her head back. Her eyes reddened and her teeth grew points.

'Arm wrestle?' she asked.

Penny wasn't interested. Dhampires all had this rush of vampire power but no real idea of what to do with it. Except nibble. They didn't even feed properly.

Most of the people at this party were drac addicts. They went for the whole bit, black capes and fingerless black widow web gloves, Victorian cameos at the throat, lots of velvet and leather, puffy minidresses over thigh-boots.

Half this lot had dracced themselves up completely for a midnight screening of *The Rocky Horror Picture Show* at the Waverly, and were just coming down, which meant they were going around the room, pestering anyone they thought might be holding out on a stash, desperate to get back up there. There was a miasma of free-floating paranoia, which Penny couldn't keep out of her head.

'Wait 'til this gets to the Coast,' said Princess Leia. 'It'll be monstrous.'

Penny had to agree.

She had lost Andy and Johnny at CBGB's, and fallen in with this crowd. The penthouse apartment apparently belonged to some political big-wig she had never heard of, Hal Philip Walker, but he was out of town and Brooke Hayward was staying here with Dennis Hopper. Penny had the idea that Johnny knew Hopper from some foreign debauch, and wanted to avoid him – which, if true, was unusual.

She was welcome here, she realised, because she was a vampire.

It hit her that if the drac ran out, there was a direct source in the room. She was stronger than any warm person, but it was a long time since she had fought anyone. The sheer press of dhampires would tell. They could hold her down and cut her open, then suck her dry, leaving her like crushed orange pulp. For the first time since turning, she understood the fear the warm had of her kind. Johnny had changed things permanently.

Princess Leia, fanged and clawed, eyed her neck slyly, and reached out to touch her.

'Excuse me,' said Penny, slipping away.

Voices burbled in her mind. She was on a wavelength with all these dhampires, who didn't know how to communicate. It was just background chatter, amplified to skull-cracking levels.

In the bedroom where she had left her coat, a Playmate of the

Month and some rock 'n' roll guy were messily performing dhampire 69, gulping from wounds in each other's wrists. She had fed earlier, and the blood did nothing for her.

A Broadway director tried to talk to her.

Yes, she had seen *Pacific Overtures*. No, she didn't want to invest in *Sweeney Todd*.

Where had anybody got the idea that she was rich?

That fat Albanian from *Animal House*, fangs like sharpened cashew nuts, claimed newfound vampire skills had helped him solve Rubik's cube. He wore a black Inverness cape over baggy Y-fronts. His eyes flashed red and gold like a cat's in headlights.

Penny had a headache.

She took the elevator down to the street.

While looking for a cab, she was accosted by some dreadful drac hag. It was the girl Johnny called Nocturna, now a snowy-haired fright with yellow eyes and rotten teeth.

The creature pressed money on her, a crumpled mess of notes.

'Just a suck, precious,' she begged.

Penny was sickened.

The money fell from the dhampire's hands, and was swept into the gutter.

'I think you'd better go home, dear,' advised Penny.

'Just a suck.'

Nocturna laid a hand on her shoulder, surprisingly strong. She retained some *nosferatu* attributes.

'Johnny still loves me,' she said, 'but he has business to take care of. He can't fit me in, you see. But I need a suck, just a little kiss, nothing serious.'

Penny took Nocturna's wrist but couldn't break the hold.

The dhampire's eyes were yolk yellow, with shots of blood. Her breath was foul. Her clothes, once fashionable, were ragged and gamey.

Penny glanced up and down the street. She could use a cop, or Spider-Man. People were passing, but in the distance. No one noticed this little scene.

Nocturna brought out something from her reticule. A Stanley knife. Penny felt a cold chill as the blade touched her cheek, then a venomous sting. The tool was silvered. She gasped in pain, and the dhampire stuck her mouth over the cut.

Penny struggled, but the dhampire was suddenly strong, juiced up by pure drac. She would make more cuts and take more sucks.

'You're his friend,' Nocturna said, lips red. 'He won't mind. I'm not being unfaithful.'

Penny supposed she deserved this.

But as the red rush dazed Nocturna, Penny broke free of the dhampire. She dabbed her cheek. Because of the silver, the cut would stay open, perhaps even leave a scar. Penny had too many of those, but this one would be where it showed.

There were people nearby, watching. Penny saw their red eyes. More dhampires, out for drac, out for her blood. She backed towards the lobby, cursing Johnny Pop.

Nocturna staggered after her.

A taxi cab stormed down the street, scattering dhampires. Penny stuck out her hand and flagged it down. Nocturna howled, and flew at her. Penny wrenched open the cab door and threw herself in. She told the driver to drive off, anywhere, fast.

Nocturna and the others hissed at the window, nails scratching the glass.

The cab sped up and left them behind.

Penny was resolved. Penance was one thing, but enough was enough. She would get out of this city. The Factory could run itself. She would leave Andy to Johnny, and hope they were satisfied with each other.

'Someday a rain's gonna come,' said the taxi driver. 'And wash the scum off the streets.'

She wished she could agree with him.

It is easy to overstate the importance of Nico to Warhol's late '60s work. She was, after all, his first 'real' vampire. Croaking, German and blonde, she was the dead image of Edie, and thus of Andy. Nico Otzak, turned some time in the '50s, arrived in New York in

1965, with her doll-like get Ari, and presented her card at the Factory. She trailed the very faintest of associations with Dracula himself, having been a fringe member of that last party, in Rome 1959, which climaxed in the true death of the Vampire King. 'She was myterious and European,' Andy said, abstaining from any mention of the v word, 'a real moon goddess type.' Like Dracula, she gave the impression of having used up the Old Worlde and moved on, searching for 'a young country, full of blood'.

In **Edie: An American Biography** *(1982), Jean Stein definitely refutes the popular version, in which the naïve, warm American is supplanted by the cold, dead European. Edie Sedgwick was on the point of turning from vampire to victim before Nico's arrival; she had made the cardinal error of thinking herself indispensable, a real star, and Andy was silently irked by her increasing need for publicity as herself rather than as his mirror. She had already strayed from the Factory and towards the circle of Bob Dylan, tempted by more serious drug habits and heterosexuality. Edie was justifiably miffed that the limited financial success of the films benefited only Andy; his position was that she was rich anyway – 'an heiress', one of his favourite words – and didn't need the money, though far less well-off folk did as much or more work on the films and silkscreens for similarly derisory pay. Edie's self-destruction cannot be laid entirely on Andy and Nico – the Dylan crowd hardly helped, moving her up from amphetamines to heroin – but it is undeniably true that without Warhol, Edie would never have become, in the English expression, 'dead famous'.*

With Nico, Andy finally had his vampire. At the back of their association must have been the possibility – the promise? – that she would turn him, but for the moment, Andy held back. To become someone's get would have displaced him from the centre of his life, and that was insupportable. When he turned, a circumstance that remains mysterious, he would do so through anonymous blood donation, making himself – as usual – his own get, his own creature. Besides, no one could seriously want Nico for a mother-in-darkness; for the rest of her nights, she drew blood from Ari, her own get, and this vampire incest contributed to the rot that would destroy them both.

Andy was especially fascinated by Nico's relationship with mirrors and film. She was one of those vampires who have no reflection, though he did his best to turn her into a creature who was all reflection with no self. He had her sing 'I'll Be Your Mirror', for instance. 'High Ashbury', the oddest segment of ******/Twenty Four Hour Movie** *(1966), places Ondine and Ultra Violet either side of an absence, engaged in conversation with what seems to be a disembodied voice. There are signs of Nico's physical presence during the shoot: the displacement of cushions, a cigarette that darts like a hovering dragonfly, a puff of smoke outlining an oesophagus. But the vampire woman just isn't there. That may be the point. Andy took photographs of silver-foiled walls and untenanted chairs and passed them off as portraits of Nico. He even silkscreened an empty coffin for an album cover.*

Having found his vampire muse, Andy had to do **something** *with her, so he stuck her together with the Velvet Underground – a band who certainly weren't that interested in having a girl singer who drank human blood – as part of the Exploding Plastic Inevitable, the club events he staged at the Dom on St Mark's Place in 1966. Amidst so much black leather, he dressed Nico in bone-white and put an angelic spotlight on her, especially when she wasn't singing. Lou Reed bought a crucifix, and started looking for a way out. The success of the EPI may well have been partially down to a wide cross-section of New Yorkers who were intrigued by Nico; most Americans in 1966 had never been in a room with a vampire, a real vampire. Andy knew that and made sure that, no matter how conveniently dark the rest of the packed club was, Nico was always visible, always the red-eyed wraith murmuring her way through 'Femme Fatale' without taking a breath. That song, of course, is a promise and a threat: 'think of her at nights, feel the way she bites . . .'*

As the Velvets performed, Warhol hid in the rafters like the Phantom of the Opera, working the lights and the projectors, cranking up the sound. Like Ulysses, he filled his ears with wax to get through the night. Behind the band, he screened his films. Often, as his real vampire paraded herself, he would show **Veneer**, *trying to project Edie onto Nico as he projected himself upon them both.*

Everybody agrees: between 1966 and 1968, Andy Warhol was a monster.
***Conklin**, ibid*

Johnny was one of the privileged few allowed into Andy's town house to witness the artist's levée. At high summer, it was impractical to wait for sundown before venturing out – so Johnny had to be ferried the short distance from the Bramford to East 66th St in a sleek limo with polaroid windows and hustled under a parasol up to the door of Number 57.

With the Churchward woman's desertion, there was a blip in the smooth running of Andy's social life and he was casting around for a replacement Girl of the Year. Johnny was wary of being impressed into taking too many of Penny Penitent's duties. There were already so many demands on his time, especially with that mad Bella Abzug whipping the NYPD into a frenzy about 'the drac problem'. It wasn't even illegal yet, but his dealers were rousted every night, and his pay-offs to the Families and the cops ratcheted up every week, which pushed him to raise the price of a suck, which meant that dhamps had to peddle more ass or bust more head to scrape together the cash they needed. The papers were full of vampire murders, and real vampires weren't even suspects.

The two-storey lobby of Number 57 was dominated by imperial busts – Napoleon, Caesar, Dracula – and still-packed crates of sculptures and paintings. Things were everywhere, collected but uncatalogued, most still in the original wrapping.

Johnny sat on an upholstered chaise longue and leafed through a male pornographic magazine that was on top of a pile of periodicals that stretched from *The New York Review of Books* to *The Fantastic Four*. He heard Andy moving about upstairs, and glanced at the top of the wide staircase. Andy made an entrance, a skull-faced spook-mask atop a floor-length red velvet dressing gown which dragged behind him as he descended, like Scarlett O'Hara's train.

In this small, private moment – with no one else around to see – Andy allowed himself to smile, a terminally ill little boy indulging his love of dressing-up. It wasn't just that Andy was a poseur, but that he let everyone know it and still found the reality in the fakery, making the posing the point. When Andy pretended, he just showed up the half-hearted way everyone else did the same thing. In the months he had been in New York, Johnny had learned that being an American was just like being a vampire, to feed off the dead and to go on and on and on, making a virtue of unoriginality, waxing a corpse-face to beauty. In a country of surfaces, no one cared about the rot that lay beneath the smile, the shine and the dollar. After the persecutions of Europe, it was an enormous relief.

Andy extended a long-nailed hand at an ocasional table by the chaise longue. It was heaped with the night's invitations, more parties and openings and galas than even Andy could hit before dawn.

'Choose,' he said.

Johnny took a handful of cards, and summarised them for Andy's approval or rejection. Shakespeare in the Park, Paul Toombs in *Timon of Athens* ('gee, misa-anthropy'). A charity ball for some new wasting disease ('gee, sa-ad'). An Anders Wolleck exhibit of metal sculptures ('gee, fa-abulous'). A premiere for the latest Steven Spielberg film *1941* ('gee, wo-onderful'). A screening at Max's Kansas City of a work in progress by Scott and Beth B, starring Lydia Lunch and Teenage Jesus ('gee, u-underground'). A night-club act by Divine ('gee, na-aughty'). Parties by and for John Lennon, Tony Perkins ('ugh *Psycho*'), Richard Hell and Tom Verlaine, Jonathan and Jennifer Hart ('ick!'), Blondie ('the cartoon character or the band?'), Malcolm McLaren ('be-est not'), David JoHansen, Edgar Allan Poe ('ne-ever-more'), Frank Sinatra ('Old Hat Rat Pack Hack!').

The night had some possibilities.

Andy was in a sulk. Truman Capote, lisping through silly fangs, had spitefully told him about an Alexander Cockburn parody, modelled on the lunch chatter of Warhol and Colacello with Imelda Marcos as transcribed in *Inter/VIEW*. Andy, of course, had to sit down in the middle of the party and pore through the piece. In Cockburn's version, Bob and Andy took Count Dracula to supper at Mortimer's Restaurant on the Upper East Side and prodded him with questions like 'Don't you wish you'd been able to spend Christmas in Transylvania?' and 'Is there still pressure on you to think of your image and act a certain way?'

Johnny understood the real reason that the supposedly unflappable artist was upset was that he had been scooped. After this, Andy wouldn't be able to run an interview with Dracula. He'd been hoping Johnny would channel the Father's ghost, as others had channelled such *Inter/VIEW* subjects as the Assyrian wind demon Pazuzu and Houdini. Andy didn't prize Johnny just because he was a vampire; it was important that he was of the direct Dracula line.

He didn't feel the Father with him so much, though he knew he was always there. It was as if he had absorbed the great ghost almost completely, learning the lessons of the Count, carrying on his mission on Earth. The past was fog, now. His European life and death were faint, and he told varying stories because he remembered differently each time. But in the fog stood the red-eyed, black-caped figure of Dracula, reaching out to him, reaching out through him.

Sometimes, Johnny Pop thought he *was* Dracula. The Churchward woman had almost believed it, once. And Andy would be so delighted if it were true. But Johnny wasn't *just* Dracula.

He was no longer unique. There were other vampires in the country, the city, at this party. They weren't the Olde Worlde seigneurs of the Transylvania Movement, at once arrogant and pitiful, but Americans, if not by birth then inclination. Their extravagant names had a copy-of-a-copy paleness, suggesting hissy impermanence: Sonja Blue, Satanico Pandemonium, Skeeter, Scumbalina. Metaphorical (or actual?) children-in-darkness of Andy Warhol, the first thing they did upon rising from the dead was – like an actor landing a first audition – change their names. Then, with golden drac running in their veins, they sold themselves to the dhamps, flooding to New York where the most suckheads were. In cash, they were richer than most castle-bound TM elders, but they coffined in camper vans or at the Y, and wore stinking rags.

Andy snapped out of his sulk. A vampire youth who called himself Nothing paid homage to him as the Master, offering him a criss-crossed arm. Andy stroked the kid's wounds, but held back from sampling the blood.

Johnny wondered if the hook he felt was jealousy.

Johnny and Andy lolled on the back seat of the limo with the sun-roof open, playing chicken with the dawn.

The chatter of the night's parties still ran around Johnny's head, as did the semi-ghosts he had swallowed with his victims' blood. He willed a calm cloud to descend upon the clamour of voices and stilled his brain. For once, the city was quiet.

He was bloated with multiple feedings – at every party, boys and girls offered their necks to him – and Andy seemed flushed enough to suggest he had accepted a few discreet nips somewhere along the course of the night. Johnny felt lassitude growing in him, and knew that after relieving himself and letting the Good Catholics go to work, he would need to hide in the refrigerated coffin unit that was his New York summer luxury for a full day.

The rectangle of sky above was starless pre-dawn blue-grey. Red tendrils were filtering through, reflected off the glass frontages of Madison Avenue. The almost-chill haze of four a.m. had been burned away in an instant, like an ancient elder, and it would be another murderously hot day, confining them both to their lairs for a full twelve hours.

They said nothing, needed to say nothing.

Valerie Solanas was the founder and sole member of the Society for Killing All Vampires, authoress of the self-published **SKAV Manifesto**. *In bite-sized quotes, the* **Manifesto** *is quite amusing – 'enlightened vampires who wish to demonstrate solidarity with the Movement may do so by killing themselves' – but it remains a wearisome read, not least because Valerie never quite sorted out what she meant by the term 'vampire'. Of course, as an academic, I understand entirely the impatience she must have felt with what she considered irrelevances like agenda-setting and precise definitions of* *abstruse language. In the end, Valerie was a paranoid sociopath, and the vampires were her enemies, all who were out to get her, to stand in her way. At first, she didn't even mean* **nosferatu** *when she referred to vampires, but a certain type of patriarchal oppressor. At the end, she meant everyone else in the world.*

She is in one of the little-known films, **I, Vampire** *(1967) – mingling briefly with Tom Baker as the vampire Lord Andrew Bennett, and Ultra Violet, the wonderfully named Bettina Coffin and a Nico-shaped patch of empty screen. She had various grudges against Andy Warhol – he had lost a playscript she sent him, he wouldn't publish her book, he didn't make her famous – but no more than any one of a dozen other Mole People. Billy Name has said that he was never sure whether he should kill himself or Andy, and kept putting off the decision. Oliver Stone's* **Who Shot Andy Warhol?** *is merely the culmination of thirty years of myth and fantasy. It bears repeating that the conspiracy theories Stone and others have espoused have little or no basis in fact, and Valerie Solanas acted entirely on her own, conspiring or colluding with no one. Stone's point, which is well-taken, is that in June 1968,* **someone** *had to shoot Andy Warhol; if Valerie hadn't stepped up to the firing line, any one of a dozen others could as easily have melted down the family silver for bullets. But it was Valerie.*

By 1968, the Factory had changed. It was at a new location and Warhol had new associates – Fred Hughes, Paul Morrissey, Bob Colacello – who tried to impose a more businesslike atmosphere. The Mole People were discouraged from hanging about, and poured out their bile on Andy's intermediaries, unable to accept that they had been banished on the passive dictate of Warhol himself. Valerie turned up while Andy was in a meeting with art critic Mario Amaya and on the phone with yet another supervamp Viva, and put two bullets into him, and one incidentally in Amaya. Fred Hughes, born negotiator, apparently talked her out of killing him and she left by the freight elevator.

It was a big story for fifteen minutes, but just as Andy was declared clinically dead at Columbus Hospital news came in from Chicago that Robert Kennedy had been assassinated. Every news-

paper in America remade their front pages, bumping the artist to 'and in other news . . .'

Kennedy stayed dead. Andy didn't.

***Conklin**, ibid*

The Halloween party at 54 was desperately lavish, and Steve made him Guest of Honour, naming him the Official Spectre at the Feast.

In a brief year, Johnny had become this town's favourite monster. Andy was Vampire Master of New York, but Johnny Pop was Prince of Darkness, father and furtherer of a generation of dhamps, scamps and vamps. There were songs about him ('Fame, I'm Gonna Live Forever'), he had been in a movie (at least his smudge had) with Andy (Ulli Lommel's *Drac Queens*), he got more neck than a giraffe, and there was a great deal of interest in him from the Coast.

Cakes shaped like coffins and castles were wheeled into 54, and the Man in the Moon sign was red-eyed and fang-toothed in homage. Liberace and Elton John played duelling pianos, while the monster-disguised Village People – the Indian as the Wolf Man, the Cowboy as the Creature From the Black Lagoon, the Construction Worker as the Frankenstein Monster, the Biker as Dracula, the Cop as the Thing From Another World, the Soldier as the Hunchback of Notre Dame – belted out a cover of Bobby 'Boris' Pickett's 'The Monster Mash'.

The day drac became a proscribed drug by act of Congress, Johnny stopped manufacturing it personally and impressed a series of down-on-their-luck *nosferatu* to be undead factories. The prices of the product shot up again, as did the expense of paying off the cops and the mob, but his personal profits towered almost beyond his mind's capacity to count. He knew the bubble would burst soon, but was ready to diversify, to survive into another era. It would be the eighties soon. That was going to be a different time. The important thing was going to be not drac or fame or party invites, but money. Numbers would be his shield and his castle, his spells of protection, invisibility and fascination.

He didn't dance so much, now. He had made his point. But he

was called onto the floor. Steve set up a chant of 'Johnny Pop, Johnny Pop' that went around the crowd. Valerie Perrine and Steve Guttenberg gave him a push. Nastassja Kinski and George Burns slapped his back. Peter Bogdanovich and Dorothy Stratten kissed his cheeks. He slipped his half-caped Versace jacket off and tossed it away, cleared a space, and performed, not to impress or awe others as before, but for himself, perhaps for the last time. He had never had such a sense of his own power. He no longer heard the Father's voice, for he was the Father. All the ghosts of this city, of this virgin continent, were his to command and consume.

Here ended the American Century. Here began, again, the Anni Draculae.

Huge, lovely eyes fixed him from the crowd. A nun in full penguin suit. Red, red heart-shaped lips and ice-white polished cheeks. Her pectoral cross, stark silver against a white collar, smote him with a force that made him stagger. She wasn't a real nun, of course, just as the Village People weren't real monsters. This was a party girl, dressed up in a costume, trying to probe the outer reaches of bad taste.

She touched his mind, and an electricity sparked.

He remembered her. The girl whose name was Death, whom he had bitten and left holding a scarf to a leaking neck-wound. He had taken from her but now, he realised, she had taken from him. She was not a vampire, but he had turned her, changed her, made her a huntress.

She daintily lifted her crucifix and held it up. Her face was a gorgeous blank.

Her belief gave the symbol power and he was smitten, driven back across the flashing dance floor, between stumbling dancers. Death glided after him like a ballet dancer, instinctively avoiding people, face red and green and purple and yellow with the changing light. At the dead centre of the dance floor, she held her cross up high above her head. It was reflected in the glitterball, a million shining cruciforms dancing over the crowds and the walls.

Johnny felt each reflected cross as a whiplash. He looked about for help.

All his friends were here. Andy was up there on a balcony, somewhere, looking down with pride. And Steve had planned this whole evening for him. This was where his rise had truly begun, where he had sold his first suck, made his first dollars. But he was not safe here. Death had consecrated Studio 54 against him.

Other vampires in the crowd writhed in pain. Johnny saw the shredded-lace punk princess who called herself Scumbalina holding her face, smoking crosses etched on her cheeks and chin. Even the dhampires were uncomfortable, haemorrhaging from noses and mouths, spattering the floor and everyone around with their tainted blood.

Death was here for him, not the others.

He barged through the throng, and made it to the street. Dawn was not far off. Death was at his heels.

A taxi was waiting for him.

Inside the hack, he told the driver to take him to the Bramford.

He saw the nun step out of 54 as the vehicle moved off. He searched inside himself for the Father, willing the panic he had felt to subside. His flight from the party would be remembered. It did not do to show such weakness.

Something was still wrong. What was it?

The nun had shaken him. Had the girl become a real nun? Was she despatched by some Vatican bureau, to put an end to him? The Church had always had its vampire killers. Or was she working with the Mafia? To evict him from the business he had created, so the established crime families could claim drac fortunes for their own. Perhaps she was a minion of one of his own kind, a catspaw of the Transylvania Movement. At the moment, Baron Meinster was petitioning the UN for support, and TM elders considered Johnny an upstart who was bringing vampirism into disrepute by sharing it so widely.

Throughout the centuries, Dracula had faced and bested enemies almost without number. To be a visionary was always to excite the enmity of inferiors. Johnny felt the Father in him, and sat back in the cab, planning.

He needed soldiers. Vampires. Dhampires. Get. An army, to protect him. Intelligence, to foresee new threats. He would start with Rudy and Elvira. It was time he gave them what they wanted, and turned them. Patrick Bateman, his young investment advisor, was another strong prospect. Men like Bateman, made vampires, would be perfect for the coming era. The Age of Money.

The taxi parked outside the Bramford. It was full night, and a thin frost of snow lay on the sidewalks, slushing in the gutters.

Johnny got out and paid off the taxi driver.

Familiar mad eyes. This was someone else he had encountered in the past year. Travis. The man had changed: the sides of his head were shaved and a Huron ridge stood up like a thicket on top of his skull.

The cabbie got out of the taxi.

Johnny could tear this warm fool apart if he tried anything. He could not be surprised.

Travis extended his arm, as if to shake hands. Johnny looked down at Travis's hand, and suddenly there was a pistol – shot out on a spring device – in it.

'Suck on this,' said Travis, jamming the gun into Johnny's stomach and pulling the trigger.

The first slug passed painlessly through him as if he were made of water. There was an icy shock, but no hurt, no damage. An old-fashioned lead bullet. Johnny laughed out loud. Travis pulled the trigger again.

This time, it was silver.

The bullet punched into his side, under his ribs, and burst through his back, tearing meat and liver. A hurricane of fire raged in the tunnel carved through him. The worst pain of his *nosferatu* life brought him to his knees, and he could *feel* the cold suddenly – his jacket was back at 54 – as the wet chill of the snow bit through his pants and at the palm of his outstretched hand.

Another silver bullet, through the head or the heart, and he would be finished.

The taxi driver stood over him. There were others, in a circle. A crowd of Fearless Vampire Killers. The silent nun. The black man with wooden knives. The black man with the crossbow. The cop who'd sworn to break the Transylvania Connection. An architect, on his own crusade to avenge a family bled dead by dhamps. The ageing beatnik from the psychedelic van, with his smelly tracking dog. A red-skinned turncoat devil boy with the tail and sawn-off horns. The exterminator with the skull on his chest and a flame-thrower in his hands.

This company of stone loners was brought together by a single mission, to put an end to Johnny Pop. He had known about them all, but never guessed they might connect with each other. This city was so complicated.

The cop, Doyle, took Johnny's head and made him look at the Bramford.

Elvira was dead on the front steps, stake jutting from her cleavage, strewn limbs like the arms of a swastika. Rudy scuttled out of the shadows, avoiding Johnny's eyes. He hopped from one foot to another, a heavy briefcase in his hands. The arrow man made a dismissive gesture, and Rudy darted off, hauling what cash he could take. The Vampire Killers hadn't even needed to bribe him with their own money.

There was a huge crump, a rush of hot air, and the top floor windows all exploded in a burst of flame. Glass and burning fragments rained all arond. His lair, his lieutenants, his factory, a significant amount of money, his coffin of earth. All gone in a moment.

The Vampire Killers were grimly satisfied.

Johnny saw people filling the lobby, rushing out onto the streets.

Again, he would have an audience.

The Father was strong in him, his ghost swollen, stiffening his spine, deadening his pain. His fang-teeth were three inches long, distending his jaw. All his other teeth were razor-edged lumps. Fresh rows of piranha-like fangs sprouted from buds he had never before suspected. His nails were poison daggers. His shirt tore at the back as his shoulders swelled, loosing the beginnings of black wings. His shoes burst and rips ran up the sides of his pants.

He stood up, slowly. The whole in his side was healed over, scabbed with dragonscales. A wooden knife lanced at him, and he batted it out of the air. Flame washed against his legs, melting the snow on the sidewalk, burning away his ragged clothes, hurting him not a bit.

Even the resolute killers were given pause.

He fixed all their faces in his mind.

'Let's dance,' Johnny hissed.

Now Andy was really a vampire, we would all see finally, doubters and admirers, what he had meant all along.

It has been a tenet of Western culture that a vampire cannot be an artist. For a hundred years, there has been fierce debate on the question. The general consensus on many careers is that many a poet or a painter was never the same man after death, that posthumous work was always derivative self-parody, never a true reaction to the wondrous new nightlife opened up by the turning. It is even suggested that this symptom is not a drawback of vampirism but proof of its superiority over life; vampires are too busy **being** *to pass comment, too concerned with their interior voyages to bother issuing travel reports for the rest of the world to pore over.*

The tragedies are too well known to recap in detail. Poe reborn, struggling with verses that refuse to soar; Dali, growing ever richer by forging his own work (or paying others to); Garbo, beautiful forever in the body but showing up on film as a rotting corpse; Dylan, born-again and boring as hell; de Lioncourt, embarrassing all **nosferatu** *with his MOR goth rocker act. But Andy was the Ultimate Vampire before turning. Surely, for him, things would be different.*

Alas, no.

Between his deaths, Andy worked continuously. Portraits of queens and inverted Tijuana crucifixes. Numberless commissioned silkscreens of anyone rich enough to hire him, at $25,000 a throw. Portraits of world-famous boxers (Mohammed Ali, Apollo Creed) and football players (O. J. Simpson, Roy Race) he had never heard of. Those embarassingly flattering likenesses, impossible to read as *irony, of the Shah, Ferdinand and Imelda, Countess Elisabeth Bathory, Victor Von Doom, Ronnie and Nancy. And he went to a* **lot** *of parties, at the White House or in the darkest dhampire clubs.*

There's nothing there.

Believe me, I've looked. As an academic, I understand exactly Andy's dilemma. I too was considered a vampire long before I turned. My entire discipline is reputed to be nothing more than a canny way of feeding off the dead, prolonging a useless existence from one grant application to the next. And no one has ever criticised elder vampires for their lack of **learning**. *To pass the centuries, one has to pick up dozens of languages and, in all probability, read every book in your national library. We may rarely have been artists, but we have always been patrons of the arts.*

Among ourselves, the search has always been on for a real vampire artist, preferably a creature turned in infancy, before any warm sensibility could be formed. I was tempted in my reassessment of Andy's lifelong dance with Dracula to put forward a thesis that he was such a discovery, that he turned not in 1968 but say, 1938, and exposed himself by degrees to sunlight, to let him age. That would explain the skin problems. And no one has ever stepped forth to say that they turned Andy. He went into hospital a living man and came out a vampire, having been declared dead. Most commentators have suggested he was transfused with vampire blood, deliberately or by accident, but the hospital authorities strenuously insist this is not so. Sadly, it won't wash. We have to admit it; Andy's best work was done when he was alive; the rest is just the black blood of the dead.

Conklin, *ibid*

Johnny lay broken on the sidewalk, a snow angel with cloak-like wings of pooled, scarlet-satin blood. He was shot through with silver and wood, and smoking from a dousing in flame. He was a ghost, locked in useless, fast-spoiling meat. The Father was loosed from him, standing over his ruin, eyes dark with sorrow and shame, a pre-dawn penumbra around his shoulders.

The Vampire Killers were dead or wounded or gone. They had not brought his true death easily. They were like him in one way; they had learned the lesson of *Dracula*, that only a family could take him down. He had known there were hunters on his track; he should have foreseen they would band together, and taken steps to break them apart as the Father would have done, had done with his own persecutors.

With the New York sunrise, he would crumble to nothing, to a scatter of drac on the snow.

Bodies moved nearby, on hands and knees, faces to the wet stone, tongues lapping. Dhampires. Johnny would have laughed. As he died, he was being sucked up, his ghost snorted by addicts.

The Father told him to reach out, to take a hold.

He could not. He was surrendering to the cold. He was leaving the Father, and letting himself be taken by Death. She was a huge-eyed fake nun.

The Father insisted.

It wasn't just Johnny dying. He was on the last link with the Father. When Johnny was gone, it would be the end of Dracula too.

Johnny's right hand twitched, fingers clacking like crab-claws. It had almost been cut through at the wrist, and even his rapid healing couldn't undo the damage.

The Father instructed.

Johnny reached out, fingers brushing a collar, sliding around a throat, thumbnail resting against a pumping jugular. He turned his head, and focused his unburst eye.

Rudy Pasko, the betrayer, the dhampire.

He would kill him and leave the world with an act of vengeance.

No, the Father told him.

Rudy's red eyes were balls of fear. He was swollen with Johnny's blood, overdosing on drac, face shifting as muscles under the skin writhed like snakes.

'Help me,' Johnny said, 'and I'll kill you.'

Rudy had boosted a car, and gathered Johnny together to pour him into the passenger seat. The dhampire was on a major drac trip, and saw the light at the end of his tunnel. If he were to be bitten by Johnny in his current state, he would die, would turn, would be a dhampire no longer. Like all the dhamps, his dearest wish was to be more, to be a full vampire. It wasn't as easy as some thought. They had to be bitten by the vampire whose blood they had ingested. Most street drac was cut so severely that the process was scrambled. Dhampires had died. But Rudy knew where the blood in him had come from. Johnny realised that his Judas had betrayed him not just for silver, but because Rudy thought that if he spilled enough of Johnny's blood, he could work the magic on his own. In the British idiom he had learned from Sid, Rudy was a wanker.

They arrived at Andy's town house just before dawn.

If Johnny could get inside, he could survive. It wasn't easy, even with Rudy's help. During the fight, he had shape-shifted too many times, sustained too many terrible wounds, even lost body parts. He had grown wings, and they'd been shredded by silver bullets, then ripped out by the roots. Important bones were gone from his back. One of his feet was lopped off and lost in the street. He hoped it was hopping after one of his enemies.

He has tasted some of them, the Vampire Killers. In Doyle's blood, he found a surprise: the drac-busting cop was a secret dhampire, and had dosed himself up to face Johnny. The knifeman, who had vampire blood in him from a strange birth, had stuffed himself with garlic, to make his blood repulsive.

The blood was something. He was fighting now.

Rudy hammered on Andy's door, shouting. Johny had last seen Andy at 54, at the party he had left. He should be home by now, or would be home soon. As dawn approached, Johnny felt himself smoking. It was a frosty all Hallows' morn, but the heat building up like a fever inside him was a monsoon-oppressive and threatened to explode in flames.

Johnny's continued life depended on Andy having made it home.

The door was opened. It was Andy himself, not yet out of his party clothes, dazzled by the pinking end of night. Johnny felt waves of horror pouring off the artist, and understood exactly how he must look.

'It's just red, Andy. You use a lot of red.'

Rudy helped him into Andy's hallway. The gloom was like a welcoming cool in midsummer. Johnny collapsed on the chaise longue and looked at Andy, begging.

Only one thing could cure him. Vampire blood.

His first choice would have been the Churchward woman, who was almost an elder. She had survived a century and was of a fresh bloodline. But Penny was gone, fleeing the city and leaving them all in the bloody lurch.

It would have to be Andy. He understood, and backed away, eyes wide.

Johnny realised he didn't even know what Andy's bloodline was. Who had made him?

Andy was horrified. He hated to be touched. He hated to give anything, much less himself.

Johnny had no choice. He reached out with what was left of his mind and took a hold of the willing Rudy. He made the dhamp, still hopped up on prime drac, grab Andy by the arms and force him across the lobby, bringing him to the chaise longue as an offering for his Master.

'I'm sorry, Andy,' said Johnny.

He didn't prolong the moment. Rudy exposed Andy's neck, stringy and chalky, and Johnny pounced like a cobra, sinking his teeth into the vein, opening his throat for the expected gush of life-giving, mind-blasting vampire blood. He didn't just need to take blood, he needed a whole ghost, to replace the tatters he had lost.

Johnny nearly choked.

He couldn't keep Andy's blood down. His stomach heaved, and gouts poured from his mouth and nose.

How had Andy done it? For all these years?

Rudy looked down on them both, wondering why Johnny was trying to laugh, why Andy was squealing and holding his neck, what the frig was going down in the big city?

Andy wasn't, had never been, a vampire.

He was still alive.

Johnny at last understood just how much Andy Warhol was his own invention.

Andy was dying now, and so was Johnny.

Andy's blood did Johnny some good. He could stand up. He could take hold of Rudy, lifting him off his feet. He could rip open Rudy's throat with his teeth and gulp down pints of the dhamp's drac-laced blood. He could toss Rudy's corpse across the lobby.

That taken care of, he cradled Andy, trying to get the dying man's attention. His eyes were still moving, barely. His neck-wound was a gouting hole, glistening with Johnny's vampire spittle. The light was going out.

Johnny stuck a thumbnail into his own wrist and poured his blood into Andy's mouth, giving back what he had taken. Andy's lips were as red as Rita Hayworth's. Johnny coaxed him and finally, after minutes, Andy swallowed, then relaxed and let go, taking his first and final drac trip.

In an instant, as it happens sometimes, Andy Warhol died and came back. It was too late, though. Valerie Solanas had hurt him very badly, and there were other problems. The turning would not take.

Johnny was too weak to do anything more.

Andy, Warhola the Vampyre at last, floated around his hallway, relishing the new sensations. Did he miss being a magnificent fake?

Then, the seizures took him and he began to crumble. Shafts of light from the glass around the door pierced him, and he melted away like the Wicked Witch of the West.

Andy Warhol was a vampire for only fifteen minutes.

Johnny would miss him. He had taken some of the man's ghost, but it was a quiet spirit. It would never compete with the Father for mastery.

Johnny waited. In a far corner, something stirred.

He had written his own epitaph, of course. 'In the future, everyone will live forever, for fifteen minutes.'

Goodbye, Drella. At the end, he gave up Dracula and was left with only Cinderella, the girl of ashes.

The rest, his legacy, is up to us.
***Conklin**, ibid*

Rudy could have been a powerful vampire. He rose, turned, full of *nosferatu* vigour, eager for his first feeding, brain a-buzz with plans of establishing a coven, a drac empire, a place in the night.

Johnny was waiting for him.

With the last of his strength, he took Rudy down and ripped him open in a dozen places, drinking his vampire blood. Finally, he ate the American boy's heart. Rudy hadn't thought it through. Johnny spat out his used-up ghost. Sad little man.

He exposed Rudy's twice-dead corpse to sunlight, and it powdered. The remains of two vampires would be found in Andy's house, the artist and the drac dealer. Johnny Pop would be officially dead. He had been just another stage in his constant turning.

It was time to quit this city. Hollywood beckoned. Andy would have liked that.

At nightfall, bones knit and face reforming, he left the house. He went to Grand Central Station. There was a cash stash in a locker there, enough to get him out of the city and set him up on the Coast.

The Father was proud of him. Now, he could acknowledge his bloodline in his name. He was no longer Ion Popescu, no longer Johnny Pop, he was Johnny Alucard.

And he had an empire to inherit.

michael marshall smith

the vaccinator

Walk North up Duval Street in Key West, past the restaurants, fruit juice stands and T-shirt emporiums, and pretty soon you'll come to the Havana Docks. It's a tourist harbour, quite small, bordered on both sides by restaurant piers and not much used for seafaring beyond a couple of glass-bottom boats and a jetski concession. Mainly it's there for looking at, and eating by, and watching the sun set over. Also, stuff swims in it. Some days you'll see a manatee down in the water around the pier supports, and there's generally some Yellow Tail and Black Fin flicking around. You'd think fish would have the sense not to swim right up close to seafood restaurants, where people can look down at them and think 'I'll have one of *those*, please, with broccoli and a cold glass of wine' but evidently not. At night little sharks swarm in the underwater lights, so many and moving so fast that it makes you wonder if the whole sea is like that, right out to the invisible horizon, a twisting mass of creatures who barely know we're here and won't miss us when we're gone.

On this particular morning a man called Eddie was sitting alone on the upper level of the East pier, feet up against the wooden railing and a cup of iced tea cradled in his lap. He was watching one of the tan jetski assholes going through his chops in the bay, showing the sparse tourists how much noisy fun they could have for a mere fifty bucks an hour. The skier hadn't fallen off yet, but there was still room for hope. Eddie was thinking that it would be best if it happened out in the bay, a long way from shore, and that if anybody asked he'd say he hadn't seen anything. It was early yet, barely ten o'clock, and the sun was just getting into its stride, glinting off the weathered wood of the pier, the swirls in the water below, and the fading edges of Eddie's hangover.

After a while, another, older, man climbed the steps up to the pier. He walked along the deck until he was level with where the Eddich was sitting, and then ground to a halt.

'Are you Eddie?' he asked eventually.

'I am,' Eddie said, without turning. He took another sip of tea. It was warm already, the ice long gone. 'And you would be George?'

The other man nodded jerkily, realised he couldn't be seen, and said that he was. Then carried on standing there.

Eddie levered himself upright in the chair, turned and looked him over. George was tall, late fifties, spreading around the stomach and thinning on top. Neatly pressed grey shorts, a blue short sleeve shirt with razor creases, dinky white socks – in general not the most hip person in the Keys that morning.

'Sit,' Eddie suggested. 'Standing there, you look like some kind of Illinois realtor on vacation.'

'Uh, I am.' George frowned, stepping back to perch on the edge of the nearest chair. 'That's what I am.'

'I know. That was a joke, to set you at ease. Didn't work, evidently. You want a cigarette?'

'No, thank you. I don't smoke.'

'Right,' Eddie nodded equably. 'You and everyone else. May you all live forever.'

George watched while the man lit up. Eddie was wearing jeans, cowboy boots, a loose jacket and an expensive-looking T-shirt that didn't proclaim him a member of the Conch Republic or have a picture of a very specific breed of dog on it or say that while he was only one year old, he had an 'attitude' – so it couldn't have been bought in Key West. He had short dark hair and a trim goatee beard, deep and sharp blue eyes. He looked late thirties, was lean but broad in the shoulders, and gave the impression that whatever he did, he did it fast and well.

'Okay,' Eddie said. 'All I know is what Connie told me. You sell land up North, and might have an unusual kind of problem.'

'Connie? That guy's name was Connie? Isn't that a girl's name?'

'Usually, yes. In this case it's short for "Conrad". You want to take the issue up with him then be my guest, but I wouldn't advise it.'

George nodded, looked down at his feet, quiet for a moment. His mouth opened after a while, but then closed again, tight enough to make a popping sound.

For the time being, that appeared to be it. Eddie watched as some seabird – he'd never been able to figure the difference between the types, or why it would be worth knowing – dropped chaotically out of the sky and snatched something from out of the swell. George meanwhile remained silent.

'Here's what you're thinking,' Eddie prompted, quietly. 'You got involved in a conversation last night with a barman you never met before. You let something slip. A matter you can't even talk to your wife about, and now here you are, sitting with another guy you've never met, and you don't think you can tell him about it either even though you want to.'

'How did you know I was married?'

'Look in the mirror some time, George. I never seen a man look as married as you. Which is a good thing, incidentally.'

'I'm glad you think so.'

'Right. Approval's very important. Plus that's not exactly a small ring you've got on your finger.'

'So – am I going to tell you these things?'

'You are. Because you don't like hiding stuff. Like the fact you told your wife you were going out to bring back pastries or something this morning as an excuse to come here alone. But lying's becoming a habit, because you don't want to worry her, and that's making you do things like go out to bars when she's asleep in bed in your nice hotel room. And that's a dubious way of life, George, because sometimes bad accidental things happen to guys in bars, and then it's going to look like you got some whole secret history you wouldn't even want.'

George smiled with half his mouth and one eyebrow. For a moment he looked like a man who closed a lot of prestige sales and was a local legend for giving junior realtors merry hell when they stepped out of line. 'Thanks for the advice. So why don't you tell me what my problem is?'

Eddie shrugged. 'You're afraid.'

'Of what?'

He obviously needed to hear someone else say it. Eddie said it. 'You think you're going to be kidnapped.'

George's face went complex, relief and confusion vying for the same advertising space. 'Kidnapped?' he said.

'What else would you call it?'

George suddenly looked very tired.

Eddie dropped his butt to the floor, ground it out with his heel. 'Why don't you tell me what's happening, and then I'll tell you what I think and if there's anything I can do about it.'

George started slowly, but gradually gained speed and confidence. He was a man used to conveying information, and his story was short and concise. Eddie occasionally asked for clarification, but mainly just let him talk. It took maybe ten minutes, and then George stopped and spread his hands, embarrassed, like a man expecting to be ridiculed.

'Okay,' Eddie said. 'In time-honoured fashion, I got some bad news and some good news. The bad news is you are indeed shaping up to be kidnapped.'

All the breath in George's body came out in a rush. He looked like he had sunstroke. 'So what is the good news, exactly?' he croaked.

'I might be able to do something about it,' Eddie said. 'How long are you aiming to stay in Key West?'

George rubbed his hand across his forehead. 'Today's Thursday. We thought probably the weekend, leaving Monday lunchtime?'

Eddie considered. 'Should be enough. Relax for a day or two. Act like nothing's happening. You staying at the Marquesa?'

'How the hell do you know that?'

'Just a guess. It's a good hotel. I'd be staying there if I was you. You should make sure you're around late afternoon on Saturday. They sometimes have wine and cheese around the pool.'

George laughed shakily. 'I'll bear it in mind.'

'Go to Bug's Pantry on the way back: they have some nice stuff there, and it's different enough to the continental breakfast that it's not going to look weird you went out for it. Corner of Curry Street.

They sell flowers too, and newspapers. One more thing. You realise this is going to cost?'

George the businessman came back. 'How much? And what kind of guarantee do I get?'

'A lot, and no kind at all. Take it or leave it.'

Eddie watched George think about the phone calls, and the fax. About what had happened to his car. About his wife, and the things he hadn't told her.

'I'll take it,' George said.

'Need the boat tonight. A beer in the next twenty seconds.'

Connie reached for the fridge. 'He's for real?'

'I think so,' Eddie said. 'Those assholes. Jeez, my head hurts.'

It was four o'clock and Slappy Jack's was empty. It was a small bar, with lots of dark wood and battered stools and pictures of the old town in heavy frames on the walls. Was a time when Key West was the biggest town in the whole of the United States. Wasn't that way any more, not by a long, long chalk, and on afternoons like this you felt the town knew it and didn't much care either way. Big towns have to get out of bed in the mornings and go do stuff. Prove themselves. Key West just put its feet up and ate some more dressed crab and thought about having another beer.

Afternoon light slanted in through the window of the bar, twirling motes of dust and casting highlights around the room like someone was setting it up for a photograph and wanted everything just right. At this time of day, there were worse places to drink. At night it was a different proposition, packed with tourists too shit-faced or stupid to realise the name was a take-off of Papa's favourite watering hole, and not the real thing. Come to that, even the real thing wasn't the real thing any more. The real Sloppy Joe's was too small and nondescript for modern tastes, didn't look enough like the real thing should – and had been superseded by a vast hell-hole on Duval which you'd have to be out of your mind to drink in.

Connie worked both the afternoon graveyard shift and the small hours, mixing strong cocktails and stuffing green olives with almonds. Big as Connie was – and he'd been hired as a deterrent to weekend warriors with Margarita hard-ons, and had spent a long time doing successfully violent things in New Orleans – Eddie was tougher. They both knew it, so that was okay.

'You want me along?'

Eddie shook his head. 'Not tonight.'

'Need anything else?'

'Just the boat.'

Connie went off to make the call. Eddie sat at the bar, sipping his beer. Not for the first time he wondered what drew them to Key West, the people who needed him. Maybe nothing, and five in three months was a coincidence. Perhaps without knowing it they found themselves heading in the direction of the Triangle. Or it was just Eddie's long-overdue good fortune, turning up in a curious package. Whatever. They were a lot easier to deal with than his previous kind of client, the type who insisted on working in Central America and driving around in expensive company cars, or who lived in the US but were just too dumb to realise they'd accumulated enough money to make them an obvious target. Doesn't matter how you've made your pile, a fat bank account is likely to breed a confidence which is a short step away from being an asshole. His new clients were less rich and usually frightened half to death, and thus prone to do what he told them.

The problem was dealing with the kidnappers.

In the old days, when Eddie took a job, he always used to hope it was Colombians he'd be dealing with. There was a set way of doing things. You thrashed out the deal in a bar somewhere, over a few lines of coke. You negotiated for the bad guys to be paid a percentage of what they might have expected to get out of the kidnapping: in return, they didn't actually go through with it. Like a vaccine. Preventative maintenance. They got some money without all the grief, and the client got to stay at home with his family, not pose for those pictures with newspapers in your hands which are never flattering, and avoided being starved, tortured and probably killed in the end. Much more convenient for everyone concerned.

The Colombians knew the score, were professionals. You arranged the vaccine, it was a deal and it was respected. These days Eddie thought he'd settle for a bunch of whacked-out Miami gangbangers, rather than the people he actually had to deal with. They were nutcases, pure and simple.

The story George Becker had told him was similar to all the others he'd heard. At first it was an occasional feeling of being watched, and half-memories of dreams which frighened him. Then one night George had been driving home after working late and it had got a little weirder.

He and his wife lived out of town, in a nice house which had a wet bar and a media room and was far too big now both kids were out in the world making the same old mistakes and calling them their own. Half a mile away from home George had been chugging along, listening to the local radio station, when suddenly it faded out. He wasn't too bothered, it was a lousy station anyway, but then the car's lights went off and he stalled. He slammed his foot on the brake but it didn't seem to make any difference: the car just cruised to a halt and then sat there, ticking as it cooled.

Nothing happened for a couple of minutes, other than the sound of insects and wind in the trees.

Then the lights flicked back on, and the radio station faded back, as if he were driving into its signal. George tried the ignition, and the car started immediately. He drove slowly home. He told Jennifer what had happened, and she shrugged, told him to take the car down to the shop in the morning. As you would – if you didn't know about the dreams, and she didn't.

He took the car down the shop. They found something to charge him for, but it was the usual bullshit. The car was fine.

Nothing else happened for a while. Nothing to do with the car, at least. Occasionally things in his workshop seemed to have moved, but you could put that down to absentmindedness. And sometimes the phone rang at odd hours, and when George picked it up there was usually nobody there. Once he thought he heard his mother talking, but the line was very bad and she'd been dead nearly ten years, so he wasn't sure.

He put up with this for six months, and had almost got used to it, when it suddenly started to invade his work. George's office had two names above the door, and his was one of them. He and Dave Marks had built the business from nothing, and were now both immovable fixtures in the annual list of the top five realty producers in the state. He believed the building their business was conducted in to be as inviolable as their status: unbreachable, the castle that Englishmen's houses were supposed to be. George rarely called Jennifer from work, unless it was urgent, and she had visited him there only a handful of times. That wasn't what the office was for.

Then one afternoon the phone on his desk rang, and when he picked it up there was no one there – but the silence had a strange undertone that made it sound as if someone was, but they weren't saying anything. He tried to find out from the operator who'd been calling, but as usual they didn't have a number recorded.

A week later a fax arrived on the private machine in his office. There was just one line typed on it, a description of a place in a forest which at first meant nothing to him. The paper was otherwise entirely blank, without even the sender information at the very top which just about every fax machine in the world automatically provides. George threw it away, and that lunchtime found a bar a few streets away and drank vodka so no one would be able to smell it.

He was feeling hunted now, by something that wasn't even there. Thirty, forty years ago, long before he'd met his wife, he'd been unfaithful to a previous girlfriend – with a friend of hers. He was mid-twenties, he got drunk, it happened. It didn't mean anything except for how bad it made him feel. He didn't call the girl, and heard nothing from her for over eight months. He assumed she'd done the same as he had – realised it was a silliness with no future in it, and tried to forget it had happened. But he didn't know this. Not for sure. There was still the possibility that at some point, with no warning, a disaster could explode into his life. Then one night he and his girlfriend were in a bar, and they ran into this other girl. She smiled on seeing them, and he knew it was all going to be all right, and he was so relieved he spent the whole evening babbling until both girls told him to shut up.

It was like that, but a lot worse.

He started fixating on the idea of their Florida vacation, only a few weeks away. He told himself that if he could just get through until then, it would be okay. Although he'd already begun to entertain some pretty odd notions of what might be happening to him, he somehow thought he'd be safe away from home.

There were two more calls before they left – one at the office, one at home. Jen glanced at him for a moment after he told her that the second had been a wrong number – again – and then went back to finding out what dungeon of homemaker psychosis Martha Stewart was plumbing this month. Something told him that, while Jen was without doubt completely unconscious of thinking this way, he wasn't going to be allowed many more wrong numbers.

On his last night at work, the car cut out again on the journey home. At exactly the same spot, in exactly the same way. George, a cautious man, had taken the car to the shop only two days before, making sure it was in good shape for the trip down. They'd tried hard to rip him off, but only been able to find a few bucks' worth of tinkering to do. The car was fine.

The next morning they locked up the house, briefed the neighbours a final time about cat-feeding, and set off. As they pulled down the drive, George felt his heart lighten. They only did a couple hours' driving that day, to break themselves in gently, and stopped at a shiny new Holiday Inn in some little town whose name they didn't even register. The guy behind the desk recommended a restaurant a short stroll down the street, and they had a great dinner, much to their surprise – pleased to be roughing it and coming out on top.

By the time they got back to their room they were feeling the way long-term couples sometimes do when they're out of their usual environment and have had a few glasses of wine. Jen said she wanted to shower quickly, and kissed him on the lips before she went. George sat on the bed, listened to the water falling on his wife's body, and smiled a little at the pair of them. Old guys going wild in the country.

Then the phone rang, and it wasn't anyone he knew. Or anyone at all, in fact. Just the rustle of wind high up in the trees. The sound of somebody not talking.

He told Jen it had been reception telling them about check-out times, and did his best to pick up where they'd left off. He did a good job considering, but it wasn't the same.

There were no more phone calls over the next few days, as they slowly made their way to Florida, down the Gulf side of the panhandle, and then into the Keys. But increasingly George found his mind was elsewhere. The sentence about the forest, which at first he'd just dismissed, kept coming back into his mind.

He couldn't remember the place it described. Nobody would have been able to. It was both too specific and too vague – as if it were not so much a real location, as a type. It just said 'Three pines almost in line, with rocks all around and a dark mountain behind'. It could have been anywhere. The more he worried over it, however, the more it began to be associated in his mind with flashes of white light, with a sensation of breathless running, and with the idea that something may have happened a long time ago which he had simply blanked out.

In the hotel in Key Largo he woke up just after midnight. He didn't know why. There'd been no dream, no sound, nothing. He was just suddenly awake. He eased himself out of bed, swapped his pjs for shorts and a shirt, and slipped out of the hotel room. The sky was wide and very dark blue. There was nothing in it. He heard the sound of faint laughter, at a distance, and saw that a few people were still lolling around the Tiki bar by the pool. On impulse he walked over, and charged a couple of Manhattans to the room. When he returned, half an hour later, he got back to sleep without any problem.

The next day they arrived in Key West, and late in the evening George had found himself in another bar, again alone, and talking to a man called Connie.

That was his story. But Eddie knew that George was right to think he hadn't heard the end of it. The nutcases had gone easy on laying in false memory, which was good and unusually restrained, but everything else suggested they were settling for the long haul.

Connie came back. The boat would be set up, with fuel and ammunition on board. Eddie stayed a while longer, drinking beer and helping stuff olives. A couple of tourists poked their head in the door, but Connie scowled at them and they went away.

*

It was a still night. The water was flat and calm. Just after ten o'clock, Eddie cut the engine and let her drift a while. It was extremely dark, the only light coming from the boat's lamps and the stars in the deep nothing above. He was five miles out, over part of the long reef which starts north of Miami and follows the coast down into open sea. During the day you could join a cruise out of Havana Docks, come and look down at the fish and sharks swimming around over the coral. After the sun went down the only people who came out this far were marine biologists who wanted to check out the nightlife on the reef. Tonight there weren't any around, which was good.

Eddie set the radio to send, lit a cigarette, and settled down to wait. The signal was a sequence of fifty tones, repeated in an order so complex it looked random. Wouldn't mean anything except to the people it was supposed to. Meanwhile he checked his gun, which had seen service in half of Central America, two European countries and the backstreets of more than a few US cities. So far he hadn't even had to pull it on one of these jobs. But you never knew. He cleaned it, loaded it with shells, and then laid it on the table in front of him. He felt keyed up, but not nervous. Eddie had done many unusual things in his life. This was merely the latest.

Fifteen minutes later the lamp on the front of the boat flickered and then went out. Gradually the other lights started to dim, and then the boat was in darkness. Eddie picked up the gun, put it in his shoulder holster. It had occurred to him, on the first trip, in fact, that there was no guarantee it would even work. They probably had ways of affecting things like that, like the stuff they could do with electric power. But he felt better having it around.

The water around the boat started to become glassy, losing motion until it felt like solid land. Everything went quiet.

Then bang – the light went on. Eddie flinched, cursed, and refused to look up into it. The light came down like a cylinder, a circular beam that was a couple of times wider than the boat was long. Though it looked just like someone had turned the world's biggest halogen flashlamp on him, Eddie knew it was more complicated than that. The boat was now rock steady, and the sea within the beam frozen in place. The light wasn't just a source of illumination. It grabbed hold of things, and could pull them up.

'It's Edward Kruger,' he said, loudly, shielding his eyes with his hands. 'Turn that fucking thing off.'

There was a long pause, during which the light stayed exactly as bright as it had been. Then it dimmed – very, very slightly.

'I want to go to the island,' he said. 'I've got business there. And I want to go the old-fashioned way, because this isn't my boat. Okay?'

Another pause, and then the beam went out.

Eddie looked up, but as usual there was nothing to see. The boat lights slowly came back on, in the order they'd gone off. Eddie started the engines.

It took another twenty minutes before he could see the island. There was a single light at the dock, and he headed for it. The tying point was at the end of a long wooden walkway, as they often were on the Keys, because the water around the islands was so shallow.

In the old days there used to be an island on the chain called No-Name Key, a few miles north of Key West: presumably so-called because the early settlers had run dry of the creative energy required to name the hundreds of local bumps in the sea, some little bigger than sandbars with a couple of trees. That island was called something else now, he couldn't remember what. Something dull, or quaint, or both.

The island he was about to land at wasn't even called something as unimaginative as No-Name. It wasn't known as anything at all, and never had been, because as far Eddie could tell, he and Connie were the only two humans who'd ever been aware of its existence – and Connie had never actually set foot on it. It wasn't on any of the maps, and Eddie had never been able to find a reference to it in any of the painfully exhaustive quasi-literate local history books. He'd come to believe that for most of the time it simply wasn't there. Some kind of cloaking device, he guessed – in place for a very long time.

He got the boat tied up to the dock, and climbed out. Took a deep breath, looking back the way he'd come. You couldn't see the lights of Key West from here, or any of the other islands. It was very quiet, just the sound of his footsteps and a faint creak from the walkway swaying in gentle time with the water. You might just as well be on a different planet.

At the land end of the walkway was another light, which showed the path ahead through the forest. Apart from the dim lamps every couple of yards along it, the path was the only sign of artificiality on the island. As far was Eddie could tell, the rest of it was entirely covered in trees and brush. He lit another cigarette before he set off. He didn't really need it, but it was nice to have something man-made in your hand. It was grounding. Rah-rah for the humans, something like that.

After a few minutes on the path, he heard a sound over on the right, amongst the trees. He stopped, listened. Nothing. There weren't even any insects on the island and it was deadly quiet. It was much warmer than it had been on the boat, and humid.

He started walking again, and this time heard the sound from the left side, maybe five yards into the trees. He kept on walking.

And then he suddenly turned around.

Behind him on the path, caught and frozen, were three small humanoid figures. About four feet high and thin, grey in colour, with bulbous heads and large black eyes that looked like those sunglasses people were wearing a couple of years back.

He laughed. 'What's the matter, someone leave the cat flap open? Going to be trouble when they hear you're out.'

The little guys looked at each other, then back at him. One of them cleared its throat.

'Hi, Eddie,' it said. It voice was a poor approximation of human speech, more of a clicking rasp. 'You got anything for us?'

Eddie reached in his pocket, pulled out a spare pack of cigarettes. He tossed it to the nearest grey.

'Thanks, Eddie,' they said, in unison.

'Yeah,' he replied. 'Now scoot.'

They scuttled off into the undergrowth. Eddie shook his head. If they were his, he'd electrify the compound.

The path wound across the island for nearly a mile. Towards the end the ground rose slightly, and then gave out into a circular clearing. This was about fifty yards across, and was completely clear of trees and bushes. It was covered in short, manicured grass, soft like you got in Europe instead of the sharp and tough Florida scrub. In the middle were four armchairs – three of which were black leather recliners, the other the kind of worn affair you'd find in a cheap motel – and a standard lamp, which shed a warm glow for a couple of yards around. Eddie walked straight over and sat in the chair that didn't recline.

'I'm here,' he said.

They kept him waiting for a while, as usual.

George, meanwhile, was walking back to his room from the Marquesa's reception, after making a dinner reservation for the following evening. He was one of those people who really enjoy their food, and look forward to it, and take enjoyment in planning where the next meal is going to come from. That evening – after careful consideration – they'd gone to Crabby Dick's on Duval, and had good steak and blackened dolphin while sitting on the upperdeck and watching people wandering past below. The Marquesa's bistro was supposed to be pretty good, so that was where they were going to be eating tomorrow night. George didn't quite have his whole menu planned out, but he'd made some ballpark wine list plans and narrowed his appetiser options down to two. Though at the last minute he might go wild and switch to something else. You never knew.

Planning food events was also useful because it gave George something simple and practical to think about. Jen had accepted his story about getting sidetracked on the way to buy Danish, and been touched by the flowers. They'd had a nice day, just wandering around. Stood on the Southernmost point, looked at Hemingway's house and all the cats, drunk their own volume in iced fruit drinks. Then spent a late afternoon hour around the Marquesa's pools: there were two, both small, hidden in the leafy courtyards created when three wooden Victorian houses had been loosely combined to form the hotel. Jen floated around, gently paddling this way and that, while George sat in a chair wearing a T-shirt and holding a copy of the local newspaper. Though it was no longer an exactly recent development, he'd never quite got over the disappointment of finding that he'd somehow become housed in an older man's body, and preferred not to inflict the sight of it upon the world.

He watched his wife swim, glad that he'd gone to see Eddie that morning. He'd been nervous, and expecting many things: blank incomprehension, ridicule, or one of several different methods of extracting money. Instead he seemed to have been taken seriously, which for an hour or so had made him feel light-headed with relief. There was no way of telling whether the guy could actually do anything – could be that it was just a more complex scam than he'd been expecting. But he felt better for having done it, whatever happened. When your wife's touched because you bring her flowers and the only reason you did it is to cover up the fact you've been lying to her, that's a bad feeling. You realise that you should bring them more often, and that you'd like to, but somehow you don't. It mainly just doesn't occur to you. Unless you're hiding something, and the guilt that engenders makes you realise how much you love the person you're lying to. He didn't want to be covering up any more. He wondered briefly what percentage of flowers in the world were bought for the right reasons – then shitcanned that stream of thought and tried to read a story about a local group of poets. He couldn't. It wasn't interesting. If there was a local poet in the whole world who wasn't shit then George believed he must be in hiding somewhere, along with all the good local artists.

That, at least, was that anyone peeking would have found in George's mind that afternoon. He'd grown very used to covering up what was actually going on in his head, because he was finding it increasingly inexplicable and disturbing.

At night the pool area was deserted, with that strange, restful atmosphere public places get when the public isn't there to clutter them up. It was dark except for a couple of low yellow lamps, the vivid blue-green glow of the pool, and a few stars visible through the palm cover above. George was passing almost exactly the same spot where he'd been sitting in the afternoon when he thought he heard something. At first he assumed it was another guest out for a stroll, and got a smile ready. No one appeared. He stopped, looked around. Someone had put in a lot of effort growing plants in and above the courtyard, with big hibiscus and ground palms and all manner of other things Jen would know the names of. During the day you could see geckos, some of them pretty big, running all over the brickwork floor. Maybe that was what he'd heard. He began walking again, and started quietly to scale the low steps around the waterfall which was on the way to their suite.

He was still a way from home when he heard something that sounded like a door handle being turned, and then Jen's voice saying his name in the form of a question. As if someone had opened the door to her suite, and she'd looked up to see no one there, and wondered if he was playing a game.

George started to run.

'Eddie, my man – how's it hanging? How are you, guy?'

Eddie looked down from the stars, to see that the three reclining chairs were now occupied. He'd given up hoping to see how they managed to do that – being not there one minute and then there the next – but it still irritated him.

'Hungry,' he said. 'And bored. You get a warning from when the assholes shine the big light in my eyes, you got video surveillance on the pier. You must know when I get to this chair. So how come it still takes you fifteen fucking minutes to get your asses out here?'

'Touchy,' said the first alien. Yag was his name. He, like the two others, had the recliner tipped back as far back as it would go, and was lounging with his arms and legs hanging off the sides. 'Think Eddie's a little out of sorts this evening, fellas.'

'It's just rude, is all,' Eddie said, and lit another cigarette.

'You know we don't like smoking,' another of the aliens said. He was about six foot eight, thin and spidery like the others. His skin was the usual pale golden colour, and glistened wetly. The way they looked, you'd expect them to smell pretty bad. Actually, they smelled of spearmint. His head was slightly elongated but otherwise not too different to ours. He was called Fud, and he was pretty drunk.

'You don't give a shit about smoking,' Eddie said, not putting it out. 'It doesn't even do anything to you guys. You're just being a pain in the ass, as usual.'

'We do too care,' Yag said, stifling a burp. 'Everybody cares. It's a zeitgeist thing.'

'You bring us anything?' the third alien slurred. Eddie didn't know his name. The spindly fucker had always been too wasted to pronounce it. Maybe that was how that Key got called No-Name too. Always too drunk to talk.

Eddie pulled the bottle of overproof rum out of his pocket and lobbed it to the alien. It landed on his stomach and he went 'Ooof.' Then pulled off the cap and took a long pull, before handing it on to Yag.

'I had some cigarettes too,' Eddie said, 'But seeing as you guys don't like that kind of thing, I gave them to the greys instead.'

'What?' Fud demanded. 'Where were they?'

Eddie laughed. 'On the path. What's up with you guys? Masters of the universe and you can't even keep your pets under control?'

Suddenly Eddie found himself with the three aliens staring at him, and for the moment they didn't look so drunk.

'When we want a human's advice on how to run our affairs,' the un-named one said, 'You'll be the first to know, Kruger. In the meantime, shut the fuck up.'

Eddie held the stare. 'Your call. But with those animals screwing around like assholes the whole time and flashing lights over people's houses, sooner or later it's all gonna go wide.'

'It's under control,' Fud said petulantly.

'Yeah right. Like that stupid autopsy video really made everybody think it was just a hoax. You guys watch television ever? It's the greys who're flavour of the decade, not you.'

'We don't give a shit what your stupid fucking species thinks,' No-name shouted, jumping to its feet and jabbing a long finger at him. 'I've wiped my ass on brighter life-forms than you, shit face.'

The sides of the alien's head were pulsing slightly, narrow slits opening in the temples. Eddie had seen this happen before, and suspected it was a prelude to something bad. Longing for a straight-forward Colombian or two, he was glad of the gun in his jacket, even if it wouldn't work. At least he could hit one of them with it, if it came to it. He stood up.

'Gentlemen, gentlemen,' Yag said, mildly. 'Eddie, calm down. Come on. Have a drink.' He held the bottle out to him.

Eddie took it, made a couple of inches disappear, and then passed it on. Fud drank. His temples stopped bulging.

No-name glared at Eddie a final time, hiccuped, and took a drink. He sat down, then grinned. 'Give us a smoke, Eddie.'

Eddie passed him a cigarette, lit it for him, his heartbeat gradually returning to normal.

'That's better,' Yag said, and kicked the ground so his recliner span in a gentle circle, making a quiet 'wheee' noise as it went. 'So, what you want to talk to us about, Eddie? Let's do business.'

'Man called George Becker,' Eddie said, sitting down. 'Lives in Illinois. I'm authorised to buy an abduction vaccine on his behalf.'

'Excellent,' Yag said, rubbing his thin, long hands together. 'What will the market stand?'

'Looking at him, I'd say forty thousand.'

'Then that's the price. Plus five thousand dollars.'

Eddie sighed. 'Why the extra five?'

'Because we feel like it,' Fud said, and the three of them cackled. 'You got a problem with that, ape-boy?'

'No problem at all,' Eddie said, reflecting that had these guys been a crew of humans out of Miami he could have just whacked the bunch of them six months ago. 'Forty-five thousand dollars,' he continued patiently, 'in return for which you leave him the fuck alone, stop freaking him out with phone calls and screwing with his car and faxing him and putting stuff in his dreams and memory and this shit about some forest with rocks in it.'

'Sure thing,' Yag smirked.

'And, of course,' Eddie said, having been caught out this way before, 'you don't abduct him either.'

'When do we see the money?'

'This weekend. And leave the guy alone in the meantime, yeah? He's on vacation. And get a mobile phone or something. I'm sick and tired of schlepping out here every time.'

'You want us to come find you instead?' Fud asked.

'No,' Eddie said.

'So we'll see you here in a couple of days.' The alien waved a hand. Eddie was dismissed. He got up, walked away.

As he disappeared down the path No-name said, with obvious satisfaction, 'Going to have to kill him sooner or later.'

Fud and Yag raised an eyebrow each.

'Eddie's okay,' Yag said. 'Does what he's told, doesn't talk to anyone, doesn't ask the right questions.'

'What do you mean?'

'Well,' Yag smiled, 'he didn't even think to ask if it was us who were buzzing this George Becker character.'

'Isn't it?'

'Hell no,' Fud laughed. 'Never heard of the fucking guy.'

'How were the weirdos?'

'Weird,' Eddie said, accepting the beer Connie handed him. 'Tell you the truth, they're really beginning to get on my nerves.'

'Why don't you just clip them, have done with it?'

'Yeah, right,' Eddie grimaced, and glanced around the bar. 'Jesus – what the hell's got into these people tonight?'

The room was crammed with tourists, apparently at one in a desire to demonstrate how much noise the human head was capable of producing. Sweating groups of guys and girls, quite a few husband-and-wife outfits, everyone happily talking and shouting and even singing – with the exception of a peaceable and remarkably sunburnt couple sitting at the end of the bar, who appeared to be methodically establishing how many Golden Margaritas you could drink before your brain melted. Connie saw Eddie glance at them.

'From London, England,' he said. 'Just married.'

'And I would care . . . why?'

'Whatever,' Connie shrugged. 'Just filling you in.'

Eddie sat and quietly smoked a cigarette, working his way through a bowl of pistachios and piling the shells neatly where Connie could brush them in the trash with one negligent sweep of his hand. He'd told the weirdos forty thousand on the assumption he'd put his standard ten on top. Fifty felt about right. The arbitrary and fuck-ass irritating extra five they'd stipulated left him with the dilemma of deciding whether George would go for fifty-five, or if Eddie had to take half rate this time out. Wouldn't be the end of the world, what with his overheads being not much more than zero, but no one likes getting stiffed on a deal. Eddie in particular didn't like it, but he was exploring the notion on the grounds that not charging the extra might store him up some brownie points somewhere. He didn't really believe in karma, but every now and then paid lip service to it or some other edited highlight of a belief system, on the grounds that you never knew – and that someone who'd put as many people under the ground as he had did well to hedge his cosmic bets.

Meanwhile Connie served the bar sitters, kept half an eye on the customers who looked likely to be first in line to cause trouble or be sick, and filled the orders that Fran brought in from the outlying regions. Fran was a cheerful and tough 23, had big hair even by Florida standards and tattoos on her wrist, shoulder and small of her back which Connie wasn't strictly in favour of. Wasn't his business, but he hated to see lilies gilded and he was of a mind that tattooing a woman's body was like air-brushing a pair of leaping dolphins into the background of the Mona Lisa, just to perk it up a bit. Fran, though attractive, had a voice which could bend trees when she was riled and Connie elected as usual to shelve the observation. Instead he reminded the English honeymooners that it was only just after nine and the bar was open until three and thus they could afford to take it easy with regard to volume of alcohol consumption per unit time. They thanked him for his insight and consideration, and ordered another couple of Margaritas. Connie moved them up to pole position in his internal list of People Most Likely To Pass Out Before Midnight, but took comfort in the fact that at least they were likely to do it politely.

Then he noticed Eddie turn his head sharply towards the door, and glanced that way himself. Two seconds later, George, the guy from the night before, came running into the bar. His hair was awry and his face red and he was panting like his heart was considering its options and leaning towards a CVA. Eddie was on his feet before the door had stopped swinging, and flashed two fingers on the way across. Connie quickly turned and sloshed out a couple of tequilas, yelled at Janine to get her butt out the kitchen and hold the fort a minute, and took the drinks out the side door.

On the sidewalk outside, Eddie was standing in front of George. He had a hand on each of the guy's shoulders, and was talking to him in a low, even tone. George's eyes were wide and he was still breathing badly, his hands down by his side and trembling. His weight was only vaguely distributed over his legs, and if Eddie hadn't been there George would have been flat on his face in a moment.

Eddie took one of the drinks and held it in front of George's mouth. 'Drink this,' he said. George shook his head as if trying to flick water off it, eyes staring at some point on Eddie's chest.

Eddie grabbed his hair, pulled the man's head back in one sudden snap and tipped the booze straight down his throat.

George spluttered like a man pulled up out of deep water and went into a coughing jag that sounded as if tissue were coming loose. Eddie meanwhile tossed the shot glass at Connie, who caught it in one hand and handed him the second with the other. But when George stopped blinking and rubbing his eyes, they were focused back on the things in front of him.

'Sorry for that,' Eddie said. 'But things really are going to be a lot simpler if you just do as I say. You need another drink?' George coughed once more, and hiccoughed, then shook his head.

Eddie nodded, satisfied, and knocked the drink back himself. 'I take it something's fucked up,' he said.

George's finger had stolen up to his lips, and he was rubbing them like there was something ingrained there which he couldn't stand. 'They've. Oh. She's gone.'

When he'd managed these words he suddenly looked around, as if he couldn't understand what he was doing in this place talking to these people and was seized with a desire to go running away in some random direction.

Eddie reached out, grabbed his arm. 'Your wife?'

There were only two salient facts. Jennifer Becker had disappeared. George didn't know where she'd gone. In the time from him hearing her saying his name and him making it up the steps to their suite, someone had stolen her away.

'When was this?'

George looked at his watch. 'Forty, forty-five minutes ago.'

Eddie pursed his lips, looked away down the street. Two things immediately occurred to him. The second was that the woman had been taken round about the time he'd been sitting talking to the weirdos. In other words, the assholes had sat there and set a price, all the while knowing that some of their buddies were already on the way to abduct the target. As it was, they'd been too fucking incompetent – or drunk – to even get the right human, but that wasn't the issue. The issue was that they were jerking him around. No one had ever successfully jerked Eddie around before, no matter what planet they were from. Not for long, anyhow, and never for long enough to tell the tale.

George started slightly when Eddie swung his gaze back at him. For a moment there was something in the younger man's eyes, something that made it very clear that Eddie wouldn't be your first choice of guy to have a fight with, unless you were a SWAT team on the top of your game. George didn't know it, which was probably just as well because it was the last kind of thing he needed at that time, but he was one of only two people who'd seen that look in Eddie's eyes and lived to see the next hour. The other person had been Eddie's father, a long time ago, and he'd since died of his own accord.

'Well, George,' Eddie said, his voice eerily calm, 'looks like we've got a situation. They sent some guys already, you weren't there, they got your wife.'

George pulled his hand away from his lip, visibly tried to pull himself together. 'Has this ever happened before?'

'No. The vaccine was negotiated. Even if it were just our bad luck that the fetchers were already on the way, they should have been recalled. Hopefully it's an error. If it's deliberate, then it's moving outside the usual rules of engagement.'

'So what do we do?'

'First thing, you go in the bar and call your room. Check she's not back there.'

'But why . . .'

'They could have realised the fuck-up, dumped her back and she's sitting there not knowing what the hell is going on. Go call.'

After George had shouldered his way into the mass of people in the bar and was out of sight, Connie looked at Eddie.

'What's going on?'

'I don't know. I don't think it's a screw-up. I think it's deliberate.'

'Could be the greys?'

'I guess, but I don't think so. They usually do their own thing and don't mess with stuff the big boys have set up. Plus they know better than to fuck with me. After that last time.'

'What you going to do? Head back out there?'

Eddie shook his head. 'Not tonight. If it's a screw-up, I want to give them time to put it right. If not, then I'm surely going to have to have a word with them.'

'Want a hand?'

'Could be. You ever whacked an extra-terrestrial before?'

'Not as far as I know. They really bleed green?'

'You got me. I never whacked one either.'

They mused on the subject for a minute, then Eddie started getting a sinking feeling. They went inside and checked the public phone where it stood a noisy yard from the gents' toilets. Five minutes later the whole building had been checked, and it was for sure.

George had disappeared.

Sunrise found Connie standing out on the deck at Havana docks, on the off-chance. Eddie meanwhile was sitting on the little balcony outside the Beckers' suite at the Marquesa. He knew nobody was inside, because he'd checked. He'd also tossed the room and the luggage. Sometimes things got left behind. He didn't know whether it was because the aliens were careless, or if it was out of a desire to leave behind some kind of annoyingly meaningless clue, but on occasion you found little globules of alloy, or scraps of stuff which looked like tinfoil but wasn't, that would make a UFOlogist hyperventilate. He kept meaning to throw it out, but hadn't got around to it yet.

There was nothing in the suite, except what you'd expect two older people to take with them on a week's vacation.

At a quarter past seven on the dot he saw a guy in a white coat approaching, bearing a tray of breakfast and the morning paper. Eddie quickly dropped around the edge of the balcony, and waited until he'd heard a soft rap on the door and the footsteps walking away. Then he flipped back up and helped himself to coffee. Way things were shaping up, the Beckers weren't going to miss it and Eddie strongly believed it a shame to let good coffee go to waste. The toast, on the other hand, he let lie.

He'd had plenty of time in the small hours, and all his thinking was done. The odds were that George would be a very long way away by now, beyond reach of anything Eddie could do help him. What had to be done had little to do with his client, though obviously he'd keep an eye out for the guy and his wife. Today's dealings mainly had to do with showing some skinny-shank weirdos that you didn't fuck with the way things were done. A vaccine was a vaccine: if the Colombians could understand that, then assholes from the planet Zog could too.

When there was still no sign at a little after eight, Eddie left the hotel and went to meet Connie down at the docks and get some breakfast with meat in it.

Meanwhile, less than a mile away, George was sitting at the end of a long concrete promontory right at the opposite end of Duval street. Either side of the first half was beach, with a little restaurant down the way, but the last half poked right into the ocean and was in fact the southernmost point in the whole of the USA. That wasn't why George was sitting there, however. He'd already done the experience with Jen the day before, as a tourist thing, and actually neither of them had felt themselves come alive with excitement. It was a five-minutes'-worth kind of attraction, though as pleasant a place to sit as any. Truth be told, he had no idea why he was there, or how it had come to happen. He was just sitting, his legs dangling over the end, watching the waves.

After a while a woman came up and stood behind him. 'Come,' she said. 'It's time.'

A few hours later Connie was sitting in back of the boat, running the engine and slowly working his way through the beers in the cooler. Eddie perched up front, smoking. The sun was bright out on the water, and the ocean ran flat out as far as the eye could see. It was hot, in the dry clear way you only get when you're moving fast over water. When they were still a way from the right area, Eddie swore. He grabbed the binoculars and glared through them at a dot on the horizon.

'What?' Connie asked, speaking loud against the noise of the engine.

'Spirit of Key fucking West.'

Connie looked at his watch. It was just before eleven. 'Kind of early for them, isn't it?'

A glass-botton boat, capable of carrying fifty-odd tourists out to go stare at underwater things and be told stuff by earnest people in white shorts, the *Spirit of Key West* usually took its first cruise out of the Havana docks at around midday.

'It's coming season,' Eddie said. 'Guess Jack reckoned he could squeeze in a load of early birds.'

'It's going to fuck things up, isn't it?'

'There's no way the weirdos will uncloak in front of a bunch of assholes with cameras.'

'So what do we do?'

'Any idea how long they stay out over the reef?'

'Never been. Got no real interest in denizens of the sea, unless there's cocktail sauce on the side. Plus, like, I live here. But shit, how long can you look at some fish? Fifteen, twenty minutes? And that's assuming you're stoned.'

Eddie swore again. 'I guess we just wait.'

Connie cut the engines and they drifted for a while. It was calm and very quiet, just the hollow slocking sound of water lapping up against the sides of the boat, and a few birds running the avian commuter routes up above. The sea bed was maybe ten, twelve feet below, mainly bone-coloured sand but some white rocks and patches of weed. Eddie knew that, in a few places in the area, if you were to dig a few feet below the surface you'd find unrusting metal caskets, places where the visitors stored things that included the buried remains of both their own kind and humans. But he had no real interest in finding them.

They gave the boat twenty-five minutes, and then Connie got on the radio to suggest to Jack that maybe his clients had seen enough fucking fish and would he like to get the hell back into harbour.

After about a couple minutes of trying Connie gave Eddie a look. Eddie nodded. 'Let's go see what's going on here.'

It took them ten minutes to get within shouting distance. Neither of them especially felt like shouting, so they went in a little closer. The boat, a sixty-foot Seabreezer IV, was stationary near the reef, though a hundred yards more to the west than you would have expected. The engine was off. The boat was drifting. Eddie tried again on the radio, and got no response. Then he tried shouting anyway, in case Jack had slipped out of the control room for a cigarette while his passengers were down on the lower deck inside. Nobody shouted back.

Meanwhile Connie brought the boat in closer. 'So now what?'

'Bring us up right to the back.' Eddie already had a gun in his hand, and one of the big knives slipped down into his boot.

Connie picked up the other gun. 'And if they suddenly kick in the engines?'

'There was anybody on the bridge, we'd have spoken to them by now.'

They got the boat up flat against the stern of the *Spirit of Key West*, and tied her on. Then they climbed aboard, Eddie first, Connie second: neither of them especially scared and both reconciled to the idea of shooting someone if the need arose.

The boat was a standard of its type. Open at the back so you could catch some rays on the way to and from the reef, a covered place at the front for sitting and the eating of potato chips. At the prow, an area where you could stand and pretend you were that baby-face asshole in *Titanic*. A bridge area, and, below decks, the lower section where you leaned on rails and look down through the bottom.

There were no people in any of these areas. There were also no bags, paperback books, jackets or other signs of things having been left behind.

After checking each of the levels, Eddie climbed back up to the top and stood and looked for a while at the desk where you bought soft drinks and cookies and stuff if you really couldn't go an hour without taking on some kind of sustenance.

Connie joined him after poking around in the bridge. 'This would be unusual, I feel?'

Eddie nodded thoughtfully. 'That about covers it.'

'So what's happened to all these people?' Connie capped a beer which he'd luckily thought to bring on board with him, took a long pull, and peered out through the windows at the tinted ocean.

'Obvious answer is there's been a mass abduction.'

'Right. That was kind of what I was assuming.'

'But,' Eddie said, 'I'm not sure that's working for me as an explanation.' He accepted the beer from Connie, took a drink, and then thought some more. Then he lifted the hatch on the food desk and went behind. Opened the cupboards and fridge.

Connie watched. 'I sense the Kruger intellect working overtime here.'

'Where's the stuff? Where the cans and the chips and those boring fucking cookies?'

'They are, I take it, absent.'

'This boat's not going to come out on a jaunt without them. You take a load of tourists out here in the sun and then tell them they can't buy a soda, you're going to have a mutiny. People are going to lose their minds with worry and just go berserk.'

Connie shrugged. 'Maybe Karen didn't make it in this morning, and Jack just took a chance on doing a trip without provisions.'

'Right. Or maybe the weirdos had the munchies, and took all the stuff with them. I don't like either version.' Eddie got out his mobile phone, flipped it open. No signal. 'Go try the radio.'

Connie went forward into the bridge again. Eddie walked out back and stood on the sun deck, leaning back against the rail and watching the waves. He'd been holding a question mark in his head overnight. He was wondering if all this might provide an answer to it. Difficult to tell at this stage, but he was beginning to think it might. Trouble was, it wasn't clear what the answer might be.

Connie came out, smiling. 'Just spent a few minutes talking to a guy who was ready to shit a brick.'

'Jack's back at the harbour?'

'You got it. With Karen, and those perky dudes in white shorts from the Marine Biology place. Not to mention a muttering horde of sunburners who bought tickets yesterday afternoon and are really keen to come stare at some fish and been looking forward to it all last night, and are currently two short steps away from litigation. He's had to stand a round of free iced teas already.'

Eddie rolled his shoulders, flicked the safety back on and holstered his gun. 'There is something unusually weird going on here,' he said, 'and it's pissing me off.'

'So now what? Sorry to keep asking you questions and stuff, but this is, like, your area. Me, I'm just a spear carrier and happy that way.'

'What did you tell Jack?'

'Said we'd found his boat, it looks fine. Maybe we'd bring it back at some stage.'

'He's not barking for it now? We don't want to be dealing with some other guys come out here to fetch it.'

'Think he's sort of given up on the day. Sounded like he had started to face the situation with the aid of alcohol-based beverages.'

Eddie nodded. 'Okay. That's cool.'

'We have a plan?'

'We surely do.'

'Hurrah.' Connie neatly stowed the empty bottle in the trash and rubbed his hands together, his grey eyes sparkling with dangerous good humour. 'And what is it?'

'We leave the boat here, and get on with business. We go have a word with the weirdos, outline our displeasure at the situation in general, and if necessary kick some butt.'

'Eddie,' Connie said, 'that's a fine plan.'

*

Jennifer Becker sat as still as she could, covertly watching the two aliens. They hadn't spoken to her in a while. That was okay. She didn't want them to. In fact, she didn't think she could bear it if they did. She was only too aware that her life as it had been up until now, which she had by and large enjoyed, was over. A conversation with either of the beings who were standing a few yards from her could only rub this in further. She had also grown tired of trying to work out what they were saying. Occasional English words floated to the surface in their discussion, which otherwise sounded like the gurgling of a boisterous stream in early spring, trickle-fed out of melting snow and gathering volume and speed as it found its joyous way down a mountainside. At first she'd wondered whether this was because the aliens didn't have words in their language for what they were saying, like the French said they were going to have *un picnic* at *le weekend* while *camping*. Or whether it was more like Mrs Lal, the woman who worked at the Vietnamese grocery store in town and who'd been bilingual for so long that she seemed to forget which words belonged to which country – and who often turned to yell at her husband in a stream of gobbledygook which sounded remarkably similar to what the aliens were saying. But it was kind of an academic question and Jennifer hadn't found that she cared enough to pursue it very far.

Instead she was thinking about a friend of hers, Sally Dickens. Sally was the wife of one of the junior realtors in Becker & Marks. She was a little older than her husband Bruce, and Jen was a little younger than George, and the two had been close, up until a year ago. Then, little by little, Sally had started to act a little weird. At first Jenny had speculated her friend was having an affair, though she couldn't really get the idea to stick because while Sally was a really nice person – and great, acerbic company at a cocktail party – she wasn't what you'd think of as a hedonistic pleasure-seeker. Pretty serious, in fact, on the whole. Not the kind for sweated afternoons in darkness behind curtains in cheap hotels out by the Interstate, or hands held under the table in unpopular bars. Actually Jennifer thought that of the two of them she was more that kind of person, though of course she never had tested this theory, and had never even wanted to.

Then one afternoon the two of them had been having lunch at the quite good Italian that was part of the new mall and she'd pressed Sally a little, partly out of concern but also just a tiny bit because her friend's new twitchiness and silences had begun to get on her nerves. When your best friends start wigging out on you, it cuts at the heart of your life. Sally was already a few glasses of Chardonnay down at that point, and, after a couple more, and over the rest of the bottle, she tried to tell Jennifer a story. About something she claimed had happened one night when her husband was out of town, involving bright lights, strange noises, and a period of time out of time.

Jennifer hadn't believed her, and maybe hadn't hidden the fact too well. It all just sounded like something off a TV show, not very imaginatively adapted. The people she claimed had come to see her had been normal height or in fact a little taller, and not looked like those grey things you saw pictured everywhere. Apart from that it wasn't even a very interesting story, and Jen had smiled politely and sat there waiting for a gap long enough in which to ask for the check. Making it worse somehow was the fact that Sally had a bit of salad stuck between her teeth, which made her look vulnerable and sad. It wasn't the kind of thing you could point out, however, not while you were being told that kind of tale. Just something that could nag at your attention, and maybe make you pay an iota less mind than you should.

Over the next couple of months she saw Sally only once, at a party. She'd been drunk, and looked a little thin, but stood next to her husband listening to realtor stories and laughing at exactly the right moments. Her eyes had been flat, almost dry-looking, and when she saw Jen she smiled a small, tired smile that made Jen feel like a five-year-old, sensing for the first time that sometimes things happened to grown-ups which were too dismal and complex for children to understand. They barely spoke that evening, and when they did, Jen felt a little as if she was talking to someone who for reasons best known to themselves had decided to impersonate her friend, and had got the look more or less right but whose heart wasn't really in the rest of the job.

A few weeks after that Sally had tried to kill herself. Tried really quite hard, and only just failed. Since then she had been resident in a private place about twenty-five miles out of town. 'Depressed', was the official verdict: just sort of depressed about stuff, in general. From what Jen could gather no mention ever been made of an otherworldly fantasy being a source for the situation. Bruce Dickens was bearing up reasonably well, probably partly because he and a female client who was trying to sell her gauche mansion over at the golf course had really quite a lot of meetings out of the office. There were no children, so that was that.

One afternoon Jennifer had driven out to the Hospital or Rest Home or Facility or Nut House or whatever it termed itself. She had got as far as parking in the lot, and sat in the car for half an hour. Then she'd driven home. She'd told herself that perhaps it wasn't a good idea for Sally to see her, that an unscheduled visit might interrupt whatever programme the place had her on. Though actually Jen knew that the programme would probably entirely consist of colour-coded pills and little measures of heavily laced liquids, administered at regular intervals by brisk girls with dusty smiles. And really she just hadn't known what she was going to say, or how she should be, when the reality of the situation was that her friend had lost her mind.

Or so she'd thought. As she sat now in the grove of trees, very hot, extremely thirsty and being herself one step away from being driven insane by what was happening, Jennifer avoiding thinking about how she felt about her current situation by realising, finally, how guilty she felt about Sally. It wasn't even that she knew now that she might have been telling the truth. That shouldn't have mattered. Jen should have been a better friend to her anyway. And she wondered, pointlessly, whether she might have taken the whole thing just a little more seriously if there hadn't been that bit of salad caught between Sally's teeth, and how many of her judgement calls – and those of everyone else in the world – were made on such a trivial basis.

She wasn't surprised, only slightly relieved, when the aliens stopped talking and one of them turned and shot her in the head.

And the sad fact of the matter was that Sally Dickens hadn't been abducted. She really had just lost her mind.

'I'm hungry, is all I'm saying.'

Eddie shelved the idea of stripping his gun down. He'd already done it twice. No good could come of doing it again. No good had come of doing it the last time. He looked up at Connie. 'If you thought you were going to need to eat, you should have brought some food. That would have been the thinking man's approach.'

'Didn't think I was going to need it, mainly because I didn't think it was going to take this long. This is a protracted fucking afternoon we're having here, not to say one that's beginning to drag.'

'Really? Funny you feel like that, because I'm having a fucking ball.' He irritably started taking the gun apart again.

Connie shrugged. 'I feel like an ass sitting out here. Plus my head is getting sunburnt and that I can do without. Not to mention we're running out of beer.'

'You think things are bad now, wait until I run out of cigarettes. Then you're really going to see a downturn in the situation.'

Connie shook his head. 'This is no good, Eddie. You got to make a change in your working conditions. What kind of fucked-up deal is this, that you can't just go find the guys and whack them? Got to be the bottom line of any transaction of this nature. People fuck you around, they know they're going to get clipped. It's motivational management. Keeps them perky.'

'Connie, I run out of cigarettes, I'm going to whack *you*.'

'I'm just saying. That's all. This isn't dignified.'

It was just after five, Connie should have been at work hours before, and the sun was dipping low in the sky – but nothing was happening. Nothing had happened all afternoon, in fact. They'd sat in the right place for a while, then got so bored that they went back to the *Spirit of Key West*, tied the smaller boat on back, and taken the cruiser back to the harbour. Connie's intuition concerning Jack's coping mechanisms had proved to be correct. There was no danger he was taking the boat out again that day, unless he had some way of working it by remote control from the barstool he was already in danger of falling off of. The tourists had lost interest and gone off to spend their refund money on T-shirts and driftwood sculptures. And food, probably, Connie mused, wishing he'd had the foresight to pick something up before they turned round and came back out again, instead of wasting the time ringing the bar to warn them he was going to be late. It wasn't that he was so damned hungry, more that the idea had got into his head and, in the absence of stimuli other than waves and sunlight and seabirds, was proving pretty hard to dislodge.

Plus, actually, when he thought about it, he *was* kind of hungry. Eddie didn't seem to care either way, which Connie felt was weird. A guy had to eat, and breakfast was many hours ago and had anyway been compact and taken on the run. Eddie, on the other hand, seemed capable of existing solely on cigarettes and scowling.

'You never had to do this by day before?'

'No.'

'We can't just forget about the big light thing, go straight to the island?'

'It's just not there during the day. I've looked. It might be there at night. We have to wait and see.'

'Well, next time you'll know to bring a sandwich.'

'There isn't going to be a next time. Or if there is, it'll be a bazooka in the lunchbox, believe me. Look, eat a piece of rope or something, would you? I'm thinking here.'

Connie shrugged again, and opened one of the few remaining beers.

Meanwhile Eddie looked out over the ocean. He was indeed thinking, and what he was primarily thinking was that this would all be settled pretty soon. Once the light went, the weirdos would be sure to pick them up. They didn't like people hanging around here after dark, as a few hundred years of disappearances testified. The only reason why Eddie wasn't on that list of anomalies is that the time when they'd picked him up and dumped him on the island he'd got the measure of the spindly ones pretty quickly, and had the balls to suggest a commercial arrangement to them. He'd known ever since then that the position was a perilous one. Of the three, he hated Yag the least, but he didn't trust him in the slightest. He especially didn't trust No-name. He'd met men like No-name many times, and they always ended up fucking you around. It was in their nature, even when it wasn't in their interests.

Eddie cleared his mind, set up what he knew, and what he suspected, and left it like that. It didn't do to do be too locked in one mindset when going into situations like this. The resolutions of violent events were generally short. You got killed, or you avoided getting killed – generally by killing someone else. That was what it came down to, and neither outcome took very long or could be meaningfully prepared for ahead of time. Like a tennis player facing a serve from someone you'd never played before, the best you could do was watch the other guy's feet, be limber, and skilled enough to whack back whatever came over the net.

So instead he thought for a while about finding a new line of work, but nothing came. After a time Connie opened the last beer and offered it to him. Eddie shook his head, but winked: and everything was relaxed in the boat once more.

That evening the restaurants and bars of Key West did good business. Nothing spectacular, because it wasn't yet full season, but everyone went home pretty happy – the proprietors to nice Victorian homes in the Old Town or Scholz-designed palaces on the North of the island, the waitress and barmen to dwindling stashes of dope and rooms in ramshackle houses. Places like Crabby Dick's and Mangoes and Febe's Grill got in two solid covers of holiday spenders, and the Hard Rock Café doled out a hundred burgers or so, as an adjunct to its primary business of making people's ears bleed. The chi-chi bistros tucked away down side-streets and in hotels raked in by far the best money – the human species having lost its bearings to such a degree that it thinks small portions on big plates are the Body of Christ, and that running when you don't need to is in some way life-affirming. Meanwhile Slappy Jack's and Sloppy Joe's and Jimmy Buffet's saw good Friday night crowds, and the usual pilgrimage was made by many down to the Havana Dock to watch the night come, despite the fact that before, during and after sunset a uniquely talentless young woman armed with a battery of cheap synths polluted the air with jerky covers of the songs of yesteryear, primarily the mid-1980s, and especially those with a maritime or vacation theme, however tangential; while another woman, who had once been beautiful but was now merely frightening, served long fruit cocktails in plastic cups and glared at the leavers of tips she considered insufficiently generous.

People walked up and down Duval Street in the warmth of the early evening, peering in stores, assaying menus, enjoying the company of their companions but with part of their minds distantly worrying about the children, pets, lovers and gas ovens they'd left behind. From above, the island was a patchwork of light and dark, groves of trees with house lights twinkling, a network of lit streets, the distant thud of music. You couldn't avoid the fact that life existed there, however far back you pulled: like a corner behind the fridge which never quite gets cleaned and is host to a variety of small microbular things going about their business with the happy, unmindful concentration of children.

This, or something like it but in heavier clothes and with no Internet access, had gone on there for hundreds of years – and would go on for hundreds more. What took place a couple of miles out to sea that evening never made any difference to anybody and was, as Eddie expected, over fairly quickly.

The light came on eventually, but only for a moment and nowhere near as brightly as usual. The sea never froze. For Connie, who'd heard about the light from above but had never seen it, the experience was kind of interesting. For Eddie it merely confirmed what he'd already decided: something was notably fucked up.

They waited another few minutes to see whether something else would happen, but it didn't. Eddie cut the signal tone on the radio, and told Connie to start the engine.

'Which direction?'

'Straight ahead. That's where the island is.'

Connie peered eloquently out at the open sea. 'It's your call.'

'Yes, and I've called. Do it.'

They went fast and fifteen minutes later Eddie told Connie to slow it down a little. Connie took it back to pootling speed and watched as Eddie stood and looked ahead. There was still nothing to see. Eddie closed his eyes, got his bearings. He'd always been a good judge of space, even in the dark and in jungles and terrains he didn't know that well. It was just one of those things.

'I'd say we're a couple of hundred yards short at this stage,' he said. 'Keep taking her ahead, but slow.'

Connie drove. Eddie loaded his pockets with shells. Up above them the moon shed a cool, confident light that for several more minutes failed to reveal anything out of the ordinary.

But then, they saw something.

About twenty yards ahead. Something small and pale grey, about three feet above the ocean.

'Shit on me,' Connie said. 'What the blue fuck is that?'

Eddie didn't reply, but just waited until they were closer, by which time the question could be answered just through using your eyes. Connie slowed the boat right down, and then a quiet *thok* noise told them they'd found the walkway.

'Eddie, thank God,' the grey croaked. 'Boy am I glad to see you.'

Eddie tied the boat up, while Connie just stared up at the alien. Then he clambered onto the walkway. Not an easy task, while the pier remained invisible, but achievable.

He looked down at the creature. 'What's going on?'

'Weird shit, Eddie,' the grey said. 'That's all I know.'

'Do the tall guys know something's afoot?'

'I don't think so. They're kind of wasted. They even forgot to feed us this morning.'

'How many have you seen? What do they look like?'

The grey shook his head. 'Couple of the guys say there's four or five. Me, I only saw two. And those looked kind of like you do.'

Eddie turned back to the boat. Connie was still standing there. 'Are you coming up here, or what?'

Connie swallowed. 'Up where, man?'

'Up on the pier.'

'The invisible pier, I take it? The one where you're chewing the rag with something out of the fucking X-Files?'

'That'd be the one.'

'You know what? I'm wondering whether this is something I'm truly going to be up to on an empty stomach.'

Eddie leant down without a word and proffered a hand. Connie grabbed it, and scrabbled with relative grace up unto the walkway. He dusted off his hands and looked down at the alien, who looked back up at him.

'Hi, Roswell dude,' Connie said eventually. 'I come in peace.'

'That wasn't us,' the grey snapped, 'and I'm tired of taking flack for it.'

'Let's get on with this,' Eddie said, and started walking. The grey skittered round to trot in front. Connie took the rear. It felt like a good place to be for the time being. They walked the length, towards a yellow light. This, Connie observed, was also hanging a few feet above the sea. The situation didn't seem to be bugging Eddie, however, so he guessed it was okay. A couple of yards before they reached it, he got a flicker in his eyes. For a moment it looked like there was something behind the light, a body of land. Then the impression disappeared, to be replaced by a couple of oval heads around the light. There was some excitable chattering in a language that was neither English or Spanish, the only ones Connie had any real acquaintance with.

'Okay guys,' the grey said to them, as they got to the end. He nodded in the direction of the three other greys, who'd appeared from behind the light. All of them either waved or nodded at Eddie. 'What you have to do is get land-side of my buddies here.'

Eddie walked past the little aliens. Connie followed. The moment his back foot was past them, a whole island flicked into view. And this time, it stayed there. Connie shook his head.

'How the hell'd you do that?'

'Our science is many centuries ahead of yours,' intoned one of the greys. 'Do not adjust your television set.' The others giggled.

Eddie shushed them, and explained his plan.

Minutes later the greys quietly led Connie towards the path, and Eddie slipped alone into the trees. He waited until they were out of sight around the corner, and then cut a wide path around the island. Partly this was because it would probably turn out better if they didn't all approach the centre from the same direction. Partly it was to see if there was any evidence to bear out a hunch which had been slowly gaining hunchiness all afternoon.

In a grove close to the shore on the East side he found the body of someone he thought very likely to be Jennifer Becker, lying awkwardly on the ground. Eddie didn't bother to check for a pulse. She'd evidently been shot by a weapon of non-human provenance, which had punched a hole right through her head. A sad, crumpled end for someone who'd never really understood the situation she'd found herself in, but then Eddie could have said the same for many people he'd known, who'd fallen in the kind of fights that got covered on CNN, and then been buried with full military honours. All around her in the sand were two sets of footprints of pretty normal shape and size. One of them bore the logo of a prominent earthling casualware manufacturer. The other showed all the signs of having been made by flip flops of equally terrestrial provenance.

Eddie decided he finally knew what was going on.

'So who the hell are you?' Fud demanded, glaring at Connie.

Connie looked right back at the alien. He'd already endured having his monkey-derived ancestry cited, and was rapidly discovering the truth of something Eddie had once told him: it didn't take very long in the company of these people before you started really, really wanting to kill them.

'Friend of Eddie's,' he said. 'He sent me here.'

'Eddie's an asshole,' slurred the No-name alien. 'I always said so. You're probably an asshole too.' He coughed, and then added in a wheedling voice: 'Did he send any smokes with you?'

Yag, who'd yet to say anything, shushed his colleague with a thoughtful wave of his hand, and carried on looking at Connie.

No-name hiccoughed and stomped away to flop down into one of the reclining chairs. The greys meanwhile were standing together in a protective huddle a few feet away, under the standard lamp as if for warmth. Most of them were casting wary glances into the trees which stood all around the grassed clearing. The one who'd met them on the pier, who so far as Connie could tell was entirely indistinguishable from the others except that he was a little bit braver, coughed nervously.

'He told us to come warn you,' the little alien said to Yag. The others stopped peering around and gathered behind him, for moral support. 'Some bad stuff is happening. The guy he was arranging a vaccine for has disappeared. Plus his wife.'

'Wasn't us,' Fud said. 'We never heard of the guy.'

'He knows,' said the grey. 'Think he's going to want a word with you about that. And you know what he's like when he's pissed off.'

'So who was it?' Yag asked.

'Us,' said a voice, and three species whirled at once.

Standing at the edge of the clearing was a man. Tall, dressed in grey shorts and nothing else. He'd lost the rest of his clothes during the day, no longer able to remember why he had to wear them. Only a shadowy vestige of an old propriety had kept the shorts in position. He stood in shadow, and at first Connie couldn't see his face. Then he took a couple of shambling paces forward, legs twisting as if he'd been knee-capped but was still somehow able to support his weight, a gun pointed in the general direction of the spindly aliens. Yag and Fud took small steps backwards.

No-name peered at the human and belched quietly. 'What the crap,' he rasped, 'is happening now?'

The man turned from the waist, as if he'd forgotten about his legs, and pointed the gun directly at him. 'Shut up,' he said.

'How did you get here, George?' Connie asked, his voice remarkably level. 'What happened to you last night?'

'By boat,' George said, his voice inflectionless. 'It had glass in the bottom. There were no sodas though. Jen was with us. But then she died. Well, we killed her, in fact. It was very sad.'

'Hold on,' said Yag, frowning. 'What do you mean, "us"? There's only one of you.' The alien was hungover to hell and back, and something was telling him this might be a bad time to be in that condition. Also that it would have been a good idea to have thought to bring some weapons out with them, even some teeny little ones, when the greys and human had appeared in the clearing.

If in doubt, bring a weapon. It seemed so obvious now.

'And,' Connie added, spotting another flaw, 'you're one of the people who's been kidnapped, surely.'

'He's referring to me,' said another voice, female this time. A young woman stepped out of the shadows on the other side of the clearing. She had big hair, dainty tattoos, and a gun in her hand that looked like a bunch of big spiders fighting on a frog. 'You got a gun, Connie?' she said. 'Sure you do. Take it out, slowly, and throw it on the ground.'

'Fran?' Connie asked, his voice finally cracking, 'What in Christ's name are you doing here?'

'Could ask the same of you. But I'm not going to, because to be frank I don't really care. Just lose the piece.'

Connie reached into his pocket like a man in a daze, pulled out the gun, and dropped it on the ground.

'Great,' muttered Fud. 'Thanks for your help, banana-boy.'

'Yeah?' Connie said, still staring at Fran. 'Well, you're so tough, you do something.'

'We're not good at that kind of thing,' Fud admitted.

Fran motioned George forward with her gun. George picked Connie's weapon up and held it in his hand, as if unsure how to proceed. In the light that was always present in the clearing he appeared strange, shaky, as if holding himself together by will-power alone. His face looked bulbous and pale, his skin damp.

Connie shook his head. 'Is Janine running the bar by herself?' he asked, evidently in need of clinging to something he could understand. 'It's Friday night. She's going to go ape.'

'No pun intended, presumably,' Fran smiled. 'I have no idea. I don't give a shit. I hate that bar. And those olive things you do? What are they about? Are they supposed to be food, or what? They're crap. Now, to business.' She pointed her gun at his head. 'You know too much. You have to die.' She laughed delightedly. 'Cool. I always wanted to say that.'

'I know shit,' Connie said hurriedly. 'Really.'

Fran did something to the gun which was clearly preparatory to using it to hurt people. 'Sorry, but that's the way it's got to be.'

'Seriously, it's overkill. There's fish in the bay got more idea of what's going on than me. Far as I know, you're just a waitress. A damned fine one, don't get me wrong. But a waitress, mainly.'

'Oh, I'm a lot more than that,' Fran laughed. 'In fact, I'm . . .'

There was a sudden, short cry. Everyone turned, to see that George was now lying on his back on the ground with the air of someone who would be there for a while. Standing beside him, his gun pointed unswervingly at Fran's head, was Eddie.

Connie didn't think he'd ever been so pleased to see in anyone in his life, and in that moment, in a tiny, very male way, he loved the guy to bits. Eddie looked so casual. He looked so armed. He looked so much like if Fran even twitched then she'd be missing her head before she knew it – which, though a very specific way to look, was easy to recognise and good to see.

No-name goggled. 'Are you seeing this too?' he hissed to Fud, in a low voice. 'People just keep appearing.'

'Yo, Fran,' Eddie said, carefully taking a couple of steps forward. His gun, while he did this, remained so steady that you could have rested a full beer glass on it and not lost a drop. 'If that's your real name. Which frankly I doubt. Why don't you lower the gun.'

'Fuck you,' Fran said.

There was a quick, dry cracking sound, and Fran's right hand disappeared, taking the gun with it. She blinked, and a moment later a thick black gloop began to drip from the severed wrist. 'You fucker,' she said, with quiet amazement.

'Why don't you tell Connie what you are?' Eddie suggested.

'He doesn't want to know,' Fran snarled, shaking her wrist. 'Jeez, Eddie, have you any idea how long it's going to take to grow a hand back? Fingers are really hard to do.'

'Fran's from another planet,' Eddie said to Connie, slowly letting the gun drop. His tone suggested this was no more remarkable than her being a Pisces, or lifelong Blue Jays fan.

'I see,' Connie said, nodding sagely.

'So's George, though he didn't know it.'

Connie stopped nodding and stared at Eddie, like an owl which believed someone was trying to pull a fast one on it. 'Kind of hard thing to forget, wouldn't you say?'

'I'd have thought so, but that's what happened. For the whole of his life George believed he was just a regular guy who sold people houses and land. Jen believed that too, which must have made this afternoon rather difficult for her. But recently he's started to remember – because someone began dumping clues in his head. He thought it was a memory of abduction, and I assumed it was these assholes gearing up to make a play.' He indicated the spindly aliens, who were all wide-eyed and silent. 'And you guys didn't go out of your way to correct my mistake, which pisses me off somewhat. Given that I've now saved your gill-headed asses, I think there's going to be a change in pay and working conditions.'

'Saved our asses?' Yag said. 'How so?'

'This is some kind of significant staging post or trans-dimensional transportation thing you've got going on this island, right? And it's your job to guard it.'

'There's an element of that,' Yag admitted cagily. 'How do you know?'

'Worked it out. I figure that if there's a whole universe out there, chances are there's going to be more than one type of alien and their pets around.' He nodded at the greys. 'No offence, fellas.'

'None taken,' the lead grey said. 'Hell, we like being pets. People give you food.'

'Sometimes,' one of the others added, pointedly.

Eddie turned back to Yag. 'Fran, she's not one of yours, so obviously she's one of a different type. Her attitude seems somewhat hostile. I didn't know from the beginning she was in on what's going on, but I figured someone other than George had to be – especially after George disappeared. My guess is that somehow, at some point in the past, she must have slipped through immigration and has been lying low. And last night I realised George wasn't what he seemed or even what he thought he was himself. When I asked him how long ago it was since his wife had been abducted, he told me forty-five minutes.'

'And?' Connie asked. He took a couple of steps away from Fran, who was glaring unhappily at Eddie. 'So what?'

'Takes about ten to get from the Marquesa to Slappy's,' Eddie said, 'Even if you were slow and got lost. Maybe he spent ten other minutes tearing his hair out in the hotel suite, or running around the grounds. Still leaves a block of time unaccounted for. I think he spent that time sitting staring into space in the room. I think that Fran abducted Jennifer as part of a process of getting George to remember what he really was.'

'What, like, gay or something?'

'No,' Eddie said patiently. 'George is a sleeper. An alien in disguise even to himself. She needed him to wake up, because she wanted him to help her take this base and open the floodgates.'

'So why'd George admit it was forty-five minutes?' Yag said. 'Why didn't he lie?'

'He'd stopped being wholly human,' Eddie shrugged. 'But hadn't yet reverted to his real type. He was confused. He no longer really understood what to say, or how to say it. When we saw him at the bar, the human part was temporarily back in control again. He didn't understand what the hell was going on, and he was afraid, and he told the truth because he thought it would help. He'd lost his wife. He wanted her back.'

'Hang on,' Connie said. 'Fran was in the bar at the time. How'd she do the Mrs Becker thing, when she was carrying drinks in front of my eyes?'

'I don't know,' Eddie admitted irritably. 'I also never understood the appeal of Seinfield, and the whole grassy knoll thing is a mystery to me too. I haven't got the complete thing worked out. But that's basically how it happened, right, Fran?'

Fran had stopped shaking her hand. She looked calmly back at Eddie.

'Four hundred and fifty years,' she said, eventually. She didn't look defeated, or worried, or frightened. 'I volunteered. I came ahead. I knew Florida when it was just a big swamp, just a few Indians wandering around. It seemed like a good place to wait for backup. It was quiet. It was hot. Then the white guys showed up. Decided this was Heaven on Earth. Whacked the first lot of Indians, and then let some more in and called them Seminoles. Let them stay. For a while, and then whacked them for the most part too. Meanwhile drained and farmed and did stuff, turning the mainland into a zoo. Then there was that stupid-ass fight about whether you were allowed to own other humans or not, so I came down the

Keys to get out of the way. Watched the hotel guy, what was his name, Flagler? – lousy lay, whatever he was called – build the bridge right down through the Keys. Then the hurricane took it a couple years later. Then another got built.'

Eddie was keen on the idea of a cigarette by this point, but knew it would ruin Fran's sense of occasion and he figured that after a few centuries she had a right to that. Plus he was running very low. He just listened. The others did too. You sort of had to.

'All the time,' Fran said, shaking her head. 'You guys have no idea that you're all just barely tolerated guests, and that these guys,' – she indicated Yag and Fud with distaste – 'have already laid claim. I wait, and I wait. They said they were going to send more after me. That there'd be enough for us to take this ridiculous island, which small though it is, is very fucking important in the general scheme of things. That was my job. But no one appeared. No one. For year after year after year. Until finally I learned what had happened. I got a message.'

'How?' Eddie asked, intrigued.

'They're beamed in, coded into the Jerry Springer Show,' Fran said. 'What else do you think is the point of that shit? Anyhow, the message told me that the controls had been tightened. They had managed to get someone over, but up in the North – and he'd only been able to stay for less than five hours. So he'd popped through, made a baby with a human, and then slipped back again. That baby was George, and he had no idea who he was. Until I finally found him, and started floating things into his head, waking him up to the way he should be. He got drawn down here, as all the sad abductee fucks do because they know something's going on around here and they think it's going to help them to be near. He still wasn't really getting with the programme until last night, when I got a wino to go around to the Marquesa and grab the little woman out of her suite. And that about brings us up to date.'

Everyone looked at her for a moment. Then Eddie spoke again. 'All that waiting, just for one more guy to arrive?'

'One is all I need,' Fran said. 'Hell, one good man is all anyone needs.'

'And now it's all screwed,' Connie said, with satisfaction.

Fran laughed, with a kind of quiet contentment. 'Screwed? I don't think so.' She nodded at where George was lying prone. 'I really don't think that at all.'

Eddie was quick. He turned, stepped back and put three shells into George before anyone else had even moved. But it made no difference. By the time the erstwhile realtor was on his feet, his body was already halfway to changing. His knees had swollen to twice their usual size, and the skin was splitting like a dropped fig. The rest of his body was swelling too, unevenly but very quickly – some parts looking like their were about to explode, others dwindling to twig thickness.

'Oh, shit,' Yag said, in a quiet, aghast voice. 'It's one of *them*.'

Eddie popped a measured three shells directly into what had been George's head, but was now a huge twisted thing that look like an old tree trunk covered in moss. It made no difference. Then he heard the greys gasp, and turned to see the same thing was happening to Fran. She was getting bigger. She was expanding and contracting in the same way George was, but as part of the process both of them were simply acquiring more mass. Somehow, drawn from somewhere, more stuff was going into them – and they were getting larger and larger. Both were making a low keening sound, though it wasn't clear whether this was coming from what was left of their mouths or if it was part of the process of change, flesh and bone screaming as it was pulled agonisingly into a configuration never meant to spend time on this planet or in our reality. It looked like something that Hellraiser dude might have come up with, the morning after far too much Mexican food.

As the creatures got bigger and bigger, and started to vibrate like gross, blood-spitting tuning forks, everyone suddenly drew breath and realised they wanted to be somewhere else. Yag and Fud ran to a point on the left-hand side of the clearing and started hammering their fists on something Eddie couldn't see, but assumed was the means of going back whence they'd come. Evidently it wasn't opening. The greys meanwhile ran in five random directions, got scared after a couple of yards, and then all hurtled back again to crash together in the middle. The two weirdos gave up on the invisible door and tried to go sprinting off into the trees, only to find that something had happened to the air there and it had become an invisible wall. No-name, meanwhile, was evidently trying to crawl underneath one of the reclining chairs. Connie just stood, hands down by his side, watching events unfold with the air of a man who'd decided that if the world was going to drive him stark raving mad he might as well go along for the ride, and get the full value out of the experience.

Within two long minutes Fran and George stood ten feet high, looking like twisted figures painted by Francis Bacon around an idea by Miro, rendered in blood and bloat. They took a few shambling steps towards each other. Then stopped, at what looked like a prescribed distance, and stretched out to each other with what had once been hands.

Eddie knew what was about to happen, and emptied his gun into various parts of their anatomies, without much hope but knowing that he had to prevent the two of them becoming one. Fran had said that's all she needed, just one other of her species. Eddie didn't want to see, didn't want the *world* to see, what happened when two of these guys conjoined. He sensed it would be a bad thing.

He shouted at Connie and Connie slowly drew his eyes from the spectacle, realised what Eddie wanted, and pulled his gun.

They fired and reloaded, fired and reloaded, picking small divots out of the aliens' flesh but doing nothing to stop the inexorable progress of each's flesh towards the other's. The two bodies were now of slightly different shape, like halves of a biological jigsaw puzzle waiting to be fitted together like sperm and egg.

The greys and the weirdos stopped trying to run and just watched transfixed, as the two humans stood mere yards from the twisting nightmare and fired and fired and fired. In Eddie's mind everything in the world had disappeared. Everything within vision, everything he had seen and done and heard about, everyone he had known and killed and kissed and loved and found merely irritating. All he could see were two lumpen hands, straining towards each other, warm, glistening knobs of flesh yearning to become one thing and grow together. He hit the knobs time and again, but within seconds they were back again: while human fingers might be difficult to do, these creatures' real shape could evidently heal and regrow almost instantaneously. Eddie was coldly aware that such a species would be impossible to fight, once they came through, and that the fate of the whole planet might depend on him doing something now, that his mother's son held the future of the world in his hands.

He gave it his best shot. He tried. He couldn't do it.

And so it was just as well that, as the bridge was made and the two hands became one with a sound that was like a hundred happy people sighing at once, there was the sudden noise of a vicious, fizzing explosion. At that very same moment the whole collective top half of both what had once been George and what had never been Fran disappeared like dirt scraped off a windshield.

The remaining four-foot-high pieces shuddered, squirmed like sentient piles of shit, and then were blown to dust by two further explosions of the same kind.

The clearing was utterly silent for a moment. Everyone stood and stared at where the action had been, seeing only a large circle of scorched grass.

Then they turned.

Standing off to one side, each holding a complex-looking weapon and still looking sunburnt, were a pair of English honeymooners.

'Sorry we're late,' they said.

About half an hour later Eddie and Connie stood at the end of the pier. The greys were gone. They'd been sent back to their compound and had complied with reasonably good grace, largely because of the promise of some extra food and being allowed to stay up late. The weirdos were also absent. The two young English people had taken them off to one side in the clearing and had a long conversation with them, during which there had been much kicking of heels, sulky nodding and general averting of gaze by the spindly ones.

Eddie and Connie stood right where they'd been, guns still in hand, waiting for everything to start making sense. Eventually the weirdos had come reluctantly over, obviously sent by the young couple. They'd mumbled short and insincere apologies for any inconvenience they'd caused, and then tramped in a line back over to the far side of the clearing, where this time the invisible door was evidently working again. Then the English couple had invited Eddie and Connie to accompany them back to the pier.

'So,' Connie said, after a while of standing looking down at the boat. 'Guess you're not from London, England after all.'

'Oh, no,' said the male one. He was wearing a white Gap T-shirt and khaki shorts, and had engaging green eyes. 'Well, not originally. Though we do have a small place in Islington at the moment. A *pied-à-terre*, really. Very convenient for the centre of town.'

'Where are you really from?' Eddie asked.

'Oh, quite some distance away. Miles and miles. I'm not sure you chaps have even found it yet.'

Connie swallowed. 'Do you look as gross in your dimension as Fran did?'

'Hardly,' the female one laughed. She had a neat blonde bob, and was slim and pretty. 'Actually we look exactly the same as we do here, but a couple of inches taller. No idea why.'

Eddie nodded. 'So what happens now?'

'Well, basically,' the male one said, glancing at his watch, 'we're all free to get on with our evenings. The invasion threat's been averted and, well, the night is yet young. Sorry to have involved you in so much trouble. Wished we'd known that Fran was the spy. Could have sorted the whole thing out last night – though to be honest we were a little tipsy by the stage it all went off.'

'What are you?' Connie asked.

The woman shrugged. 'Police, angels, inspectors,' she said. 'Pick your metaphor. We sort things out. Though to be frank, at the moment what I mostly am is starving. It's probably about time for some dinner, isn't it, darling?'

'Absolutely,' the male one said. 'Now: the gatekeepers have been told not to mess around with this whole abduction nonsense any more, but of course they will. Incidentally, Eddie, you shouldn't really have been doing what you've been doing without a licence.'

'Well, you know how it is, out in the sticks,' Eddie said. 'We don't always do things by the book. But we generally get by.'

'Quite. Well . . .' The man dug around in his pocket, and pulled out a thin black piece of paper. 'Here's a licence. With our thanks.'

Eddie took it, turned it over. It had no writing on either side. 'This is it?'

'I'm afraid so. I suppose you could get it laminated if you wanted. One final favour: we're thinking of zipping up the coast tonight, Gulf side, maybe Sarasota and its environs, checking out some new restaurants. Any recommendations?'

'You could try Tommy Bahama's,' Eddie said, eyeing them carefully. 'That's pretty good.'

'What kind of food is it?'

'They specialise in a Floridian/Caribbean cuisine. Kind of a "Floribbean" thing, I guess you'd call it.'

The man frowned. 'Which is?'

'American. But with fruit in it.'

'Sounds perfect,' the woman beamed. 'Thanks awfully.'

The two aliens thanked Eddie and Connie once more, took each other's hands, and then vanished into thin air with a quiet pop.

Eddie and Connie stood in silence for quite a while.

Then Eddie coughed quietly. 'Sorry about Fran,' he said.

'She was a good waitress.'

'You didn't . . .'

'Actually, yes, we did, a couple of times. I'd rather not think about it right now.'

Eddie nodded for a while, and let quiet settle once more. Then: 'Can I buy you a beer?'

'Hell, no. I'll buy the beer. What you're buying me is food.'

'Crabby Dick's?'

'You read my mind.'

They climbed down into the boat, took a look back at the island before it disappeared, and then set off across the calm, flat water towards Key West and food and drink and the things we do so well. They figured they might as well make a night of it. It was only just after eight o'clock.

*

Couple of weeks later, Eddie was standing on the upper deck of the Havana Dock early one evening, bathed in soft peachy light and waiting for the sun to go down. Even after seven months on the Key, he liked to watch it, and for the time being he liked living there too.

All around were couples and small groups, dressed smart casual for the evening, sitting in warm expectation and sipping at fruity drinks. Many were tourists, but there was a good sprinkling of locals, come to enjoy a thing of beauty because living with it hadn't staled them to its charm. There was a hum of loose chatter, but mainly it was quiet, largely because the female synth player was taking one of her all-too-infrequent breaks. Eddie hoped that by the time she came back, and discovered that someone had removed the fuses from each and every one of her keyboards, they would all have been able to watch the sunset in peace.

He was sipping his Margarita, which was punishingly strong because the woman who made them had a frightening crush on him and was also in his debt because he'd sorted out a problem she'd had involving the most psychotic of her many ex-husbands, when he saw a young woman walking up the way. She had long brown hair and was pretty, but her eyes were watchful and there was something in the set of her shoulders which said she wasn't here for the sunset but rather because she was worried and afraid and had heard in a bar there might be a man on the dock who could help do something about it.

Eddie lit a cigarette, and settled down to wait for her to find him.